PRAISE FOR IMPENDING STRIKE

Impending Strike grabs you on the first page and takes you along on a twisting, edge-of-your-seat story that will keep you flipping pages to find out what happens next.

— PATRICIA BRADLEY, AUTHOR OF THE NATCHEZ TRACE PARK RANGERS SERIES

Fans of the Elite Guardians world will love this story. Charlie and Lizzie overcome their painful pasts and find their happily ever after in this explosive, high-stakes story. I was sucked right in!

— LISA PHILLIPS, USA TODAY BESTSELLING AUTHOR OF THE LAST CHANCE COUNTY SERIES

Impending Strike has everything I look for in a romantic suspense novel—page-turning suspense, great romantic chemistry between Lizzie and Charlie, and a familiar cast of characters from previous books in the series. Don't miss this fabulous addition to the Elite Guardians collection!

— LISA HARRIS, USA TODAY BESTSELLING AUTHOR

IMPENDING STRIKE

AN ELITE GUARDIANS NOVEL

LYNETTE EASON

SAMI A. ABRAMS

A NOTE FROM LYNETTE

Hey everyone!

I'm so excited to be introducing you to the second book in the second Elite Guardian Collection. When I read Sami's premise for this story, I was super excited.

Charlie and Lizzie were meant to be together, but neither one would admit it. It takes a conk on the head, a concussion, and more, to bring Charlie to his senses. And Lizzie, too.

When she's sitting in the hospital with him, waiting for him to wake up, it really hits home how much she cares about this man. Of course that scares her to death since she doesn't have a great track record with love! And boy do things get interesting when Lizzie is assigned to bodyguard the bodyguard!

So, strap on your seatbelt for a non-stop ride full of thrills, chills, and romance. I truly hope you enjoy the story. I know I did!

God Bless,

Lynette

A special thanks to my parents for supporting me and telling me I can do anything I set my mind to. To my sister Jeanine, and my brother Craig for encouraging me on this journey. And to my brother Bruce, who is with Jesus. I miss you every day.

1

THURSDAY, 11:00 P.M

Did the crazy girl want to get herself killed?

Elite Guardians Agency bodyguard Lizzie Tremaine parked her older model silver BMW out of eyeshot of the biker bar and hefted herself from the driver's seat. She'd bought the car for the safety ratings but had to admit the sleek design gave her a sense of luxury. Not exactly the type of vehicle that one drove around these parts of Columbia, South Carolina—but with no time to exchange it for a rental, she didn't have a choice.

Lizzie strode toward the entrance of Dirty Dogs, her boots crunching on the gravel. The song "Welcome to the Jungle" poured from the open door. She slowed her approach. *Jungle is right.* The bar was known for more than bikers looking for a good time. Rumor had it that girls disappeared from the establishment on a regular basis, but the cops had no evidence to close the place down.

The interior lights flowed from the building, glowing

against the dark veil of night. The seedy bar on the outskirts of town was not one anyone in their right mind would pick for a nice evening out. Bridget Rutledge, the underage daughter of Lizzie's recent celebrity client, Bodie Rutledge, had chosen the place as a slap in her father's face.

The rumble of Harleys in the parking lot threw off the rhythm of Lizzie's heart. Or maybe it was Mr. Tall Dark and Scary bouncer guarding the door. She craned her neck and caught a glimpse of the missing sixteen-year-old.

Go in or wait? She'd called one of the other agency bodyguards, Charlie Lee, for backup, so help was on the way. And while Lizzie hated pulling him from his undercover assignment as a drug dealer, going into *that* bar without a male counterpart equaled foolishness. Just as she'd set herself up to wait on Charlie, a hard-eyed, tattooed man moved in on Bridget.

Fabulous. If someone pulled the girl out the back door... Nope. Charlie or not, she had to get in there before the girl got herself killed—or worse.

Lizzie tugged at her too-short leather skirt and steeled her spine. She hated undercover assignments in places like this but refused to let Bodie down. The man was beside himself with worry for Bridget. With good reason. Lizzie stepped forward. The bouncer held up his hand, inches from her chest. Inked numbers adorned his fingers, and the three teardrop tattoos next to his right eye told her the man had seen the inside of a prison.

Shoulders back, Lizzie smiled. "I need to see my friend." She motioned inside.

"Don't think so." The man crossed his tree-trunk-sized arms over his chest. "Lady doesn't want to be bothered."

"Is that so?" Lizzie leaned in. "Listen, I really don't think you want cops showing up. I'm guessing someone in there isn't twenty-one." Lizzie raised her chin. She'd studied her opponent. He had weaknesses, but she'd rather not explore them.

A low growl rumbled in the bouncer's throat, and his glare zinged daggers at her. "Fine." He stepped aside.

She brushed past him and released a long breath. Once inside, she meandered her way across the postage stamp room. The smoky haze stung her eyes.

"Hey, baby."

Lizzie raised a brow at the man clad in black leather, who, by the looks of him, had joined the three hundred club years ago. "Not your type."

He belly laughed. "Maybe. Maybe not." He slid a rough knuckle down her cheek.

The mixed scent of body odor and beer curdled her stomach, but she refused to cringe at his touch.

Hurry up, Charlie.

She jerked her face away from the man. "Paws off."

"Feisty little thing, aren't you?" He reached for her again.

She didn't have time for this. Lizzie snatched his thumb and twisted it to the breaking point. He let out a howl. "You don't want to find out." A quick push and the man stumbled. Lizzie took advantage of the opportunity and found a stool at the bar with a perfect view of Bridget.

The Dirty Dogs bar, small compared to the local places in downtown Columbia, had four red plastic booths that lined the far wall and six four-topper tables in the center of the room. Easy enough to keep her target in sight.

The bartender slid a glass of amber-colored liquid in front of her then continued wiping the bar top with a white cloth.

She sniffed the drink. Whiskey. "Excuse me. I didn't order this."

He jutted his chin at the guy wearing a black doo-rag skull

cap with red and yellow flames. Skull and rose tattoo sleeves covered both arms.

Great, another one. A single woman in a bar full of testosterone and attitude—there'd be more. And it was the entire reason she'd called Charlie. Where was he, anyway? She lifted the glass in a silent toast, then brought it to her lips and pretended to take a sip. Her gaze zeroed in on Bridget. The young girl sat between two men in a booth, flirting like her last meal depended on it. Lizzie had to get her out of here before one of the big dudes took Bridget up on her unspoken offer.

The thump of the bass increased, and the murky cloud of cigarette smoke around her thickened. A massive hand landed on Lizzie's shoulder. Her eyes trailed the meaty fingers and up the thick inked arm to a bearded face. The same doo-ragged man that had bought her a drink peered down at her.

He stepped into her line of sight of Bridget and leaned down, pressing his hand on the bar top, trapping her. His rancid breath brushed across her cheek. "Drinks aren't free around here."

Lizzie's patience waned. What was it with this type of neanderthal? She had no doubt about her abilities to handle him, but getting physical might encourage him to bring his friends into the action. And as skilled as she was in self-defense, not even she dared to take on the whole pack. She gritted her teeth and focused on a spot on the far wall, forcing in three shallow breaths, pushing her anxiety aside.

"Then stop buying drinks." With a flick of her hand, she flipped her long hair over her shoulder. "Not interested."

The man rose to his full six-foot-plus height. "I think—"

"Hey, gorgeous." Lips pressed against her temple. "This guy a problem?"

Charlie. Her partner of three years had never looked so

good, even in his scruffy undercover state with that wicked temporary dragon tattoo on his forearm.

"Hi, baby." Her sickening sweet drawl made her want to gag.

His hand wrapped around hers, Charlie tugged her behind him and widened his stance. "I think you better leave my woman alone."

His woman? Lizzie refrained from rolling her eyes.

After a long stare down, the man rejoined his friends.

She pivoted and gazed up at Charlie. *Play the part, Lizzie.* She let a coy smile curve her lips, and she ran her hands down his arms. "Thanks, Drago."

He pulled her in close and nuzzled her neck. "Why didn't you wait?"

"Bridget's playing a dangerous game. I couldn't leave her alone."

"Where is she?" He kissed her behind the ear.

A jolt of electricity zipped down her spine, muddling her train of thought. "At your four o'clock."

"Got her." Charlie slipped his hands to Lizzie's waist, pressed the Glock 43 she had tucked in the waistband of her leather skirt against her skin, and grinned. "Nice."

"I don't leave home without it." She winked.

"Uh oh, looks like Tiny and friend are planning to make their move." Charlie shifted and slid his hand into hers and squeezed.

Tiny scooted from the booth and hauled Bridget up next to him. His partner slipped from his seat and exited out the back door of the bar.

"Showtime." Lizzie sauntered toward Bridget. "Hey, girl! Haven't seen you in forever."

Wide eyes of the sixteen-year-old stared at her, lower lip quivering.

Tiny's beefy hand clutched Bridget's thin bicep.

Charlie's warm touch on the small of Lizzie's back centered her. His quick tap on her right side indicated she go for Bridget while he took care of the big man. Her focus tunneled in on the task at hand and even the loud music faded into the background.

Charlie brushed past her and bumped into Tiny.

"Watch it, boy." Tiny's deep timbre rose above the din.

"Boy?" Charlie's fists rested on his hips. "Don't think so, dude." Without warning, Charlie's hand chopped against the pressure point on the side of Tiny's neck, and his knee connected with the man's stomach. Tiny lost his hold on Bridget and staggered backward.

"Let's go!" Sending up a quick prayer for Charlie, Lizzie grabbed Bridget and pushed her out the backdoor. Lizzie blinked, forcing her eyes to adjust to the dark alley. She scanned the surroundings. Dumpsters to her left with cardboard boxes lining the brick exterior walls. The exit to her right. A dim streetlamp glowed at the end of the alleyway.

"Come on." She dragged the girl toward the parking lot.

Bridget's hand trembled in hers, but she stayed with Lizzie.

Tiny's partner stepped from the shadows. "And where do you think you're going?"

"Get in that alcove," she whispered to Bridget.

The girl rushed to the opening while Lizzie kept her eyes on the man in front of her. Charlie had better not have gotten himself killed.

The huge man rushed her. She stepped back and spun with a roundhouse kick to his face. His head snapped back. He staggered. Lizzie grabbed his shoulders and brought her knee up full force. With a howl, the guy dropped like a rock to the pavement.

Lizzie yanked her Glock from her holster and aimed it at

him. She sucked in air, trying to catch her breath. "Don't move." She shifted, but never took her eyes off the man lying on the ground. "You okay, Bridget?"

"I-I think so."

The back entrance to the bar crashed open, and two figures fell out into the alley. Tiny and Charlie. Tiny took a swing, but Charlie dodged it. He grabbed the man's arm, wrenched it behind him, and shoved him against the dumpster. Charlie whipped out zip ties and secured his attacker to the metal handle.

He pivoted and took in the scene. "Y'all good? No problem taking him down, right?"

Brat. "Nah. Six-five and two hundred eighty pounds is a walk in the park. Come secure him so I can get Bridget out of here, will you?"

Before Lizzie got her Glock holstered and helped Bridget to her feet, Charlie had the guy flex-cuffed next to Tiny.

"Let's get your package in the car."

Sandwiched between her and Charlie, Bridget shuffled, head down. Lizzie held on to the girl's arm and led her toward the vehicle.

Lizzie opened the passenger door and all but shoved Bridget in. If the night's events didn't open the young lady's eyes, Lizzie didn't know what would. She shut the door and turned, coming nose to nose with Charlie. A little too close for her sanity after the canoodling in the bar. She had no business being attracted to any man, especially not Charlie.

Lizzie skirted around him and headed for the driver's side. "Thanks for the assist."

"No problem." He scratched his beard and grimaced.

"Ready to see the light of day again?" Lizzie grinned and lowered herself into the vehicle. She rolled down the driver's window then hit the locks.

"More than." Charlie rested his forearms on the top of the car and leaned in. "You take the princess back to her tower, and I'll take out the garbage."

"Deal. See you in the morning?" Each week, the agency had a team meeting, and Charlie had been hit and miss lately due to his undercover assignment.

"Unsure. Now, get out of here. Kiss Addy goodnight."

Her twelve-year-old daughter. Once again, Lizzie had left her mother to watch over Addy while Lizzie rescued someone else. Her pulse raced, and her breathing shallowed. She struggled to tamp down her reaction. No one could know about her condition. Not now. Not ever. She swallowed hard and peered up at Charlie. "As soon as I drop off Bridget. Stay safe."

His knuckles rapped on the roof. "Always." Charlie sauntered off into the shadows. He'd call Detective Quinn Holcombe to pick up the two jerks from the bar and head off to his undercover world of drug deals. And she'd drop Bridget into the hands of her worried father, then head home to Addy.

She glanced at her passenger and tightened her grip on the steering wheel, causing the laces to dig into her fingertips. "That could've ended badly."

Tears trailed down Bridget's cheeks. "I know." The mousy voice surprised Lizzie. She prayed the young lady had learned her lesson.

"Good."

Only one thought entered her mind as she drove through town in silence. What if it had been Addy in that bar, and Lizzie hadn't arrived in time?

Charlie hated living within the depths of depravity.

And yet, that's where he found himself once again. God

had called him to a life of service and protection, so here he was. He just wished it didn't include undercover work.

Charlie slinked past the dingy apartment that Mayor Eliza Baker had arranged for him and sauntered down the sidewalk, aiming toward his next drug deal—one that might land him the big fish and stop the new flood of drugs into Columbia, South Carolina.

The fingers of moonlight touched the neighborhood, creating eerie shadows along the edges of the street. Poorly lit streetlamps gave no relief in illuminating the dark corners. Why must the big deals take place in the dead of night? The temperatures had dropped but the humidity hung on, causing sweat to bead on his upper lip.

Three warm blocks later, he slipped into the opening of a dark alley. The stench of vomit and alcohol turned his stomach. One of the many effects of the drug-invaded world that he hated.

Two years ago, his sister Olivia Edwards Savage—one of the founders of the Elite Guardians Agency—had assigned him to guard Darrell Hewitt, the son of the biggest crime boss on the East Coast. Due to Charlie's contacts from that assignment, the mayor had begged him to use his former police training to go undercover and help shut down the newest influx of drugs coming through Columbia. She'd confided in EGA and two detectives, his friends Quinn and Steven, that she felt if they stopped the drug flow, the uptick in gang activity might slow. The mayor wanted the best for her city, but she worried about a leak in the office and had kept the operation under wraps.

He leaned against the building, folded his arms, and closed his eyes, relishing the cool brick on his back. A skitter at the back of the alley had him searching the darkness for the little four-legged critter that had captured his attention. Unsuccessful in his visual hunt, he turned away from the distraction.

He strained to peer around the corner and settled back in. Where was his contact?

Charlie ignored the nighttime noises and allowed his mind to wander to earlier that evening. He'd chanced sneaking out of the neighborhood and going to the bar. But Lizzie had called, so he'd gone. The image of the large man's hand on Lizzie popped into his mind. His teeth clenched. If that man had hurt her... He shook off the direction of his thoughts. She'd handled herself like a pro. Always did.

Petite, full of spunk and deadly skills described Lizzie perfectly. She never backed down from a challenge and loved to learn new things. Everything from archaeology to computers to the latest in self-defense techniques. Something that had captured his attention when she'd started working for EGA. But he'd never acted on his interest. As the only male on the team, he refused to put his coworkers, especially Olivia or Lizzie, in an uncomfortable position. Besides, getting his heart stomped on once in life was more than enough.

Friends. That's where Lizzie landed, and that's where she'd stay. He liked her way too much to ruin their friendship. But if he ever wanted to wade into the dating pool again, Lizzie would be the girl.

Shoes shuffled on the pavement. A grunt and thud echoed through the night air. Charlie jolted. He instinctively went for his weapon at the small of his back, but suppressed the reflex to yank it from the holster. He squinted into the darkness. A drunk had fallen and lay curled in the fetal position at the end of the passageway.

Get your head in the game, man. Now wasn't the time to lose focus. No more thinking about Lizzie. He settled back against the brick wall and waited for his new *friend*.

The sticky August humidity continued to hang in the air.

Sweat trickled between Charlie's shoulder blades and his tattered black T-shirt stuck to his chest like a second skin.

Thirty miserable minutes later, Jimmy appeared from the shadows and made Charlie a drug deal offer that he gladly accepted. One that would clean up more filth from the streets.

"You got a deal, bro." Charlie gave the drug runner the required gang-type handshake. The glint of the streetlight illuminated the flaming skull and crossbones tattoo covering the man's forearm. Its glowing eye sockets gave Charlie the creeps. He retracted his hand and had a strong desire to shower away the slimy feeling from dealing with the lowlife.

Jimmy grinned, revealing several missing teeth. "Thanks for the business." With a nod, the man disappeared around the corner.

Charlie released the proverbial breath he'd held during the transaction. His shoulders sagged. With his forearm, he wiped the sweat from his brow. One more successful deal for a delivery made him that much closer to ending the undercover charade of drug dealer.

Each planned drug buy raked on Charlie's nerves. The lifestyle wore on him. After a year of setting up his presence in the drug scene and five weeks of full work undercover, he wondered how much more he had in him to continue.

He shoved his hands in his pockets and fiddled with his burner phone. His touchstone. His lifeline to the safe world. No names, only speed dial numbers of his Elite Guardians Agency teammates and Quinn. The women had insisted that he include their numbers. He'd resisted, not wanting to put the members of the agency in danger. But they'd reminded him that's what a team did. They had each other's backs. He was honored to be included among the top bodyguards in the nation, even if he was the only male. Not that he had a problem with that. He trusted them more than he trusted the police officers he'd served with on the Atlanta PD. And that said something.

Knowing that God was watching over him and that the team was a phone call away allowed him to maintain his calm demeanor and play the part of the cocky, confident dealer of his alter ego, Rod. He left the phone in his pocket and strolled down the sidewalk like he owned the neighborhood.

"I can do the hit." A gruff voice drifted on the night air.

Charlie froze and scanned the area, searching for the source of the words.

"Not so fast," a second man argued. "You can't mess this up. We have one shot at killing her, and if we miss, they'll close ranks."

The hair on the back of Charlie's neck rose. He ducked behind a row of trash cans next to an apartment building, grimacing at the strong garbage odor, a mixture between fish and rotten eggs. Forcing himself to focus, he strained to hear the conversation, but the men moved out of earshot.

Charlie slipped from his hiding spot and clung to the shadows on the edge of the street, following his targets. His ratty shirt and stained jeans, not to mention his unkempt hair, gave him the ability to blend into the neighborhood, but a hinky feeling of being watched crept in and stayed.

He itched to call his sister and Quinn for backup, but he shoved the desire away. His imagination had kicked into high gear. That was all. With the Crips territory only a couple blocks away, it was probably some gangbangers planning their next attack.

A light breeze cut through the warmth, rustling the leaves on the trees that lined the street. Shouts and raised voices filled the night. A baby cried in the distance. Typical evening sounds for this part of town. Why didn't that fact comfort him?

Charlie made a left turn at the corner and glanced at the

path he'd taken. He caught a glimpse of two figures slipping into the tree line.

Ah ha. Gotcha.

Charlie backtracked and edged closer. The voices rose. He held his breath and listened.

A twig snapped behind him.

Charlie spun.

Something connected with his midsection, and he dropped to the ground, gasping for air. Another hit caught him in the ribs. He cried out and threw up his arms to cover his head, then twisted as his attacker connected with a third blow to his temple.

Lightning arched through his skull with piercing brightness. Then the world dimmed.

Charlie's eyes fluttered, and he floated in and out of consciousness. He lay curled up on his side, blood pouring from a gash on his head. Eyes closed, he tugged his phone from his pocket. The movement sent pain shooting through his torso and he moaned. His brain and stomach swirled.

He laid the cell phone beside his face and struggled to get his fingers to cooperate. He made contact with the buttons and tapped a speed dial number.

"You've reached Lizzie. Please leave a message." The female voice swam in the distance.

"Help," he gasped through the agony. "Help me."

Charlie struggled to hold onto the present—but failed.

2

FRIDAY, 7:00 A.M

Rushed. That's how Lizzie's day had started after a fitful night's sleep. Guilt had plagued her for not tucking Addy into bed. Missing one night was a major deal to Lizzie. She wouldn't have much longer before her twelve-year-old refused the nighttime ritual. And then there was Charlie. She'd taken a huge risk pulling him from his undercover work, but she'd needed a man to play the part of a biker couple. Within EGA, Charlie was it. Besides, he was her partner and she trusted him. And trust wasn't something that came easy for her.

An extra-large coffee in hand, she meandered down the Elite Guardians Agency office hallway and waved at Angela Malone, EGA's administrative assistant. She pushed open the conference room door and the empty room greeted her. First one to the meeting, she plopped down in her favorite cushiony office chair positioned at the end of the oval table and inhaled the bold aroma of her morning brew. She took a long sip, letting the caffeine infuse her body. Her world settled. At least a little. Lizzie leaned back against the headrest and allowed the calming light blue walls and Monet-style paintings hanging around the room to soothe her.

"They're back!" Olivia ushered Haley and Steven into the room, followed by the rest of the crew, minus Maddy, who had a few more weeks of her maternity leave after the birth of her and Quinn's daughter, Stacy, four months ago.

Lizzie scanned the small crowd of her coworkers. Her shoulders drooped. No Charlie. He hadn't guaranteed to show, but she'd hoped.

"So, how was the honeymoon in Ireland?" Laila tossed her notepad on the table.

Haley blushed. "Good."

Steven drew his new bride to his side. "Better than good."

Haley buried her bright red face in Steven's chest, and the group laughed.

"I'm happy for you two." Lizzie rose and hugged her friends.

Katie, Christina, Laila, and Olivia joined in the hug-fest.

"I better let you ladies get to work," Steven said. "I need to go save my partner. I think Quinn is about to have a coronary with all the paperwork."

"Thanks for the ride. Zeke really wanted to see his friends and I couldn't say no." Haley smiled at her husband. Married life and the adoption of their teens, Zeke and Micah, seemed to agree with her.

"You know I'm okay with that. Now that Zeke is driving, we'll look into getting another car." Steven kissed his new wife and exited the room.

After a round of goodbyes, Olivia motioned to the seats. "Let's get started." Everyone settled in and for the next two hours, they discussed the current cases and new assignments.

Katie finally leaned back in her chair. "If things keep up, we'll have to contract out a few jobs."

"Agreed." Olivia tapped notes into her phone. "Christina, I'll call Alana and also reach out to Noelle." They could really use the skills and help of Alana Flores, Christina's foster sister, and Noelle Burton, a friend of Lizzie's, if they said yes. "Let's see if they want a few side jobs. I'll also check with Juliette Montgomery, one of the new Bodyguard Academy graduates that I've had my eye on." She aimed her gaze at Katie. "You think Daniel would be interested?"

"I don't know. Steven and Quinn keep hounding him to join Columbia PD, and he hasn't bitten yet. But the man is a bundle of energy. His restaurants keep him busy occasionally, but he's finally got a great staff, so he needs something to occupy his time. In other words, I can ask." Katie's eyes twinkled with mischief when she talked about her husband.

"Go for it. I'm sure Charlie would welcome another guy into the mix, even if Daniel's only willing to help out on occasion."

Katie scribbled on her pad of paper. "I'll let you know what he says."

"Sounds good." Olivia folded her hands on the table. "The mayor called. Mayor Pro Tem Jacob Stone is planning a rally for his new community Mental Health Awareness project. Mayor Baker asked us to provide security for the event."

"I heard about that." Laila leaned forward. "It's in honor of his sister-in-law if I remember correctly."

Christina nodded. "I saw his interview on Channel 10 last Friday. Six years ago, his nephew was killed. Stone said his sister-in-law suffered from horrible depression and his brother, Parker, pretty much became a recluse. He wanted to do something to help others, to present the message that there is help out there, that they don't have to fight depression alone."

"Kudos to him," Lizzie said, and if she wasn't a coward, she'd do more than support Stone's efforts. She'd stand up and tell her story. Not happening. Her mother didn't even know about her struggles. Deep breath in, she fought the familiar tightening of her chest.

"I'm assuming everyone's on board to help?" Olivia asked.

A chorus of yeses filled the conference room.

"All right then, next point of business. Mayor Baker's birthday party." Olivia smiled. "The mayor requested a contingent of State Law Enforcement Department agents. SLED can handle security during the event, since she'd like us to attend and enjoy the festivities."

"That's nice of her." Katie sighed. "An evening out sounds amazing."

Olivia reviewed her notes and scanned the room. "Anything else?"

Lizzie rubbed her hands together. "Let's talk about the important stuff. It's time to start an annual EGA family summer BBQ. Not like we need help getting together, but with our family growing, it'd be nice to have something preplanned."

"I think that's a great idea." Haley flipped to a clean sheet of paper. "We can have it at our place and have a country theme, or at Olivia and Wade's and do a pool-slash-lake party."

Olivia nodded. "I'm sure Wade would agree."

"I vote pool party." Christina fanned her face. "August and water go together. We can go to Haley and Steven's for a fall shindig."

"Two parties. I love it." Haley jotted down ideas for food as everyone pitched in their opinion.

"Anyone heard from Charlie?" Katie rubbed her rounded belly. She and Daniel were over the moon about her pregnancy.

Lizzie rested her forearms on the table. "I saw him last night."

"Oh, reeeally?" Olivia's eyebrow arched.

"Knock it off. He helped me retrieve Bodie Rutledge's daughter from Dirty Dogs."

"A girl can hope."

Lizzie shook her head. "Not happening." If Olivia only knew how she'd tossed and turned last night remembering Charlie's touch, she'd press for more information.

"How is he?" Laila tapped her pen on the arm of her chair.

"He looked ragged. This job is taking a lot out of him."

A rap on the conference room door caught the team's attention.

Angela stood in the doorway. "Olivia, Lizzie, can you *please* check your phones? Quinn's been trying to reach you both and keeps getting voicemail."

"That's weird." Lizzie dug her phone out from her purse and groaned. "I forgot to charge it. It's dead. Hang on." She connected the charging cord to the battery pack she kept with her.

Olivia shook her head. "Oops, I left mine on silent. Sorry."

A few seconds later, Lizzie's device pinged. Three missed calls from Quinn and a voicemail from Charlie. Her stomach bottomed out. Charlie never called during his time undercover. She'd been fortunate he'd answered last night.

"Lizzie, what's wrong?" Olivia shifted to face her.

"Charlie called."

Olivia dropped her phone on the table and gripped Lizzie's arm. "That's not good."

She retrieved the voicemail and listened.

"Help. Help me."

The call went dead. "No. No. No." Lizzie jabbed Charlie's burner contact number.

It rang several times.

"Come on, Charlie, pick up." All eyes were on Lizzie.

"Hello?"

"Charlie?"

"Lizzie? It's Quinn."

She put the call on speaker. "Quinn, why are you answering Charlie's phone?"

"I'm at the hospital, Lizzie. Charlie's been hurt. He's pretty bad." Quinn practically growled the last word. The man had softened since he and Maddy married and recently welcomed their first child, but the old grumpy Quinn resurfaced on occasion.

"Is he going to be okay?" She squeaked out the question.

"He's got a huge gash on his head, at minimum bruised ribs, plus other scrapes and cuts. And that's what we can see. Who knows about internal injuries, brain damage—"

"Stop!" Tears flooded her eyes. She sucked in a breath. Due to past experiences and career choices, she'd witnessed horrible scenes, but this was Charlie. Her coworker. Her friend. "I get the picture."

"Sorry."

She shook her head, dislodging the path her mind had traveled. "What happened?"

"Not sure. 9-1-1 got a call about an injured man. When the patrol officer arrived, he happened to recognize Charlie, knew we were friends, and called me. By the time I got there, the paramedics had loaded him in the ambulance. I jumped in with him and came to the hospital. The doc hasn't updated us yet, but he looked awful. I let Steven know a little while ago, and he's here to relieve me so I can check out the scene."

Olivia leaned in. "Where'd they take him, Quinn?"

"Baptist Hospital."

"On our way." Olivia shoved her phone into her pocket, collected her notes, and stood.

Lizzie ended the call. Standing, she swayed and clutched the arms of her chair. *Come on, Lizzie, you're stronger than this.* She found her balance, grabbed her purse, and followed Olivia out of the office to the parking garage.

The twenty-minute drive dragged on and on. The interior of the car closed in on her. Memories of her fiancé's death filled her brain. A raid gone bad. The gunshot. Blood flowing from a bullet wound. The ride to the hospital. The doctor informing her that the man she loved had died. She struggled to pull air into her lungs, fighting the familiar sensation. She walked herself through her coping steps. She was fine. She wasn't going to die. *Just relax. Breathe.* Charlie would be all right... He *had* to be. Lizzie couldn't live through that again.

She pulled into a law enforcement reserved parking spot next to Olivia's vehicle and slapped her special permit on the dash.

A few minutes later, she paced the waiting room while Olivia gathered information from the nurse. Lizzie spotted Steven and rushed to him. "What did you find out?"

Steven escorted her to the seats lining the wall. "Have a seat. We don't have anything yet."

She scowled at him but gave in and plopped down. "Why—"

He held up his palm. "Hold on. Quinn left a little bit ago and is working on it, but from what he said, there's little evidence."

"How little?"

"Without the full crime scene report ready yet, we're only making an educated guess. But it looks as though he was jumped and beaten. Nothing to suggest anything more than a mugging. No weapon or even shoe prints. But..."

She narrowed her gaze. "Steven? What aren't you saying?"

Steven ran his hand over his mouth. "He was found not even a block from Crips territory. Plus, the gang unit discovered two more bodies dumped in the Crips' backyard, so to speak."

"You think this is a gang thing?"

"I don't know, Lizzie. It just seems too coincidental it happened on the same night."

"So, someone retaliated? But for what?"

Steven shrugged. "I'm just not sure what to make of it."

Lizzie dropped her head in her hands. If someone suspected him of being a cop... "I did this to him."

"What are you talking about?"

She peered up.

Olivia had cocked her head to the side and raised her brows.

Lizzie bit her lip. "I called him in for backup. I blew his cover."

Steven clutched her hand. "Doubtful. From what Quinn told me, Charlie's beyond careful when he comes and goes from his undercover world. He doesn't carry ID, and they found his cell phone lying next to him."

The same phone he'd called her from, asking for help. And she'd let him down.

"Lizzie." Olivia lowered herself onto the seat beside her. "Stop feeling guilty. You did nothing wrong. You did what had to be done. Charlie's good at his job. Bodyguard *and* undercover work. He's not careless."

"But I missed his call." A blanket of darkness hovered over her. She sensed that all too common pit of despair swallowing her whole. "He lay there half the night beaten and left for dead."

Olivia flinched.

Okay, so her imagination had gotten the best of her. "Sorry." *Shake it off, Lizzie.* Here she sat, feeling sorry for herself when it was Olivia's brother they talked about.

"Nothing to be sorry for. You two are close." Olivia wrapped an arm around Lizzie's shoulder. "The nurse told me he lost a lot of blood from his head wound and has a concussion, a bruised bone in his arm, and a couple of bruised ribs. He'll be sore and have a massive headache, but he'll survive."

Lizzie's heartbeat whooshed in her ears. She closed her eyes and let the good news wash over her.

"Let's go see him." Olivia patted Lizzie's leg and rose. "Steven, will you watch for the others? I have a feeling the team will descend upon this place pretty quick."

He smiled. "Of course."

Lizzie and Olivia walked down the stark hospital hallway to Charlie's room. The disinfectant odor soured her stomach. She swallowed the bile building in the back of her throat. She hated hospitals. Too much pain. Too much death. Her fingers trailed the plain cream-colored walls, anchoring her in the moment.

Hand on the door to room 208, Olivia paused. "I've no doubt he looks pretty rough."

Lizzie nodded and steeled herself.

Olivia pushed the door open, and Lizzie eased inside. Her boss and friend entered behind her.

The white sheets, a huge contrast against Charlie's bruised arms and face, weakened Lizzie's knees. The strong, silly man she knew lay silent and motionless on the bed. His heart monitor beeped at a steady rhythm, giving her a bit of comfort.

"Hard to believe that's my brother behind all those bruises." A noticeable quiver lined Olivia's statement.

Lizzie gripped her friend's hand and squeezed. No idea what to say, she chose silence.

Olivia stepped forward and kissed Charlie's forehead. "I'll go call Mom and Dad. If you know what's good for you, you'll wake up and call them yourself. You know Mom. She'll smother you, and you won't be able to breathe without her fussing." Olivia turned to face Lizzie. "You'll stay with him?"

"I'm not leaving his side."

Tears pooling on Olivia's lashes, she forced a smile and patted Lizzie on the shoulder as she exited the room.

Lizzie scooted the easy chair closer to Charlie and sat on the edge. She eased her hand beneath his and leaned forward. "I'm here, Charlie. Everything's going to be fine."

She wrapped her fingers tighter around Charlie's. *God, please.* Would He listen? She'd lost her dad, her daughter's father, and her fiancé. Three men she'd loved—gone, all due to her poor choices. She still believed in God, but had quit trusting Him to listen to her prayers years ago and protect those she loved. But in times of desperation, she couldn't help herself from trying. Could she trust Him now? Or would He continue turning His back on her? She might not be in love with Charlie, but he was a dear friend who she had no desire to lose. *Please help him. I can't bear the idea of life without him. If not for me, do it for Olivia. She would be devastated. And what about little Chaz? He needs his uncle. Don't make Charlie's namesake live without him like my daughter has had to live without her dad.*

Lizzie laid her cheek on her and Charlie's clasped hands and gazed up at his face. Tears slid down her temple and onto the bed beneath. "Please, wake up and tell me you're okay."

Those idiots. He'd left clear instructions to kill the man, but they'd failed.

His phone rang, and he swiped it from the table and answered. "What?"

"Boss, the guy's dead," the minion declared, like he'd won a prize fight.

"Try again." He practically growled the words at the incompetent fool.

"What? Of course he is. I mean, yeah, we ran when we heard someone coming, but there's no way he survived the beating we gave him. He had to have bled out."

He closed his eyes and pinched the bridge of his nose. "He survived. And is expected to live."

"I don't know how. But we'll take care of it," the man rushed to assure him.

"See that you do. I'm paying you a hefty amount for the job. Don't screw it up—again."

"No, sir. Consider it done."

He disconnected the call, unwilling to listen to the guy's drivel. He paced the small living room and ran a hand through his hair. Where had his contact come up with these two buffoons? He had a plan in play and couldn't take the chance that the guy in the hospital had overheard his conversation.

Dumb and Dumber better take care of business or he might eliminate them as well.

He lowered himself onto the recliner, retrieved his glass of whiskey from the side table, and took a swig. The liquid burned a path down his throat. He closed his eyes and let the ambrosia take effect.

Soon, his problems would all be over.

Grit cemented Charlie's eyes shut. He struggled to pry them open but failed. His head pounded, and fire shot through his torso with every breath. His stomach churned and nausea threatened to overtake him. Every part of his body throbbed with a vengeance.

What had happened?

He dug through his foggy memory. Oh yeah, he'd been shot. How had he forgotten that?

Wait. His leg didn't hurt. Well, it did, but not like he remembered. He scrunched his forehead. An icepick jabbed his temple. His heart raced and he moaned against the pain.

The beeping beyond the darkness intensified.

"Calm down, Charlie. I'm here. Everything's going to be okay." A sweet voice carved through the hurt and soothed the agony exploding through him.

The beeping slowed, and the pain eased to some degree.

He forced his heavy lids open. The most beautiful angel stood over him. Her dark brown hair with an unusual purple streak flowed over her shoulders. And her brown eyes. They glowed as bright as her halo.

The angel brushed the hair from his forehead. "There you are." Her smile was one of pure bliss.

Charlie tried to lift his hand to touch her face, but his arm refused to cooperate. The shimmering aura around her thickened. He blinked the haze from his vision. Not an angel. A gorgeous woman.

Wow, the pain meds must be pretty good if he thought he'd seen an angel.

She cupped his cheek. "Can I get you anything?"

He relaxed into her touch and shook his head, instantly regretting the movement. He clamped his eyes closed and begged the contents of his stomach to stay put.

"Stay still."

As if he had a choice. The pounding in his head intensified. He shifted to ease the ache in his ribs. Fire shot through his torso, sending the world spinning at an alarming rate.

"I said not to move. You never listen, do you? I'll get the nurse to bring you some pain meds."

She was a demanding little thing. But whether he admitted it or not, the lady was right. Minutes later, with meds injected into his IV port, the universe—and his stomach—settled. He glanced up at her and smiled. At least, he tried, but the desert inhabiting his mouth made it nearly impossible for him to be sure.

"Here."

A straw rested on his lips. He sucked in the cool liquid, and the water unstuck his tongue from the roof of his mouth. "Thank you," he whispered.

"No problem." The brunette sat the cup on the tray and plopped into the easy chair beside his bed. "What were you thinking, getting yourself hurt? You were supposed to be careful. You promised. I can't believe I missed your phone call..."

Charlie struggled to follow the monologue. The last thing he remembered was chasing after the suspect. Then the gun went off, and he collapsed on the ground with a bullet wound in his right thigh. He'd had surgery to repair the damage and was in the hospital recovering. Funny. His leg didn't hurt. Not like a bullet wound. About the only place on his body immune to pain.

"...and you should have seen Haley and Steven this morning. Apparently, their honeymoon was amazing. As if we all expected anything less..."

The fog continued to lift, but her words didn't click. What had he missed? Charlie scanned the room, searching for anything to grasp on to. Tan walls with a TV opposite him. A huge window to his left and the door to his right. A smaller passage he assumed contained the bathroom. Nothing to give him a clue as to where he was besides in a hospital.

"...anyway. Olivia should be back in a minute."

His foster sister's name jerked him from his musing. "Olivia? What's she doing here?" Wonderful. His Christian Bale Batman imitation had nothing on the rasp in his voice.

"She's your sister. Where else would she be?"

"But she—"

"Charlie, you're awake."

He rolled his head to face the doorway, taking care not to rattle his brains. "Olivia?"

"Hey. How are you doing?"

"Been better."

His foster sister chuckled. "I'd say. I haven't seen so many bruises since you were hit by that car when you were twelve."

Oh, he'd never forget that summer. The ache in his chest had never truly disappeared from all those years ago. "Hurts worse this time."

"I don't doubt it." Olivia patted his shoulder. She pulled a chair close to him and sat. "I've waylaid Mom and Dad, so you should have peace for a little while. However, Mom will probably make Dad drive straight through from Yellowstone."

"Yellowstone?"

"That's where they are in their two-month-long vacation, traipsing all over the countryside."

Wonderful. Another opportunity to disappoint his parents. Mom would fuss, and Dad would let her. Just what he needed. Not. "Liv. I love you, turkey, but why are you here?"

She tilted her head. "Where else would I be? You're my brother."

Her brother? It was true, but she'd never fully acknowledged it before. Something wasn't right. He strained to put the pieces together. His head hammered in time with his heartbeat. He swallowed hard to force down the bile crawling up his throat.

"Stop trying to think. Everything will be okay. I'll go update the team and keep them at bay so you can get some rest." She kissed his forehead. "I'll be back in a little while."

The team?

Before he responded, Olivia waltzed out of the room, leaving him with the chatty woman on the other side of his bed.

"I know you're in pain, but that's no way to treat Olivia. She's finally put the past behind her. Don't you dare hurt her." The spirited little brunette crossed her arms over her chest and glared at him.

"Sorry."

"You should be. Now, where was I? Oh yes, Bridget is fine. Her dad has grounded her for a year, but we all know that won't stick." The woman grinned. She had an amazing smile. "Anyhoo, so I went home..."

A smile that reminded him of Susan. Where was his fiancée, anyway? She should be here next to him. The thought of her presence eased a bit of his pain. He'd ask Olivia when she returned. His thoughts took a dark turn. Had Susan been hurt? If so, how? Not by the gunman. So, why wasn't she here? He lifted his hand, careful not to aggravate his injuries, and pinched the bridge of his nose. The woman's incessant chatter finally got the best of him.

"Stop."

The chatterbox raised a brow. Dark brown eyes stared at him.

"Look, I appreciate your concern." Charlie studied her, praying for clarity, but he drew a blank. "But who are you? And where is Susan?"

3

FRIDAY, 2:00 P.M

Lizzie's jaw dropped. The hum of the IV infusion pump filled the otherwise silent room. She swore her heart thumped loud enough to be heard.

Susan? Who is Susan? And better yet, what did he mean by who was she?

She searched her memory for anything Charlie had told her over the last few years and came up with nothing. She rubbed her forehead, trying to make sense of his words. A lightning bolt of realization zapped Lizzie, and her heart sank.

"Charlie, what's the last thing you remember?" She bit her lower lip, waiting for his answer.

He shifted and groaned.

"Here, let me help." Lizzie adjusted his bed and blanket.

"Thanks." His eyes closed.

For a moment, Lizzie thought he'd fallen asleep, then he licked his lips and spoke again. She leaned forward, straining to hear his soft voice.

"I ran after the suspect, and he fired at me, hitting me in the leg. I went down and woke up here."

She'd witnessed his slight limp from time to time, but he'd never confided in her and told her the cause. It seemed off-limits, so Lizzie hadn't pressed. She wondered how long ago it had occurred. More than three years. Of that, she was certain.

"Why don't you get some rest while I go check-in with Olivia?" Lizzie intended to unearth answers about his leg and this Susan woman. Guilt tugged at her, but she had to have the information if she planned to help him. Right? *Nice try, Lizzie. You're just miffed he never said anything.*

"All right." His words slurred, and within minutes his breathing evened out.

Lizzie ambled to the door. She glanced over her shoulder at the battered man beneath the covers. The bruises on Charlie's body and the white bandage over the gash on his temple... She swallowed the lump that had taken up residence in her throat. "Get some sleep, Hotshot," she whispered.

She pushed open the door and eased it closed with a soft snick.

Lizzie rounded the corner of the waiting room and marched up to Olivia. "When was he shot? And who is Susan?"

Shock crossed her boss's face. Olivia wilted and dropped into a chair. "How did you find out?"

"He thinks he has a gunshot wound in the leg and asked about Susan by name." Lizzie crossed her arms, too tired and worried to have more tact. Not to mention a little hurt that he'd kept such huge secrets from her.

The team crowded around, questioning looks bounced between them.

Laila's brow furrowed. "Gunshot?"

"Susan?" Haley gaped.

At least Lizzie wasn't the only one in the dark. It helped in the margins, but the lack of trust from her partner stung.

Wade sat beside Olivia, wrapped an arm around her, and pulled her close. "Go ahead, honey. Tell them. I think Charlie will understand."

Olivia chewed on her bottom lip, clearly debating what to say then sighed. She rested her head on her husband's shoulder. "Four years ago, Charlie had a fiancée named Susan."

Laila's eyes widened. "Fiancée? Our *I'm having too much fun to settle down* Charlie?"

"Yes. One and the same." Olivia made eye contact with each one of them. "They planned to have a spring wedding, but Charlie got injured. He received a call out to a robbery at a liquor store. He and his partner responded. They chased the suspect for several blocks. No one told dispatch the guy had a gun, only that he had a knife. The man turned and fired, hitting Charlie in the thigh."

Christina tilted her head. "That explains his uneven gait, but not the missing fiancée."

Lizzie's gut told her she knew what Olivia would say. Charlie's actions all made sense now. The *fun for a night* dates. The intense focus on work. She held her breath, hoping she had it wrong.

"Susan went to the hospital. But when she saw him lying there a few hours after surgery, she told him she couldn't be a cop's wife." Olivia twisted the ring on her left hand and shrugged. "That's the basics anyway."

Heat crawled up Lizzie's neck. "Right after surgery? That rotten, horrible woman." Other words crowded her brain, but she refused to stoop to Susan's level of nastiness. That woman didn't deserve him. Poor Charlie. How could anyone throw him away like that? No wonder he never took things seriously.

"I'm glad you're all here." Quinn strode over, a scowl on his face.

Olivia stood. "What do you have?"

"Not much. But I have officers searching the neighborhood. We should have something soon."

"Any idea why someone used him as a punching bag?" Lizzie continued to worry that she'd blown his cover, adding another tragedy to her long list of bad decisions.

"Nothing yet." Quinn narrowed his gaze at her. "I know that look."

"What?"

"Steven told me about last night. And no. You had nothing to do with this."

She bit her lip. "How can you be sure?"

Lizzie scanned the group. No one said a word.

See, they couldn't confirm her actions hadn't put him in danger. Only one way to get the information she needed. Last night had disaster written all over it. Charlie had taken a chance to help her and ended up saving her bacon. She owed him. "I'm going undercover as his girlfriend. I intend to find out if his cover is intact."

"Lizzie."

"No, Olivia. We need to know."

Quinn grumbled under his breath. An improvement from a year ago. "Let me get you a burner phone with my number programmed in it. You aren't going in there without a handler, especially after the two gang killings last night. It happened a little too close to the neighborhood for comfort."

She'd accept the offer. No need to be careless about it. And she had no intention of straying near Crips territory. The farther away, the better.

The doctor entered before Lizzie responded. "Lee family?"

"That's me." Olivia strode over, and the others followed.

"I examined his CT scan. Everything says he'll make a full recovery. But as you might have noticed, his memory's been affected. He has post-traumatic retrograde amnesia. He seems to have lost a few years, but that should clear up with rest and time. However, I can't guarantee it."

"I understand." Olivia shook the man's hand then addressed the team. Tears shimmered in her eyes. "I want his attacker."

"We're on it." Lizzie clapped Quinn's shoulder. He harrumphed. Too bad. She had to make sure she wasn't to blame. "I'm going to check on Charlie then head home to get changed." She thought her biker babe getup had seen the light of day for the last time, at least for a while. Apparently not.

She made her way to Charlie's room and knocked before pushing the door open.

"Knock, knock." Lizzie peered in. "I came to see—"

A man covered in tattoos stood over Charlie. Arm against Charlie's chest, the assailant pinned him down, pushing against his hurt ribs.

Charlie let out a guttural moan.

Syringe in hand, the stranger grabbed Charlie's forearm and aimed.

"Stop!" Lizzie flung herself at the man, grabbed his wrist, and tackled him to the floor. His hot rancid breath fanned her face before he slipped from beneath her and aimed the needle in her direction. She twisted and landed a blow to his solar plexus. The air whooshed from his lungs. Without giving him a chance to recover, she slammed his hand against the tile. The syringe rolled under the bed.

Lizzie shifted to restrain him, but he recovered from her hit and threw her to the side. She crashed into the wall, the back of her head hitting first. Fireworks exploded behind her eyes, and she collapsed to the floor, blinking in a desperate effort to clear her vision.

The attacker scrambled to his feet and stumbled from the room.

Dazed, Lizzie punched the emergency call button on Charlie's bed and crawled to the doorway. "Quinn. Steven." Her breathy words no more than a whisper. She had to get their attention. She filled her lungs and tried again. "Quinn! Steven!"

The two detectives sprinted down the hall. Quinn reached her first. "Lizzie! You okay?"

"Attack. Suspect. Go." She pointed in the direction the tattoo man had fled.

Quinn took off after him. Nurses rushed past her into Charlie's room. Good. He had help, because at the moment she was worthless.

Steven yanked his cell phone from his pocket and informed security of the attack. He hung up and knelt beside her. "Are you sure you're okay?"

She rolled to a seated position and scooted against the wall, rubbing the knot on the back of her head with a grimace. "I've had worse. What about Charlie?"

Olivia appeared out of nowhere. "Come on, let's get you off the floor."

The two helped Lizzie into Charlie's room, and she dropped into the easy chair.

"I'll get an ice pack," one of the nurses offered.

"That'd be great."

"The doctor should be here in just a few minutes. I'll let him know he needs to check you out too."

Before Lizzie could assure the woman she didn't need a doctor, the nurse hurried from the room only to return a short time later with the promised ice pack.

"Thanks." Lizzie held it to her head. The cold was a welcome relief to the growing goose egg. She pointed to the syringe under the bed. "Grab that, will you?" she said to Steven. "See if you can get prints?"

Steven crawled under the bed and collected the evidence, while Olivia hovered. "Got it."

"Thank you." Charlie's quiet voice almost didn't register.

"How are you doing?" Lizzie scooted forward until her knees touched Charlie's bed. The attacker had pressed down on him when she'd walked in. His ribs had to be killing him.

"Hard to breathe, but I'll live. Thanks to you." The corner of his mouth hitched.

Her heart rate ran wild. What if she'd left without coming to check on him?

"I guess you heard that my brain is mush." He glanced between her and Olivia. "Sorry if I can't remember things I should."

Lizzie lowered the ice and shifted forward in her seat. She cupped his cheek. "Don't worry. You'll be up harassing us in no time."

He leaned into her touch and nodded. Charlie's reaction stumped Lizzie, yet delighted her. He was the same old Charlie, yet there was something different about him—a seriousness that tugged at her.

Lizzie shook off the odd sensation. She stood and pivoted to face Olivia. "I'll be back once I have answers."

"Be careful, Lizzie." Olivia edged next to her brother.

"Will do." She jutted her chin toward Charlie. "Take care of him." She hurried out and spotted Quinn, storming toward her. "Any luck?" she asked.

"No. He got away," he groused. "You ready to play *Rod's* arm candy?"

More than. She nodded.

"Steven will get you set up."

"I'll find him." She rubbed the knot on the back of her head. She wanted the guy responsible for the recent attack—bad—but confirming Charlie's cover was intact and gathering information came first.

"I'll be ready to join you as soon as I hear from the lab."

Whoever had hurt Charlie would regret the day he'd laid a finger on her friend. "Let's go hunting."

So, his beating wasn't a fluke. Someone had tried to kill him—for real.

Charlie shifted on the hospital bed in search of a comfortable position. Attempted and failed. His head pounded, and his body ached. Not to mention the throbbing in his chest where the attacker had pinned him to the mattress. He'd have more bruises to add to his collection. If the chatterbox hadn't come in...

He closed his eyes and let the truth wash over him. Trouble had found him, and he had no clue who or why. So many questions and so little brain power. Four years gone, according to Olivia.

Trapped in time, he'd never wanted to crawl under the covers and escape more than he did right now. No. That wasn't right. A vague recollection tapped at his brain. A dark hole of some kind. But the memory refused to surface.

He opened his eyes and shifted his gaze to the doorway. He wanted the intriguing woman to return. The whirlwind brunette had left Charlie reeling. The guys at the Atlanta PD had nothing on her. Of course, he wasn't with APD anymore. Not if he believed Olivia, which he did.

A hand slipped into his.

He jerked and groaned.

"Sorry."

His sister stood next to him, holding his hand. "No. My fault," he said. "I kinda forgot you were here."

"Thanks a lot, bro." Her cheesy grin flashed.

"Trust me, you aren't an easy person to ignore."

She scowled, but mirth shimmered underneath. "And again, thanks for that."

"Anytime. You can always count on me." His gaze traveled back to the door. "Who is she?" He smirked. He was starting to like his Batman voice.

"That, my dear brother, is Lizzie."

Interesting. The way Lizzie had stayed with him, then called him out about Olivia, triggered a curiosity about her. "I take it we're close?"

Olivia chuckled. "You might say that. I tend to pair you two for assignments. You work well together."

Careful not to move too quickly, he raised his hand to his face and rubbed his eyes. "Okay. Back up. What kind of assignments and why you?"

"Oh, my dear Charlie, we need to talk." Olivia scooted the chair closer and eased onto it.

His foster sister had changed from his last memory to now. She used to have a hard edge about her, a distance. But something had softened her no-nonsense ways. "What happened to you?"

"Well, I discovered that I had a family all along and finally quit holding back from Mom and Dad."

Whoa. That was huge. He readjusted his position to look at her. "So, you're saying you come to Sunday dinners?"

"Sure do. So does my husband, Wade, our teenage daughter, Amy, and our nine-month-old little guy, Chaz—your namesake."

"You're married and have a son, and you named him after me?"

Olivia nodded.

Charlie never imagined Olivia letting go of the memories that had plagued her for so long. He'd loved her like a sister since the day she came to live with his family, but she'd always held herself at arm's length, especially after his sister, Shana died. Olivia had finally put the past to rest. His sister, married with kids. Wow. A lump lodged in his throat. And she'd named her son after him.

He froze. "Wait. Teenage daughter?"

Her smile widened. "She's Wade's daughter, and she's pretty amazing. You adore her." Olivia filled him in on the family updates over the past four years.

How had he forgotten his niece and nephew? It didn't matter that he had gotten his brain scrambled—a doting uncle would remember. Wouldn't he? What else hid in the recesses of his mind? He had questions. Lots of them. But he hesitated to ask, unsure he wanted the answers. He inhaled and winced at the jab of pain from his bruised ribs. "Susan's really gone? And I don't work for Atlanta PD?"

"I'm sorry, Charlie. Yes. After you got hurt, Susan decided she couldn't be a police officer's wife." Olivia shifted and tucked her legs under herself. "And you left Atlanta PD soon after your injury."

Unbelievable. The woman he'd loved and his dream job—poof. Gone. His heart and mind struggled to keep up. Olivia had stopped talking, allowing him to process the information. The news of Susan leaving him hurt, but somewhere deep down he must've known, because after letting the words of her abandonment sink in, they didn't have a stranglehold on him like he expected. Otherwise, why would he find Lizzie so fascinating?

"What happened with APD, and what do I do now?"

"As for Atlanta, you had a hard time with your recovery. I asked..." She paused. "Okay, more like *pushed* you to come work with me as a bodyguard. I—along with Maddy, Haley, and Katie—started the Elite Guardians Agency. You enjoy being the token male on the team." She beamed with amusement.

"After meeting one of your employees, I have no doubt." If all the women were as kind—not to mention as good looking—as Lizzie, he was a very fortunate man.

"Wipe that smug look off your face."

"What?" He pursed his lips, keeping his grin in check.

"They're all taken except Lizzie and Laila."

"Hmm, Lizzie's unattached, huh?"

Olivia rolled her eyes. "Give it a rest, Romeo."

He loved bantering with her. Besides, it kept the emotional hurt from rising to the surface. He adjusted the sheets and stared at his arm. For the first time, the dragon tattoo registered. Not something he would have picked. At least he didn't think so.

He pointed to the ink. "Mind telling me when and why I got this?"

"It's temporary." She trailed her finger over the gnarly tail. "You've been deep undercover for the past five weeks."

"I thought you said I wasn't a cop anymore." The whole thing made his head hurt, literally.

"You're not. EGA works with Mayor Eliza Baker. She's given us law enforcement authority, and requested you for a special assignment. Only a couple of people on the Columbia PD know about it—Quinn and Steven being two. You met them earlier."

Charlie had, but don't ask him to pick them out of a lineup. He hoped this amnesia thing went away fast. He hated living with a black hole where the past four years existed. "Keep it coming."

"You are undercover setting up drug stings. The mayor wants the newest influx of drug dealers taken down before they get a handhold in the city, with the hopes it'll decrease the gang activity as well. She thinks there's a mastermind behind it. Someone's giving these guys unfettered access. The PD can't get a handle on locations, or the people involved."

"Can't blame her for that." He'd seen too many overdoses during his time in uniform. "Do you think my cover was blown?"

"Quinn's confidential informant says no. But..."

He narrowed his gaze at his sister. "Go on."

"Lizzie's not so sure. She pulled you in for backup last night at Dirty Dogs. Let's just say, she's worried that she compromised you."

The possibility of his cover jeopardized sat on his stomach like a bag burrito. "What do you think?"

"I'm not sure. She's going undercover as your girlfriend to see what she can find out."

"She's doing what?" Charlie's head exploded in pain. His senses went into overdrive. The scent of the hospital disinfectant roiled his stomach, and the whirl of the infusion pump hammered his ears. He lay still, praying the onslaught ceased.

Olivia stood, leaned over him, and brushed the hair from his forehead. "Chill, bro. Just breathe. Lizzie can handle herself."

He might not remember his current assignment, but he knew the dangers of undercover work in the drug world. During his stint with APD, they'd pulled him in on multiple assignments. Undercover work was not his favorite thing to do, but his superiors had praised his work and had practically begged him to do it full-time. But he'd known his limits, and those jobs had pushed him to the edge of his sanity.

The agony subsided, and Olivia returned to her seat and continued with her info dump of his life. Her words were as foreign to him as if she spoke another language, but at least he had context for the present.

When she stopped, she patted his hand. "You're exhausted. Go to sleep—I'll be here if you need anything." Olivia snuggled deeper into the easy chair.

The door burst open. "I don't believe it," Quinn said.

"Shh. Tone it down. Don't you know what it's like to have a concussion?" Olivia pierced the other man with a glare.

"Sorry." The big guy cringed.

"Spit it out, Quinn." That was his sister's no-nonsense attitude Charlie remembered.

"I have the lab results. The syringe had a lethal dose of heroin. If that guy succeeded, you'd be dead, dude."

"And that, Charlie, is our tactless Quinn," Olivia huffed.

"So, Lizzie's out there with a killer." Charlie's mind whirled from the hit on the head and the fact that the sweet woman who'd sat beside him and comforted him had put her life on the line to find the person who wanted him dead.

"Maybe." Quinn rubbed the stubble on his jaw. "I'm just not sure."

Great. If his carelessness had compromised his cover, and Lizzie approached the wrong person...

4

FRIDAY, 6:00 P.M

How had Charlie lived with this scum for so long? The sour smell of the garbage-lined streets was enough to send Lizzie running—forget about the drugs around every corner.

She took a deep breath to settle her racing pulse then put an extra swing in her step and popped her gum like she hadn't a care in the world. Her short leather skirt rode high on her thighs. Of course, that attracted the attention of the local gross boys. Their inspecting gazes gave her the willies. She cringed and resisted the urge to race home and put on sweats even in the eighty-degree weather with high humidity.

"If those guys don't stop looking at you like a slab of meat, I'm going to have to come in and haul you out of there." Quinn's grumble filtered through the earpiece that Steven had given her.

The men had set up surveillance in an empty storage room above the store in the middle of the block and had eyes and ears on her. She was grateful for the backup, but if Quinn didn't rein in his irritable self...ugh.

She flipped her hair and chomped her gum, hiding her words from the neighborhood riffraff. "Get a grip, dude."

"Don't dude me. Maddy will kill me if something happens to you."

Lizzie grinned. The man had a point. Mr. Big Bad Detective was afraid of his wife's temper. She didn't blame him. Maddy was a force to be reckoned with if someone threatened her family. And EGA, beyond everything else, was family.

A catcall halted her stroll down the sidewalk.

"Hey, hot stuff." The man who'd whistled leaned against a brick building, arms crossed over his chest.

She looked the grungy man up and down. "Hey, handsome." Lizzie swallowed a gag.

"A pretty thing like you shouldn't be walking the streets alone. Maybe I can help with that." He pushed off the building and sauntered toward her.

Her fingers twitched to slide her hand behind her back and grab her Glock. But since the guy was talking, she might as well see if he knew anything. "Don't think I need help..." She raised a brow in question.

"Lucas."

She added a little sultry to her tone. "Well, Lucas. I'm looking for my boyfriend. Rod."

"Shoulda known. That guy has all the luck."

And what did Lucas mean by that? The idea of women throwing themselves at Charlie irritated her. "Have you seen him?"

"Sorry. Haven't done business with him in several days."

"Guess I'll keep looking."

"Let me know if you need a shoulder to cry on." The guy looked like a lion, ready to devour his prey.

She smiled and gave him a small wave, then continued down the street. "Can I just say...ick."

Quinn snorted. "Lucas is on my radar, but I can't see him lying about seeing Charlie. He's a dealer, but low level from what we can tell."

"Got it." Lizzie scanned the area. A couple of alleys she'd investigate, but the normal trash and nasty smells filled her path. "Heading into that side street."

"Be careful. If you go in, we won't have eyes."

She rolled hers. "Yes, Dad."

Steven chuckled in the background. Quinn's partner and Haley's new husband's calm demeanor was a nice contrast to Quinn's grizzly bear attitude.

Lizzie rounded the corner and peered down the dimly lit alley—a dumpster and wooden crates, the perfect places to hide. After only few steps in, the hair on her neck prickled. Her gaze roamed the shadowed corners. She spun to leave and bumped into a man's chest. When he grabbed her upper arms, she bit back a scream.

A wicked skull and crossbones tattoo on his forearm stared back at her.

"Lizzie, what's happening?" The worry in Quinn's voice was evident. She had to respond before the guys rushed in.

Sweat beaded at her hairline, and her heart raced. "Oh, sorry. I didn't mean to run into you." Lizzie focused her attention on the man staring at her.

His hands remained on her biceps. "My bad. You look lost." The man's eyes narrowed.

She forced the corners of her mouth into a smile. "Lookin' for my man. That's all."

"And who might that be?" The steel in his voice sent shivers darting up her spine.

Get it together, Lizzie. Do your job.

"Rod." She huffed. "He took off yesterday and hasn't come home."

"Is that right?" The guy loosened his grip but didn't remove his hands.

Get the info and get out. "Have you seen him?"

"Yup."

She waited for more details, but he stood there. His silence upped her irritation. "So. Are you going to tell me where?"

"Maybe. Depends."

Oh, for heaven's sake. Lizzie yanked away. The man had gone from frightening to infuriating. "On what?"

"Easy, Lizzie."

She snapped her arms across her chest to cover her flinch at the voice in her ear. She'd forgotten all about Quinn.

"On if I believe you're his girlfriend." The man's muscles flexed under his black T-shirt.

"Listen. Your glowing-eyed skull and crossbones look really tough and all." She popped her head to the side and gave him a sassy look. *Come on, Quinn, a name to go with that tattoo would be good right about now.*

"Jimmy. His name is Jimmy. Big dealer in the area."

Thank you, Quinn. "But I'm sure Rod wouldn't like you harassing his woman. Would he, Jimmy?" She drew out his name.

Jimmy smirked. "No, guess not." He relaxed and leaned his shoulder against the building. "Funny. He never mentioned a girl."

Lizzie let out a long sigh. "I've been in Atlanta on and off, firming up some, shall we say, business." She glared at him and added attitude to her words. "Not my fault you haven't seen me when I've been in town."

"Yeah, you're Rod's girl all right. Only he'd put up with a sass like you."

"What can I say? I'm worth it." She smoothed her hair. "Now, are you going to answer my question or not. Have you seen Rod?"

"My apologies. Needed to make sure you were who you said you were. Can't have him exposed, if you know what I mean."

She tapped her foot, unwilling to say more and make Jimmy suspicious.

"Saw him around midnight last night. When we parted ways, he went that way." Jimmy pointed down the street toward Charlie's undercover apartment.

"Now, see? Was that so hard?" Lizzie popped her gum. "Thanks, Jimmy." She waggled her fingers and put distance between herself and the drug dealer. Half a block later, she released a pent-up breath.

"I'd prefer you didn't do that again." Quinn's words raked across her nerves.

"You and me both." She hadn't given Charlie enough credit for his ability to work in these conditions. "Hey, we got somewhere. Sounds like Jimmy might have been the last person to see Charlie before his attack."

"Maybe. But I agree with my confidential informant. I think Charlie's cover is intact. Once Jimmy was convinced you were Rod's girlfriend, he cooperated."

She agreed with Charlie. She, too, hated undercover work in the drug world. "Unless he's setting me up."

"Nah. Jimmy likes to handle things himself."

"Oh, that's nice to know." Lizzie's imagination ran wild at all the horrible things Jimmy would do and had to get a grip on those thoughts. "Hold on. I see Charlie's car." She took a couple steps closer. What if it *was* a setup? Only one way to find out. She moved to the vehicle and peered into the sedan.

"Anything?"

If Quinn didn't stop with the chatter, she'd make his life miserable. "Stop bugging for a second. Let me do my job."

"How does Charlie put up with her?" Quinn grumbled.

"I heard that."

"Wasn't trying to hide it." His snarky teasing tone made her smile.

Her gaze traveled over the small parking area and caught sight of a man standing next to the apartment building on the far side. Had she seen him before or were her eyes playing tricks on her? She shook off the odd sensation and continued her scan of the shops lining the opposite side of the street. A couple mom-and-pop-type establishments with bars over the windows. *Ah ha.* A liquor store with an ATM. She meandered to the entrance. Yup. Just as she suspected. A camera.

Time to put Quinn and Steven to work getting the recordings. She passed on the information and took one last look around. Something about the man in the distance continued to nag at her. Her gaze drifted in his direction, but he was gone.

Lizzie retraced her steps to her rental car, acting like she didn't have a care in the world. But something was off. Her sixth sense had kicked in two blocks back. In her line of work, she'd learned to trust those internal warnings. She slowed. Her burner phone in hand, she itched to call for backup. Instead, she dropped her hand into her bag and pulled out a tube of lipstick. She punched the camera button on the phone, switched it to face her, and lifted it. With a clear view behind her, she swiped the purple color over her lips, searching the area.

She came up empty.

But she knew, without a doubt, eyes followed her every move.

Once his body agreed to let him, Charlie planned to get out of here and go back to his job. Whatever that meant. A bodyguard? Really? His entire life, he'd wanted to be a cop. Olivia *had* said the mayor granted them law enforcement privileges, and that gave him a sense of relief about his new choice in careers.

His body aches had nothing on his brain fog. How did someone forget four years of his life? Charlie adjusted the head of his bed and groaned. The gunshot wound hadn't hurt this bad. He froze. A flicker of recollection danced on the edge of his memory. Being shot, his time in the hospital, and his ex's grand exit had poked through the haze. Not the greatest of moments from his past, but at least *something* had returned. He dug the heels of his palms into his eyes, pushing against the pulsing ache.

Charlie grasped the TV remote looped around the bed rail and stared at the black screen on the wall. The temptation to turn it on and lose himself in mind-numbing drivel had him pondering the sensibility of the action. Doc said low lighting and no screens. Yeah, well, what was he supposed to do? Sit here and wonder about his life? That made his brain hurt too. Charlie gave the remote a toss. It clanged against the metal rail, sending daggers shooting through his head. *Don't do that again.*

"Quit tearing up the hospital equipment."

Charlie shifted his gaze to the doorway. "Hey, Olivia."

"Hey, yourself. What did the remote do to you?" His sister strolled in and plopped on the chair beside his bed.

"I'm just sick of lying here doing nothing." Charlie picked at the medical tape on his arm that held the bandage in place.

Olivia rested her hand over his. "I heard Lizzie and the guys are on their way to the hospital. You up for shop talk?"

As if he'd even know what they were talking about, but it

was better than staying in the dark. He might as well get a handle on what his life looked like now. "Of course."

The door burst open. A short brunette with purple streaks in her long brown hair and a shorter than appropriate leather skirt came stomping in.

"Now I remember why I hate undercover drug ops." The woman shuddered.

He squinted, getting a better look. "Lizzie?"

"Hey, Hotshot. Looking good."

He narrowed his gaze. "Yeah, and the Queen of England is twenty-five."

Lizzie rolled her eyes. "Same old Charlie."

"Thank you."

"It wasn't a compliment." She folded her arms across her chest. "Olivia, do something about your brother."

His sister chuckled. "It's nice to see that some things never change with you two."

Charlie's lips curved upward. Bantering with Lizzie felt familiar, and he'd take anything that fell into that category.

He flicked his finger up and down at her outfit. "I'm assuming you don't normally dress that way."

She smoothed her skirt and flipped her hair over her shoulder. "What? Don't like it?"

"I..." How did he answer that? He had to admit, he liked it a little too much. "Um..."

Olivia snorted.

He looked at her silently, begging for help. "Olivia?"

"Nope. You're on your own there, little brother."

Lizzie waved her hand, seeming oblivious to his internal struggle. "Don't answer that. I feel like I'm on display. Sure hope Addy doesn't see me like this."

"Addy?"

"My twelve-year-old daughter."

She had a kid? Olivia said Lizzie wasn't married, so there had to be a story there. "Yeah, that wouldn't be good." He shifted on the bed and bit back a moan. Stupid bruised ribs.

A knock on the door and Quinn stepped in. "Hey, man. These two driving you crazy yet?" Mischief twinkled in his eyes.

"Huh-uh, no way. I'm not going there." He had no recollection of Lizzie, but he knew Olivia. Not stepping in that pile of doggie doo.

Quinn nodded. "Smart man."

Charlie relaxed onto his pillow and returned his attention to Lizzie. "Did you find out anything while playing my girlfriend?"

"You sure you're up for this?" Lizzie collapsed against the wall.

"I might not remember my assignment, but at least I can start from here and be helpful."

"I ran into several of your *good buddies* out there. Can I say, *yuck*? Anyway. I met Jimmy. From what I can tell, I think your cover is intact."

"I concur," Quinn said. "Word on the street is that you've gone dark, but no one seems to know that you were attacked."

"That's a relief." From what Olivia had told him, his assignment held high hopes for taking down a major drug ring.

Lizzie pushed off the wall and paced the small room. "If your cover wasn't blown, then who did this?" She turned to Quinn. "Could it be the two guys from the bar?"

"I don't see how. They were in custody when it happened." Quinn scratched the stubble on his jaw. "Unless they called in reinforcements, but I can't see it. They don't want the attention."

"Any news from the gang unit? Does it have anything to do with the two dead guys?"

Quinn shook his head. "Not that they can find. The two events seem to have no connection. Just odd timing."

Lizzie threw her hands in the air. "So, some random dude walks up to Charlie and beats him for no reason?"

"Lizzie." Olivia's warning tone halted Lizzie mid rant.

Lizzie bit her lip. "Sorry. What about the video footage? Any luck getting your hands on that?"

"We're working on it," Quinn said.

"Wait. What video?" Charlie glanced at Olivia.

She shrugged.

Good, he wasn't the only one clueless here.

Lizzie moved next to Olivia, making it easier for him to focus on her. "I spotted an ATM with a camera across the street from your car. I'm hoping it'll give us a clue as to who did this to you. Or at least help narrow down the time you were attacked."

Wouldn't that be nice? "I want to see it."

Olivia grasped his hand. "Doc said no screen time."

"Don't play mom with me. I want to watch it. I'm a part of this whether I like it or not." His voice rose, and the tension in the crown of his head tightened like a vise.

"I know you are." She squeezed his hand.

His sister was only trying to help. But the blank gap in his memory made him edgy. "Maybe it'll help me remember."

"I'll make a copy and send it to Lizzie," Quinn said, "and cc you as well."

"Thanks." Charlie appreciated the man's willingness to include him.

A nurse pushed a wheelchair inside the room and eased the door shut behind her. "Olivia, you asked me to keep an eye out. There's a man out there asking about a drug dealer that was brought in this morning."

Olivia rose, her body rigid. "Did you tell him anything?"

The nurse shook her head. "No way. Rhonda told him she couldn't divulge any information about patients, but he hasn't left. He keeps watching the hallway."

Lizzie hurried to the door and peeked out. She spun. "We need to get Charlie out of here."

"What's wrong?" Quinn stood toe to toe with her.

"I have a bad feeling this guy followed me to the hospital."

"Why do you say that?"

"I swear I saw him while I searched Charlie's undercover neighborhood. I never talked to him. He stayed on the periphery. There's something about him that caught my attention, but I can't put my finger on it."

Olivia turned to the nurse. "Dani?"

"I have room 302 on the third floor that you can move him to." The nurse pointed to the wheelchair.

"Thanks, Dani."

"Charlie?" Concern laced Olivia's features.

Charlie had no idea how he'd make it out of bed without falling, but what choice did he have? "Let's do it."

"Quinn, help him get situated in the wheelchair. Lizzie, you're now officially his bodyguard."

"I don't think—"

"It's not up for discussion, Lizzie. You're his partner, and he needs someone who can help him with his memory. And that's you."

Lizzie's shoulders drooped. "You know I'll do everything in my power to keep him safe."

Charlie wanted to protest his need for protection, but his sister's tone told him he'd waste his breath with that argument. Besides, he wouldn't mind time getting to know Lizzie...again.

Olivia and Lizzie huddled by the door and talked, giving him privacy while Quinn helped him into the wheelchair and nurse Dani fixed his IV and covered him with a blanket. Sweat beaded on Charlie's forehead, and his stomach did flip-flops.

Quinn knelt beside him. "You okay? You don't look so hot."

"Just get me upstairs," Charlie snapped. He hadn't intended to bite Quinn's head off, but he was miserable. Bruised ribs were annoying, but concussions were the worst. "Sorry."

Quinn chuckled. "Trust me. I was much worse after my legs were smashed under that backhoe. Just ask everyone at EGA."

Another story Charlie couldn't remember. He'd ask later, but right now, he wanted to be horizontal in a bad way.

Quinn stood and took charge. "All right, ladies, here's the plan. Olivia, you, Dani, and I will go out and keep the creep's attention away from this room. Lizzie, since you're still dressed in your getup, you get Charlie upstairs. If you're caught, you can pretend to be his girlfriend again."

"Sounds like a plan." Lizzie moved behind Charlie.

Olivia pinned him and Lizzie with a glare. "Don't get caught." She grabbed Quinn's arm. "Come on."

Alone in the room with Lizzie, he tucked his chin and closed his eyes. "I hope this works."

"You and me both." She wheeled him to the doorway and peered out. "Keep your head down."

"As if I can do anything else." He prayed he'd make it to the third floor without losing his lunch.

"Hang in there, Hotshot. It's show time." Lizzie pushed him out of the room.

He hoped the man didn't notice them leave. Because Charlie didn't have it in him to do much more than hold on and pray that they made it to their destination unnoticed.

He slammed his hand on the kitchen counter and pressed the phone to his ear. "What do you mean, you failed—again?" How hard was it to kill someone?

"A girl came in and caught Donny before he injected the heroin into the dude's arm."

"That's no excuse." He ran a hand through his hair. "If he regains his memory and identifies me or remembers hearing the plan, you're dead. Even if I have to do it myself."

"Donny was freaked out and couldn't tell me the room number. I went back later and asked around, but never found him."

"You asked around?" He was surrounded by incompetent fools. "I suggest you figure out how to finish the job." He jabbed the end button on his phone and threw it across the room. The device landed on the couch and bounced to the floor. He placed his hands on the counter and hung his head. How had his life ended up here? He missed his family something fierce.

The men who'd started the chain of events he was living deserved to pay. Along with the prosecuting attorney who'd dropped the ball and let the slime bags walk.

Not enough evidence to convict.

As if.

They should have created the evidence and taken those punks down.

Anger bubbled and heat climbed up his neck. The pressure built in his head like a volcano ready to explode.

He vowed to get revenge even if it was the last thing he ever did.

5

SUNDAY, 4:00 P.M

Grateful the doctors had released Charlie to her care, Lizzie relaxed as she drove through town. The past two days had been the longest of Lizzie's life. Once she'd moved Charlie to the undisclosed room, the team had provided around-the-clock hospital protection as he recovered. Each member had taken turns monitoring the hallway, but she and Olivia had had the task of sitting with him in his room. The poor guy hadn't had a moment of peace since he'd arrived at the hospital.

The man they'd spotted asking about Charlie had disappeared, but no one had let their guard down.

The nurses had given a description of the man, but nobody had paid enough attention until it was too late. And the fact he'd worn a baseball cap that hid a good look at his face hadn't helped. Steven had checked the security footage and found nothing to go on. The attacker had avoided the cameras, and the video only caught a partial view of him when he'd tilted his head. The man remained a mystery. Even Quinn hadn't recognized him.

Lizzie pulled into her drive and put her car into park. The team had decided that since Charlie's undercover work had no connection to her and her security system was one of the best, he'd be more comfortable at her house. Plus, it allowed her to be with Addy and not in a safe house away from her daughter.

She placed her hand on Charlie's arm. "Wait. I'll come around."

"I'm not an invalid." Charlie's bruises and the pain lingering behind his eyes told a different story.

"Humor me." She slipped from the driver's seat and jogged around the car.

He'd already opened his door and swung his legs out.

"I see some things haven't changed." She held out her hand. He took it and pulled to a standing position. "You still don't listen."

"I listened." His grip tightened, and he clutched the doorframe with his other hand.

"Keep telling yourself that." The crazy man would have been out of the car, or at least tried to be, if she'd hadn't hurried around. She scanned the neighborhood. Doubtful danger lurked around the corner, but Olivia had trusted Charlie's safety to her and Lizzie refused to take the job lightly. "You ready?"

"Yeah. I think so." After a few steps, he found his balance and walked up her pink azalea-lined pathway without assistance.

"Let me." Lizzie unlocked the door and swung it open. "Go on in."

He cautiously stepped over the threshold. Charlie had told her that his ribs and other bruises ached, but it was the headache from his concussion, along with occasional issues with balance, that hung on. Plus, the doctor warned of fatigue for a few days due to the blood loss from the gash on his head and the delay in treatment. So, she stayed by his elbow to intervene just in case.

Once inside, she shut the door and flipped the lock. Some called her paranoid, but she'd seen too much on the job to be lax about something like leaving an entrance unlocked.

Charlie scanned the interior. "Nice place."

She started to remind him that he'd visited plenty of times for planning sessions and EGA get-togethers but stopped herself. No need to frustrate him any more than he already was. "Thank you."

Feet pounded on the wood floors. Addy came running through the room. "Uncle Charlie!"

Her daughter flung herself at him. Lizzie caught her around the waist just in time to prevent the impact. "Whoa, girl. Remember what we talked about? Uncle Charlie isn't feeling well. We need to take it easy around him and avoid loud noises. Got it?"

"Got it," Addy whispered. "Sorry, Uncle Charlie."

"It's okay." He stuck out his hand. "It's a pleasure to meet you."

Her daughter gave him a quizzical look then shook his hand.

"Go help your grandma with dinner," Lizzie said. "I'll join you as soon as I get Uncle Charlie settled in the den." Lizzie shooed Addy toward the kitchen. "Sorry about that."

He waved a hand, dismissing her apology. "Cute kid."

"She adores you."

A flash of regret washed over his face. "The feeling is mutual, I'm sure. Just wish I could remember."

"It'll come back. Don't force it."

"Right." He didn't look convinced, and she couldn't blame him.

She motioned toward the hallway. "Come on. Let's get you settled, then I'll bring you an early dinner. I'm sure you're hungry."

"A little." Charlie followed her to the den.

"Here." She pointed to a sage green recliner that sat next to the red gingham sofa. "Thought the recliner would be best, but if you'd like, the couch pulls out into a queen-size bed."

"The recliner sounds good." He lowered himself onto the seat.

"What can I get you?" Lizzie's heart ached for the man. They had partnered enough times to become best friends. A dark cloud of regret washed over her. She'd missed his call for help all because of a careless act of not charging her phone. When would she learn to make better choices?

"Nothing for now." His eyes drooped. "Mind if I rest for a bit?"

"Go for it. I'll fix you a plate. When you're ready, you can eat."

Eyes closed, he nodded.

Lizzie watched him for a moment, then tiptoed from the room and joined her mother and daughter in the kitchen.

"What's wrong with Uncle Charlie?" Addy asked. "He looks terrible."

Lizzie choked back a laugh. "Yes, he does. But don't let him hear you say that." She snatched a slice of apple from the tray her mom had fixed. The sweet juice exploded on her taste buds. She grabbed another.

"Momma?" Addy's fists went to her hips.

"Sorry." Apparently, Lizzie was hungrier than she thought. Her gaze met Addy's. She'd promised to always be honest with her daughter. Even if she'd used age-appropriate terms during

Addy's younger years. But now that she was almost a teenager, Addy insisted that Lizzie not sugarcoat things anymore. "Aunt Olivia assigned me to Charlie. He's my client right now. He was beaten up a couple of days ago and has lost part of his memory."

"Someone beat him up? And now you're guarding him? And he doesn't know who he is?" Addy's eyes widened a fraction more with each question. "You didn't tell me all of that, just that he was hurt."

"I know. I was in a hurry when we talked. I'm sorry about that." Lizzie grabbed a grape and popped it into her mouth. "But, yes, I'm his bodyguard. He remembers who he is, he just can't remember the last few years. So, he doesn't remember us."

Addy scowled. "Will he get his memory back?"

"We hope so. He's remembered a few little things already. Just be patient with him. Treat him like the same Uncle Charlie, and he'll remember you, in time." At least Lizzie hoped so. "Just don't tackle him like you usually do."

"Got it."

The three moved around the kitchen in sync, finishing a small smorgasbord-type dinner. Lizzie loved her little family. At times she wished for more, but she'd never put another man at risk by loving him.

"Come on, Momma. Let's go see him." Addy filled her plate and one for Charlie with all his favorite things, then hustled toward the den.

"That girl." Lizzie's mother, Helen, tsked then smiled. "Charlie will have no choice but to remember her."

"I better go referee. He might have no recollection of us, but in most ways, he's still the same ol' Charlie." Lizzie grabbed her food and followed her daughter's path.

Muted chatter flowed down the hallway. Lizzie entered the den and stopped. Addy had dug out a wooden TV tray table for

Charlie and now sat crossed-legged on the floor, balancing her plate and jabbering away about her first week of school. Charlie hung on her every word, asking questions like he truly wanted to know about the life of a preteen. Not that he hadn't cared pre-beating, but she didn't remember him being so focused like this before. Lizzie continued to the couch and joined their little group.

"And then Kenny bumped into me." Addy pointed her carrot stick at Charlie. "He's not very nice." She shoved the vegetable into her mouth and chewed.

"I hate to tell you this, Addy, but he likes you." Charlie smirked.

"Well, that doesn't make sense."

"Boys aren't very smart at times."

Addy cocked her head and scrunched her forehead. A few moments later, she shrugged. "Guess not."

Lizzie bit the inside of her cheek to keep from laughing. The conversation moved from Kenny to school activities that interested Addy. Enjoying her daughter's animated explanations, Lizzie stayed quiet and listened. Charlie's unwavering attention fascinated her. In the past, he'd teased Addy and played with her, but never had he listened so intently.

After they finished their dinners, Lizzie gathered their plates.

Addy moved the TV tray to the side of Charlie's chair and pulled the lever for him to raise his footrest. "Want to play Mario Kart, Uncle Charlie?"

Her sweet girl intended to make sure her favorite uncle was well taken care of.

"I don't think Doc would be too happy with me if I played video games." Charlie took a sip of his drink and set it on the small table.

Addy scrambled to the bookcase and pulled out her go-to game. "How about a game of Uno?"

"Hold on, honey. Charlie and I have work to do. Besides, we don't want to tire him out."

"Ah, Mom." Her daughter's face fell.

"Work can wait," Charlie said.

Lizzie's jaw dropped.

"Addy here needs to feel the agony of defeat." Charlie rubbed his hands together and made the *mwa-ha-ha-ha* sound of an evil villain.

"In your dreams." Addy pulled a chair over and shuffled the cards on the TV tray.

Lizzie stared at the odd occurrence. Charlie always gave Addy attention, and the man loved to have fun, but when work called, playtime ended. Work came first. No exception. Almost like an obsession. It was the one area in his life that his serious side surfaced. The fact he'd offered to play with Addy—when he knew they had security footage to watch—puzzled her. Another mystery circling Charlie. She shook her head and returned the dishes to the kitchen.

Lizzie cleaned the counter and put away the extra food. After confirming the kitchen was tidy, she wandered back to the den and smiled at the giggles filling the room. Might as well be productive while she waited. She sat at her desk and checked her emails then prepped the video that she and Charlie planned to watch.

She rolled her shoulders and stretched her neck from one side to the other. A quick glance at her cell phone told her she'd better encourage an end to the card game.

"Woohoo! I won!" Addy jumped up and did a victory dance.

Charlie cringed at the loud proclamation. "You sure did."

"Sorry," Addy whispered.

"It's okay, kiddo. But I think it's time for a break. And your mom looks like she's ready to work."

Addy gathered the cards and put them away. "Thanks for playing with me." She kissed Charlie on the cheek then hugged Lizzie. "I like this new Charlie," she whispered in her ear then skipped out of the room.

Charlie rested his head back on the recliner and closed his eyes. "That girl has energy."

Lizzie chuckled. "That she does. You doing okay?"

"Yeah, just a little tired."

"Do you want to watch the video then take a nap, or rest first?" Lizzie knew her opinion. A few hours post hospital release, the man should rest, but she'd let him decide.

Silence filled the room. Had he fallen asleep? Lizzie rose from her seat. She'd sneak out and let him rest.

"Video."

She halted. "Excuse me?"

"Let's watch the video."

Retracing her steps, she grabbed her laptop and connected it to the TV with a long HDMI cable, then claimed the end of the couch closest to him. "I have it cued up." She balanced the device on her lap and clicked on the TV.

Charlie rubbed his temples.

The pain etched across his face worried her. "You sure about this?"

"Yes. It's only a small headache, and I want to see if I can figure out who did this to me."

Alrighty then. Lizzie hit play. "There's your car. No one appears to be anywhere near it."

The recording continued, showing nothing except Charlie's undercover sedan. Then several minutes later, he walked into view.

Charlie pushed himself forward in the chair and pointed.

"There I am. I don't seem to be concerned." The on-screen Charlie stopped and turned. He scanned the area and slinked out of sight.

She paused the recording.

"I saw or heard something over in that area." He pointed to a space off-screen. "But I have no idea what." Charlie rubbed his eyes.

"Relax. It was a long shot. Quinn and Steven have been all over this video. They didn't really think we'd find anything." Lizzie unhooked the cable and put her laptop back on her desk. "At least it gave us a feel for the situation. You need to lie low and recover. The team can investigate for you."

"No way."

Lizzie spun to face him. "No?"

"I want in. I want to go back there and see if it jogs my memory."

"That's not a good idea." In fact, it reeked of a bad one. They had no clue who had targeted him.

"Lizzie, come on. I can't live like this. I have to do something."

"Not this."

"I can call an Uber if I have to." He folded his arms across his chest, grimaced, and dropped them to his side.

She glared at him. The man was stubborn, she'd give him that. But how would she feel if it were her? She and Charlie had the same work ethic. Sitting on the sidelines was not her style or his. Lizzie finally nodded. "For the record, I'm not in favor of this. But I'll call Laila for backup, and we'll go in the morning."

"No. No backup."

"I really think—"

"Lizzie. It's bad enough that you see me like this. I don't want the rest of the team feeling sorry for me."

"They wouldn't do that."

"Maybe not, but I'd feel like they were. I don't want anyone's pity. Besides, I only want to look around. We won't stay long."

Charlie had opened up more in the last minute about his insecurities than he'd done in the last three years. Most people wouldn't think anything of his admission, but to her it was huge.

"All right, but if I say we're leaving, you won't argue."

"Deal. Thank you."

"I'll see you in the morning."

Charlie nodded. Seconds later, his eyes drooped closed, and his breathing evened out.

"Get some rest, Hotshot." She tiptoed from the room and eased the door closed. Lizzie slumped against the wall. She agreed with Addy. Lizzie liked this new Charlie. The one who admitted his feelings and didn't hide them behind humor. And the way he'd treated her daughter...

She exhaled. If her past didn't hang over her life like a storm cloud ready to burst—

No, she refused to go there.

She should ask for backup. Olivia had tasked her with Charlie's safety, and she intended to do her job. Backup was usually included in that job description. But she also trusted Charlie and if he said they didn't need backup, then she'd go with it.

She just hoped she hadn't made an irresponsible decision. If Charlie got himself killed by returning to where it all began because of her choice not to ask the team for help, she'd never recover.

MONDAY, 10:00 A.M.

Charlie took in the unfamiliar neighborhood as Lizzie maneuvered down the street. Whiskey bottles littered the gutters, drugs slipped from one hand to another, and in the distance, gang members chilled on the steps of a nearby apartment building, taunting people who walked by.

A career in law enforcement had been Charlie's choice and he'd never looked back. He had many reasons for agreeing to work in this world of immorality, not the least of which included the desire to make sure innocent people stayed exactly that way. Innocent. Untouched. With the ability to sleep at night without nightmares stalking their dreams. If he said all that out loud, it would come across as heroic and noble. And he was neither. It was just what he'd chosen to do.

Lizzie parked several spots over from his undercover sedan that he'd seen in the video. He assumed it had sat where he'd left it just over three days ago. Charlie hefted himself from the rental car, and his head pounded from the glare of the midmorning sun.

Had it really been that long? He gingerly patted the stitches on his forehead. The lump remained, but he'd discarded the bandage in an attempt not to bring more attention to his injuries. Like that was going to happen. But the baseball cap Lizzie had found for him helped conceal his stitches. He'd worn grunge clothes and Lizzie had donned her biker bar outfit in hopes they'd look like the perfect drug dealing couple.

"Doing okay over there?" Lizzie closed the driver's side door.

Not really. My head is pounding, I'm looking for the person who tried to kill me, and I can't remember the last four years of my life. Other than that, I'm perfect. He met her gaze. "Yeah. I'm good." Had she just rolled her eyes at him? "Let's do this."

Lizzie rounded the car and hooked her hand inside the crook of his elbow. "Then come on, big daddy. Your audience awaits you, Chuck."

Now it was his turn to roll his eyes before he glared at her. "I know I've never gone by that name."

She laughed then pulled a pair of sunglasses from her pocket and handed them to him. "Looks like you might need these."

"Thanks." He slid on the glasses and sighed with relief. His headache had dulled over the last day or so, but lights and loud noises continued to bother him. "Are you always this easygoing?"

She snorted. "I don't think anyone has ever called me easy-going. But if you're asking if I talk a lot, then yes. I'm pretty much a *what you see is what you get* type girl."

He studied her for a moment. "Nope. I don't think so. I think you let people see only what you want them to see."

A moment of panic flashed in Lizzie's eyes then vanished. She smiled and jerked her head toward the street. "Come on, Hotshot."

The twinkle in her eyes had him wondering about the woman next to him. Oh, she was hiding something from the world. But her sassiness intrigued him. Actually, it was more than that. He found her attractive, which confused him. Shouldn't he be pining over his ex-fiancée? But Susan had left him to fend for himself hours after surgery for a bullet wound four years ago—at least according to his sister and his muddy memories—and he felt nothing for his ex. Not even a twinge of regret for his thoughts. Another hidden piece of his life that made no sense.

Lizzie squeezed his arm and flashed him a smile. One that made his insides do funny things.

Focus, Charlie.

He walked next to Lizzie, searching for suspicious faces or anything that triggered a memory. There had to be something. The screaming baby ten feet ahead. The rotten garbage strung along the gutter. Two men huddled at the edge of a building exchanging money and goods.

An odd sense of tension built between his shoulder blades.

"I know you have bruised ribs and a concussion, but if Quinn is to be believed, Rod has swagger. You look stiff and on edge."

"Got it." Charlie rolled his neck side to side and exhaled. He'd better get his act together if they planned to pull this off. Snaking his arm around Lizzie's waist, he leaned in. His nose inches from hers. "Ah, baby, don't worry your little head." He nuzzled her cheek.

"Watch it, buster," she whispered between clenched teeth.

Charlie laughed, then grabbed his ribs and groaned.

"Glad you find this funny." Lizzie scowled. But mirth lingered behind her reaction.

"What can I say? You're fun to tease." He flicked his hand toward the corner store. "Let's stop over there and take a look at the area from that angle."

They snuggled together and meandered to the building.

Lizzie ran her gaze over the area. "We're out of the range of the camera, but there's no place to go beyond up and down the sidewalk."

"What about farther down?" He tilted his head and caught sight of an alley. "There. Let's check that out."

They stopped at the entrance and peered down the side street. Shadows danced along the edges. Wooden crates lay haphazard in the path, and the stench of stale beer and cigarette smoke assaulted his senses. But the tingle on his scalp had him on high alert.

Lizzie tensed beside him. "You remember something?"

Had he? "Not exactly. It's more of an impression than a memory."

"Go with it. Talk it out."

"Walking down the sidewalk, it felt familiar in an odd sort of way. But here..." His cop days screamed at him to put his back against the brick wall, giving him a full view of his surroundings. He shifted and listened to his instincts. "This is where my anxiety hits full force." He closed his eyes, pushing his mind to connect the dots. "I have no idea why. I just can't remember." The pounding behind his eyes increased, and the vise over the top of his head tightened. His hands flew to his head. His stomach churned.

"Charlie. Stop it." Lizzie's hands covered his. "You can't do this to yourself. It'll come with time."

White lights streaked behind his eyelids.

Arms encircled him. "Breathe through the pain."

Forming a response to her soft assurance was impossible. Charlie inhaled through his nose as deep as his aching ribs allowed and blew out air through pursed lips. If his head wasn't protesting with a vengeance, he'd be mortified at showing this level of vulnerability.

"Let it pass. Don't power through." Her petite hand rubbed circles on his back.

What seemed like hours later, still in Lizzie's arms, he opened his eyes, determined to move slowly and not set his world spinning again.

Lizzie patted his arm and took two steps back. "The doctor told you not to force the memories."

"I just hate the blank spot in my brain. It makes me feel...I don't know how to explain it."

Lizzie tilted her head. "Stick with the stuff you know and the rest will come."

A bang echoed through the alley.

Lizzie hit him with the force of a linebacker and landed on top of him with a grunt.

"Stay down. Don't move." She yanked her Glock from her waistband and scanned the area.

"Did you see where the shot came from?" He tried to twist to see what had happened, but Lizzie had him pinned.

After three deep breaths, she relaxed. "It wasn't a gunshot. It must have been a car backfiring. Sorry that I tackled you."

He looked up from his position on the ground. His heart skipped a beat. Lizzie was gorgeous, especially in protective mode. "This is working for me. I'll be in danger as long as you want us to be."

She scowled at him. "And there's the old Charlie. I had such high hopes for you." She shook her head. "You're a brat, you know that?"

Ouch. That hurt. He'd never meant to hurt her. "I'm sorry. I shouldn't have said that."

Lizzie shook her head. "Charlie, I'm used to your sense of humor."

"Still..." He'd let it drop for now. Charlie rolled his head to the side so he didn't have to look her in the eye, then blinked. A red cylindrical object lay five feet from him, partially hidden under a box. The item looked odd for the dingy alleyway.

"Lizzie, what's that red thing over there?"

She shifted, and he immediately missed her warmth. "Hang on." Lizzie pushed off him and retrieved the object by the tip. "It's a pen from Bobby T's Seafood."

Charlie used the wall to pull himself to a standing position. His head continued to throb, but the nausea had settled. "What is a pen from a high-class restaurant doing in a neighborhood like this?"

"Does seem out of place, doesn't it?"

Charlie joined Lizzie. "We should bag it just in case it's evidence."

She arched a brow. "You really think that will lead anywhere?"

He knew he was grasping at anything to find answers. "Not a clue, but it's worth a look. Let's head to the restaurant and check it out."

"You sure you're up for this? I can ask Laila to run by there."

"I want to do this. I'll be fine." *Please, God, don't make a liar out of me.* His head pounded in time with his heart, and he didn't think this was what the doc had in mind when he'd told Charlie to let his brain heal.

Lizzie shook her head. "If you insist, but I'm not carrying you if you collapse due to stupidity."

"Thanks. I knew I could count on you." He didn't think she had any idea how on target her statement was. But he had to find out who had tried to kill him before the person succeeded.

6

MONDAY, 12:00 P.M

Lizzie needed her head checked for letting Charlie talk her into coming to Bobby T's.

The restaurant buzzed with the activity of the lunch crowd. With parking at a premium, Lizzie circled the block and found a spot near the delivery dock.

"Did you see those cars out front?" Charlie adjusted his sunglasses. She assumed the constant movement kept the metal frames away from the small cut on his cheek. "I mean, I've heard of Bobby T's, but what is this place? The hangout of the rich and famous?"

She shifted the car into park and turned off the engine. "I haven't eaten here. Too pricey for me, but I hear it's good and a local favorite." Lizzie glanced at her outfit then at Charlie's and laughed. "Think they'll let us in?"

Charlie straightened his shirt. "What? Dragged behind a truck isn't fashionable?"

"Come on, smarty pants. Let's go check it out." Lizzie waited for him on the sidewalk. "Doing okay?"

He huffed. "Will you quit asking me that, Mom?"

"All right. No need to snap." The man appeared ready to fold, but refused to admit it. Lizzie promised herself that as soon as they finished, she'd take him home and insist that he rest.

The sun beat down, and the humidity made her wish for a dip in Olivia and Wade's swimming pool. Flowerpots lined the front walkway in front of Bobby T's, and a red awning with white lettering indicated the front entrance.

They strolled over, and Charlie held the door open for her. She brushed past him and perused the interior.

White cloth covered tables with black linen napkins filled the dining area. More high-end than Lizzie had thought. She stepped to the hostess sign and scanned the patrons. Businessmen and women filled multiple tables, but one group in particular caught her attention. She gently nudged Charlie's arm. "Your ten o'clock. A group of councilmen. I recognize a few others from the mayor's office too."

Charlie's gaze found the group. "I don't think any of these people would hang out where we found the pen."

"Not likely." Lizzie weighed her options. Stay and question the workers or get out before one of the councilmen looked their way?

A young lady in black slacks and a white blouse headed their direction.

Charlie placed his hand on the small of Lizzie's back. "So, what's the plan? We stand out like a skunk in a pack of dogs."

Lizzie turned from the group of men at the far table. "We have to get out of here. If I recognized those guys, I bet they'll know us. If your cover isn't blown, it will be if they see you."

"Go. I'm right behind you."

With a nonchalant stride, she pushed through the door. Sensing Charlie following her, she headed straight for her car. Her heart pounded. She sucked in air, attempting to settle her racing pulse.

"Slow down. They didn't see us." He grabbed her arm. "Hey, calm down."

Not now. Lizzie couldn't afford for her anxiety to take control.

Charlie dipped his chin and peered up at her. "What happened back there?"

Lizzie had no idea other than her gut had screamed to get out. "Let's just call it instinct. I'll get Laila to check out the restaurant. I think we should—" She spotted a delivery truck blocking the rear of her car.

"Well, that kinda halts our escape." Charlie strode to the truck and knocked on the driver's door.

The window lowered. "You mind moving?" Charlie asked. "You're blocking cars."

The door swung open, and a man with black hair and a scruffy beard dropped from the cab. "What's it to ya?" His eyes widened for a split second. Most people wouldn't notice, but Lizzie wasn't most people.

Another man with reddish blond hair and a goatee rounded the front of the truck, took a wide stance, and crossed his arms.

Charlie straightened. "For starters, we need to leave. And it's illegal to park here."

"Illegal? Are you serious? What are you, some kind of cop?"

Lizzie hustled to Charlie's side and grabbed his bicep. "Cool it," she muttered. "You're acting like one." Charlie's lack of memory could get them into trouble.

His jaw twitched, but his demeanor changed. "Nah, man. I just want to get my lady home."

The black-haired man studied them.

"Come on, baby. These guys need to get back to work and deliver that yummy seafood." She pivoted to the deliverymen. "That's what you do, right?"

"Yeah, lady, something like that." The redhead smirked and eyed his partner.

She tugged on Charlie and pulled him back to the car. Thank heaven he didn't protest.

He rested against the sedan and pulled her close. "Sorry about that."

Snuggling in, she kept her eyes on the two delivery guys. "Look, I know you don't remember, but you can't go acting like a police officer. You're smooth-talking Rod, the drug dealer."

One arm around Lizzie, he ran his fingers through his hair with his other hand. "I still can't believe I'm not a cop."

"Relax, Hotshot. No harm, no foul." Lizzie enjoyed the comfort of his arm a bit too much, but she was only playing a part in the undercover drama. Right?

"Did you see his surprise when he jumped out of the truck?"

"Yes, I wondered what that was about." Lizzie tucked away that piece of information for later.

"Don't know, but I got the license plate." He grinned like he'd won a prize.

"Perfect." She peered over his shoulder. "They pulled out. Let's go back to your undercover place. I want to make sure we aren't followed before we head to my house."

"From the video and our excursion earlier, I knew I had a secondary place but have no idea where it is beyond near my car."

"I've got that covered. Quinn gave me the address and key this morning before you woke up."

"I don't like the idea of bringing this home to your mom and daughter, so lead the way to my apartment." Charlie released her, and they got in the vehicle.

After placing a call to Steven to run the plate and one to Laila to investigate the restaurant, Lizzie backed from the parking spot and headed toward his undercover place.

A scowl creased Charlie's face.

"It's really bothering you that you're not a cop anymore, isn't it?"

"You could say that." He shifted his gaze out the side window.

Uncertainty gripped Lizzie as she drove. Had they blown Charlie's cover by going to Bobby T's, or was the pen a coincidence and had nothing to do with his attack? The councilmen worried her. No one knew of Charlie's special assignment. If the other dealers hadn't had him beaten, but they found out the two of them had snooped around, danger would return once again to find Charlie in a big way.

Not a cop. Charlie's mind struggled to accept that fact. He scanned the side mirror for tails on the way back to the rundown neighborhood, but hadn't seen anything. So why was his gut screaming at him? Someone had followed them, but he had no proof. Only his trained intuition said they hadn't left the restaurant clean.

He glanced at Lizzie. Her gaze jumped from mirror to mirror.

"You felt it too, didn't you?"

"Yes. Do you see anyone?" The muscle in her jaw twitched.

"No. But it doesn't change the fact someone's out there."

Lizzie pulled onto the street and headed in the opposite direction of the undercover neighborhood.

"Where are you going?"

"Away from your apartment. I'm not leading this nutcase to your place."

He'd thank Lizzie later, but right now, he had to help have their backs. He shifted to look out the rear window and grimaced. That wouldn't work so he straightened and focused his attention on the side mirror. Two blocks later, his fears came true. "Black SUV two cars back."

"Got it." Lizzie's hands tightened on the steering wheel.

The vehicle following them increased speed and hung on their bumper.

Charlie noted the lack of egress. "Any ideas?"

"Stay alive?"

"I like it, but I think we need more."

The vehicle behind them accelerated.

He grabbed the dash. "That plan needs to be sooner versus later."

"Call Steven or Quinn. Tell them what's happening."

"Not 9-1-1?"

She glanced in his direction then focused back on the road. "No. No one knows about your assignment. I'm not blowing your cover by pulling in the cops unless we have to. I'll let the guys make that call."

Charlie grabbed his phone, dialed Quinn, and put it on speaker.

"Hey, Charlie. How's it going?"

"We have a tail. Black SUV about ten yards back."

"Where?"

Charlie rattled off the names of the streets as they flew by.

"Keep heading straight and we'll intersect in five."

"No can do. Quinn, I'm getting us out of here. Track my GPS." Lizzie sped up and whipped a right-hand turn, taking a side street.

Tires screeched behind them. Their tormentor made the quick maneuver and stayed with them. The SUV tilted then righted.

"Quinn—you still there?" Lizzie's concentration never wavered.

"Talk to me."

"I'm taking the highway." She flashed Charlie a quick smile. "Let's use some of the semis to our advantage."

In other words, she planned to play chicken in a playground of 80,000-pound hunks of metal. *Oh, joy*. "Go."

She accelerated onto the entrance ramp and merged into traffic. The guy followed, keeping pace with her.

"Here we go." Lizzie zipped back and forth between the huge trucks, receiving horn blasts for her efforts.

"He's two truck lengths back."

"Which side?"

Charlie forced himself to pivot for a better look. "Left."

"Perfect."

She hit the gas, cut across traffic, then yanked the wheel to the right, barely catching the off-ramp.

Charlie strained his neck to get a visual of the offending SUV. "Got him. He's wedged in and couldn't make the exit." He exhaled, calming his racing pulse. "Nice driving, by the way."

Lizzie's hold on the wheel remained firm, her white knuckles a testament to her stress level.

He rested his hand on her forearm. "You can relax now. You did it. You lost him."

She nodded and eased her death grip. "Thanks. Quinn?"

"Are you two okay?"

"Fine. You have my GPS location. Meet us at the nearest Chick-fil-A parking lot."

"Be there ASAP."

Charlie melted into the passenger seat and let the adrenaline fade from his battered body. Within thirty minutes, they had met with Quinn and Steven, passed on all the information they had about the SUV—which wasn't much—and were back on their way to his undercover apartment.

How many times had he cheated death over the past few days? The thought exhausted him.

He closed his eyes. *I'm not a cat, God. I don't have nine lives, and I'd really like to stay in this world a little longer if that's okay with You.*

All he could do now was wait to see what God had planned for his life—or his death.

The car stopped and Lizzie turned off the engine. Charlie opened his eyes, and his gaze landed on her. Her wrist rested on the steering wheel. "We're here."

He straightened and peered out the front window—and cringed. "I have good taste in apartments."

She snorted. "Only the best for you."

He let his eyes roam over the rundown building. Dark images flickered in his mind but didn't last long enough for him to grasp.

"You're edgy."

"Like a cat next to a vacuum cleaner." Charlie's head had gone from a throb to an all-out assault.

She shot him a look then turned her attention back to the parking lot and surrounding area. "I want to get you inside."

"You'd make a good officer." Charlie glanced at her. "Or were you?"

"I was a detective until about three years ago." Her hand dropped to the door handle and tightened.

"What happened?"

"Long story."

"Oh, come on, Lizzie. Give me a break here. I can't remember my own life, let alone anyone else's."

"I never told you everything."

"Then tell me what I did know."

She closed her eyes briefly and exhaled. "My fiancé died in a drug raid. Shot. He never made it to the hospital."

Ouch. He was a rat. A pushy, selfish idiot. "I shouldn't have insisted." Not having a memory was his problem, not hers.

"It's okay. Like you said, you knew that before. Old news."

He studied her. "There's more?"

"For another time. I want you out of the open and tucked away."

Charlie agreed. But he wished she'd tell him about her past. "I'd like to know more about you, Lizzie. When you're ready, I'm willing to listen."

She stared at him like he'd grown another head.

"I'm serious. I hope you'll trust me with your secrets."

Lizzie opened her mouth then closed it and nodded.

Someday, Lizzie. "Come on. Let's get moving."

They exited the car and he followed her to his second-story apartment. She used the extra key she'd secured from Quinn and opened the door.

Charlie stepped inside and perused the interior. It resembled the undercover apartments he'd had in the past. He moved from the doorway and waved his hand in an arc. "Mi casa es su casa."

"Your Spanish is as bad as mine." Lizzie scooted past him and spun in a slow circle. "Love what you've done with the place." She strode to the couch and swiped a finger over the back of it. "Early century ick."

He chuckled, then held his ribs. "Please, don't make me laugh. Go ahead and have a seat. It may not look like it, but I'd bet my next paycheck that it's clean. If it's anything like my old undercover assignments, the stains on the furniture were added aftermarket."

"That's good to know." Lizzie eyed the offending piece of furniture.

"I'm serious."

"I believe you—I think." Lizzie rounded the couch and sat.

Charlie strode to the kitchen and opened the fridge. He peered over the door. "Can I get you anything? Water, tea, Coke?"

Lizzie burst out laughing.

Charlie's go-to was class clown, always had been, but what had he said that set her off?

"Please don't offer anyone Coke. That just sounds wrong coming from a *drug dealer*."

He shook his head, closed the refrigerator then made his way back to the living room. "Funny you are not. Aren't you supposed to be my straight man...er...woman?"

Lizzie tapped the cushion. "Charlie, have a seat before you fall down."

He lowered himself onto the couch and propped his feet on a coffee table that looked like something he'd picked up off the side of the road.

"You doing okay?" Lizzie patted his leg.

"I wish everyone would quit asking me that. If I say yes, I'm lying. If I say no, everyone pities me."

"Not hardly. Feel bad and want to help, but definitely not pity."

He rested his head on the back of the sofa. The concept of him not regaining his memory danced along the perimeter of his thoughts. What would he do if he never remembered the last four years? "If you say so."

"I do." She mimicked his movement. "So, why are you so fired up about not being a cop anymore?"

"It's all I've ever wanted."

"I know that. But, why?"

Could he trust her with his past?

Lizzie rolled her head to the side to look at him. "Is this about your sister, Shana?"

"Shana's death had something to do with it." His sister, a country music star, had died at the hands of her fans. The tragic accident had rippled through the music industry and had sent his foster sister, Olivia, onto her law enforcement path. He, on the other hand, had wanted to be an officer for years before that. His father's career as a detective and obsession for justice had pushed him to become a cop. But Shana's accident had only solidified the desire. Not something he shared. He let people believe Shana's death had influenced his decision because it had in a small way.

"But that's not the real reason, is it?"

To share or not to share? He and Lizzie had a thread connecting them. The question in his mind was how intimate that link was. All he knew was that he wanted a previous relationship to be true.

"No, it's not." He pursed his lips. Should he divulge the real reason? Might as well. What did he have to lose? "It started when I was ten. The summer I got hit by a car and broke my leg. The guy who ran into me took off. It happened when Dad was a detective with Columbia PD. I had to sit at home all summer while Mom went with Shana. She performed locally, but that summer she had a few opening gigs for big names. I told mom I'd be fine and insisted she go. I couldn't stand in Shana's way of launching her career. Dad stayed home with me. But in his determination to get justice, he spent every waking hour searching for the guy that hit me. Dad never found him. It was then and there that I decided to be a cop. I wanted to fight for those who couldn't fight for themselves."

"Sounds like a good reason." She reached over and grasped his hand. "Very noble."

"Right." If only it was that easy.

"What's wrong?"

The painful reality of a ten-year-old sat there waiting to burst forth. "I've always wondered why it came at such a cost to me."

Lizzie shifted to face him. "Tell me what happened."

Charlie sighed. Might as well go all in. "That summer with Shana's gigs and Dad's hunt for justice, they forgot about me. I stayed at home playing video games by myself and ended up celebrating my birthday alone." Every birthday had been a big deal. Whether a family dinner or a party. Until that summer.

"They forgot?" Her wide brown eyes stared at him.

"Yup." He squeezed her hand. He hadn't told anyone that part of the story before. Or had he? "Mom tried to make up for it over the years, but I told her not to worry. I've made peace with my role in the family. Shana needed Mom's attention. Olivia had her own struggles that my parents focused on, and rightfully so. And then there's Dad. My case was the one black mark on his record. He never solved his own son's hit-and-run. So, I guess I wanted him to feel like his efforts weren't wasted." *Even though he's never looked at me quite the same since. Like it was my fault he failed.*

"It makes sense now why you take care of everyone else first."

He shrugged. "It's what I do. It's my job in life."

"Do you remember why you quit the force?"

"I know what Olivia told me, but no..." A flash of a memory formed in his mind. Susan leaving him, the trepidation that accompanied the depression after. Similar to Lizzie's stress reaction a little while ago.

A reel of images flittered across his brain. He and Lizzie

hanging out in her backyard by the firepit. The two of them leaning together, laughing at something. Her in an emerald-green dress and heels, dancing with him at a party. The emotions different from that of losing his ex.

His feelings for Lizzie slammed into him like a two-by-four, the hit all too real. He rubbed his chest to relieve the pain and straightened.

Lizzie jerked upright and tucked her leg under her. "You remembered something."

He nodded. Why hadn't she said anything? Or had they broken up since this memory?

"Well, what was it?" She practically bounced off the couch.

"I had flashes of us having fun, and I remember Susan leaving me and the months leading up to it."

"That's good. Okay, maybe not good on the Susan front, but you know what I mean."

Yes, he did. It didn't eliminate the questions about him and Lizzie or grief from the events surrounding Susan, but it beat the black hole that had taken up residence in his brain. "I have several years that are still missing, but at least I remember something." More than she knew. He laced his fingers with hers. "Thank you."

She glanced at their entwined hands. "For what?"

"This whole thing is a minefield of emotions." He collapsed against the couch. "I appreciate you listening."

"Of course." She tilted her head. A crease lined her forehead. "You've had a rough day."

"I'd like to disagree, but I can't." He shifted. "You tackle like a linebacker."

She scrunched up her nose. "Sorry about that."

"Are you kidding? You tried to protect me. I owe you a huge thank you." He grasped her hand in a light hold. "What about you? What deep dark secrets do you have?"

Her muscles tensed under his fingers. "What are you talking about? I'm an open book."

Charlie snorted. "As if. You like to make people think that." *Come on, Lizzie, I poured my heart out to you. Don't shut me out.*

"Another time, Hotshot."

Disappointed, he laid his head back and closed his eyes. Once again, not worthy enough to confide in. *God, why can't people treat me like I'm important? I lied to Lizzie. I'm tired of always being second place.*

7

MONDAY, 3:00 P.M

He asked too much. Lizzie had no intention of revealing her weaknesses—to anyone.

But what would it be like to share her burdens and have complete trust in someone with her fears and failures? For that person to understand and not judge? Could she have that with Charlie? No. She wouldn't allow herself to go there. Charlie's life meant the world to her, and if she fell in love with him, she'd make a stupid decision and lose him like all the other men in her life.

The window unit air conditioner *thunked* and kicked on again—the blast of cool air, a welcome reprieve from the rising temperatures. Lizzie scanned the ratty apartment. How had Charlie lived here in the filth? She ran her finger over the tattered couch and paused. *Huh, not dirty.* She narrowed her gaze and took a second look. The place gave the impression of a rattrap, but in reality, it was clean and tidy except for the few well-placed items that gave it a trashed appearance. Charlie had done a great job setting up a drug dealer facade.

"This place is truly a piece of junkyard art."

He shifted to face her. "Thanks. I think."

"Listen, Charlie, I should have—"

He waved her off. "No. You don't have to explain. We all have secrets. You're allowed to keep yours."

"I appreciate that."

"Although, I'm here if you need to talk."

The sincerity in his voice surprised her. Sure, he was her friend and they'd shared before, but nothing serious. The fact he offered to listen on a deeper level warmed her heart and scared her at the same time.

Lizzie rose. "That bottle of water sounds pretty good now. Want something?"

"Nah. But thanks. I think I'm going to hit the little boys' room." Charlie pushed off the couch and headed to the opposite side of the apartment.

She strode to the kitchen, retrieved the bottle from the refrigerator, and leaned against the counter. Lizzie twisted the lid and took a swig. Charlie's shift from happy-go-lucky to serious had her mind scrambling.

A glass bottle shattered the window and exploded in the apartment.

Orange and red tentacles licked the walls and engulfed the couch they'd sat on moments ago.

A black haze filled the room at an alarming rate. "Charlie!" Lizzie coughed and covered her nose and mouth with the neck of her shirt. She couldn't see beyond a couple of feet in front of her. "Charlie!"

She lifted her arm to shield her face. The heat rolled off the flames like waves tumbling toward her. She grabbed a kitchen towel, poured the remaining water from her bottle on it, and covered her nose and mouth. She had to find Charlie and get them out before they both died of smoke inhalation or worse—burned to death.

His lungs burned, and his eyes watered. Charlie didn't want to die. Not like this. A black cloud hovered above like an incoming thunderstorm. He wheezed and choked on the tainted air and stumbled down the hall

"Charlie!"

"Here!" He broke into another fit of coughs.

A hand grabbed his arm and forced him to the floor. Lizzie slapped a wet cloth over his nose and mouth. He inhaled, finding a bit of relief from the fumes.

"What happened?"

"Molotov cocktail. Come on. We have to get out of here before we both turn into barbecue meat." Lizzie's voice filtered over the roar of the flames. "Follow me."

He wrapped the towel around his head and crawled after her through the blazing apartment and into the outside hallway.

Lizzie slammed the door shut behind him and tugged him a few feet away from the roaring fire.

He collapsed to the ground and sucked in precious oxygen.

Lizzie coughed and sputtered, clearing her lungs, then pulled her phone from her pocket and dialed 9-1-1. He hoisted himself up, grabbed the fire alarm, and pulled.

People peeked from their doorways, confusion stamped across their faces.

Charlie pointed to the stairway. "Get out! The building's on fire!"

Lizzie hung up and joined him. He took one side of the hall

and she took the other. They ran from door to door and pounded, shouting warnings to the residents, then hurried to the stairway leading to the exit.

Several men forced past Charlie as he helped a woman with a baby on her hip down the rickety steps.

When they hit the first floor, he released the woman's arm and followed her through the door. He inhaled a clean breath, but air refused to enter his lungs. Reality hit. All these people could have died because of him.

Lizzie escorted him farther from the building and leaned in close. "Calm down. Take a deep breath to clear the smoke from your lungs."

Lizzie, I can't breathe and it has nothing to do with the fire. Stars danced on the edge of his vision. "Not smoke," he choked out.

Hands cupped his face, and Lizzie's warm breath caressed his cheek. "Charlie. Try to relax. You're having a panic attack."

As far as Charlie remembered, he'd never had one before.

So, this is what they feel like. Great. His tombstone would read, *He panicked to death.*

Lizzie gripped his shoulders. "Look at me and do what I do."

He blinked and peered into her brown eyes and mimicked her breaths. A sip of air entered his lungs. Then another.

"That's it. A little deeper now." Her voice softened. "You've got it."

The streaks of white lights cleared, and his breathing evened. "Sorry."

"Don't apologize." Her sad smile said she knew exactly what it felt like to lose control.

All he could do was nod. Another round of coughs racked his body.

A paramedic stopped beside them. "Sounds like you could use some oxygen."

"He inhaled a lot of smoke." The concern in Lizzie's voice wasn't lost on him.

"I'm guessing you did too." The medic grinned at her.

Charlie took a good look at Lizzie. Black soot coated her face and arms. "Yes, she did."

"Then let's get you guys taken care of." The paramedic led them to the medic unit and sat him on the gurney in the back of the ambulance. He strapped the mask over Charlie's nose and mouth and added drops to his eyes. A few minutes later, the man left Charlie to suck in the clean air.

The paramedic's partner treated Lizzie then helped her onto the bench seat next to Charlie and eased the doors closed at her request.

"Feeling better?"

"Much, thanks. How about you?" The mask muffled his words.

She lifted the mask from her face and smiled. "This is helping."

"Good. Any idea what happened?"

"I think the guy throwing the Molotov cocktail had something to do with it."

"You're a genius." He shook his head. "I thought I was supposed to be the jokester." The smoke had added a gruffness to his voice, bringing back his Batman imitation.

The corner of her mouth curled upward. "You've rubbed off on me over the years."

And there he was, back to living in the dark, wondering about their relationship. "Think it was the guy who followed us from the restaurant?"

"It crossed my mind."

"And if it wasn't him? Then it has to be one of the drug

dealers around here." He used the gauze the paramedic had given him to wipe the moisture from his eyes.

"I'm just not sure what to think at this point." Lizzie rubbed her forehead. "I texted Olivia a few minutes ago. We're supposed to head to the office once we're cleared."

The rear door swung open.

Lizzie whipped her gun from her concealed holster and shifted in front of him.

"Whoa. Sorry." The paramedic's voice filtered through the interior of the ambulance. "Just wanted to check on my patients."

Lizzie tucked the Glock into her waist holster and returned to the seat.

"Okay, then." The medic climbed into the truck and took a seat on the other side of Charlie. "How's the breathing?" His gazed shifted between them.

"We're good." Charlie lifted the mask and handed it to the man. "We appreciate your help, but we need to go."

"I can see I'm not going to convince either of you to go to the hospital, so I'd advise watching for complications and see the doc ASAP if there are any issues." He ran down the list of all the symptoms to watch for and had them sign Treatment Refusal forms.

"Ready?" Lizzie jumped down, surveyed the scene, then held out her hand. Charlie took it, and she helped him from the ambulance. "Time to go to headquarters. I want you out of the line of fire."

Charlie walked to the car, scanning the area along the way. He trusted Lizzie, but whoever was after him had come too close this time and put others in danger. If they didn't figure out where the threat had come from, he might not survive another attack.

8

MONDAY, 5:00 P.M

Lizzie had almost lost him. Again.

She'd let her guard down and failed to keep him safe. Another bad choice that had almost cost Charlie his life.

And then there was Addy. What if they'd gone to her house instead? Lizzie had come close to suggesting it, but thankfully changed her mind. She gritted her teeth and tightened her hands on the steering wheel. Lizzie never would have forgiven herself if she'd put her mother and daughter in the middle of danger. Her chest tightened, squeezing the air from her lungs.

Stop it! Get yourself under control.

Her body ignored the command, and the panic gripped tighter. She needed to go for a walk, or sit and run through her 5-4-3-2-1 grounding technique, but at the moment neither were possible. So she tightened her hands on the steering wheel, held the tension, then relaxed for ten seconds and repeated the sequence. Finally, she took a deep breath and focused on the road.

The ride from Charlie's now-torched undercover apartment to the Elite Guardians Agency office was a quiet one. If Charlie noticed her struggle, he chose not to say anything. Which was fine with her. She had enough guilt and self-recrimination to work through.

Her cell phone beeped, jarring Lizzie from her thoughts. She tapped the Bluetooth and answered. "Tremaine."

"Lizzie, it's Steven. Got a sec?"

"Sure. You're on speaker with Charlie."

"How are you guys doing? Heard you ate some smoke."

"We'll survive," Charlie called out. "But it's not something I recommend."

Steven chuckled. "Thanks for the advice."

"Do you have anything on the unmarked delivery truck at Bobby T's?" Lizzie flipped the AC on high then lifted her long hair off the back of her neck with one hand and drove with the other. The temps had held on, and today's killer humidity had sweat trickling down her back.

"Came back to Blackwell Seafood Inc. out of Charleston. They supply seafood for multiple restaurants in the area and along the coast."

"Any red flags?"

"Not on the surface. I haven't had a chance to dig deeper."

"It's probably nothing. I'll ask Laila what she discovered."

"No need. She reported back that the councilmen and a few others from the mayor's office frequent the establishment on a biweekly basis."

"Twice a week? They must really like the food. Ever get the feeling they're doing more than eating?"

"That came to mind. The hostess was pretty open with her information, so I don't think she knows anything more than the habits of the customers and her manager."

"Thanks for taking care of that for me."

"No worries. Just be careful. I'm not liking what's going on." Papers shuffled on Steven's end. "Anything else I can do for you?"

"Not that I can think of. But if that changes, I'll let you know."

"Sounds good. I'll see you later."

Lizzie hung up and pulled into the lot next to the EGA building. She took the first spot and parked the car. Without a word, they entered the building and headed to the conference room. The scent of smoke wafted from her and Charlie's soot-covered clothes. She'd wiped her hands and face with a towel provided by the paramedic, but that hadn't removed the ashy reminder of how close they'd come to being consumed by the fire.

Once inside, Charlie spun to face her. "What's going on in that pretty mind of yours?"

She shook her head. If she gave voice to her concern, her emotions would overtake her.

He placed his hands on her shoulders, dipped his chin, and peered up at her. "Come on, Lizzie, tell me."

The vise around her chest tightened. "My lack of focus nearly got you killed. And what if we had gone to my house? Addy could have been..."

"Don't even think that."

A tear escaped her lashes and rolled down her cheek. Wonderful. Looking weak in front of Charlie was all she needed. Especially since he couldn't remember their partnership.

"Ah, honey." He wrapped his arms around her and held her head to his chest. His body and head had to ache, but he continued to comfort her. "I'm fine, and Addy's safe."

Another tear trickled down her cheek. Then another.

Finger under her chin, he lifted. His unwavering gaze

seemed to stare straight into the depths of her soul. His brown eyes shifted to her lips. Almost as if asking for permission. But this was Charlie. Her friend and partner. There was nothing between them. Right?

The world quieted around them, and Charlie cupped the sides of her face and wiped the tears away with his thumbs. Her breath caught, and she gripped his bicep. Her brain screamed at her to turn away, but her heart craved the closeness. Could she and Charlie be more than friends? Could she take the risk of loving another man?

"Momma!"

Lizzie jumped back like a guilty teenager. "Addy. Mom." She wanted to smack her forehead at the breathy way her words came out.

Her mother smiled, and Addy launched herself into Lizzie's arms. "Aunt Olivia told me what happened. Are you okay?"

Lizzie snuggled her daughter, letting the comfort of her baby in her arms wash over her. "We're good."

"Momma, you're smothering me."

Lizzie eased her grip. "Sorry."

"Hey, Addy." Charlie smiled at her daughter.

"Hi, Uncle Charlie. Did my mom really get you out of a burning building?"

"She sure did."

Lizzie shook her head. She'd come close to getting him killed, not rescuing him. She started to protest, but the look in Charlie's eyes dared her to disagree, so she kept her opinion to herself. Lizzie glanced to the doorway and found Olivia leaning against the doorjamb, arms folded across her chest. "Olivia."

"Hey, sis," Charlie said.

"Lizzie. Charlie. I'm just here to check on you and make sure you're in one piece."

Charlie lowered himself into one of the office chairs and smirked. "I think I'd like to take a year off if that's okay with my boss."

Olivia's eyebrow arched. "No, it's not. But I'll give you two weeks once we catch whoever's doing this."

"Two weeks? What a hardnose." He moaned with a ridiculous exaggeration. A seriousness washed over his expression. "I'll settle for finding this guy and getting justice."

Lizzie blinked. She'd never heard Charlie so grim. Her attention turned to her mom and daughter. What if they got caught in the killer's crosshairs? She stepped in front of Olivia and lowered her voice. "I want Mom and Addy far away from this mess. I don't care where you send them, just get them out of here."

"And I want you focused on Charlie and keeping him safe."

Lizzie mentally staggered backward at Olivia's harsh tone. "I should have been more alert. I won't make that mistake again." Charlie's life was in her hands, and she'd do everything in her control to protect him.

Olivia studied her a moment then nodded.

"What about my family?"

"I agree. Are there friends your mom and Addy can visit for a few days?"

Lizzie considered the options. "I hate to split them up, but yes. Mom has a lady from church she could stay with, and Addy's friend Kathy is a good choice. Her mom's a deputy sheriff. I trust her to protect my daughter."

"Then it's settled. I'll work with your mother to make the arrangements and keep your family safe."

"Thank you."

Olivia gripped her shoulder. "Please, do the same for me."

"You have my word." The weight of the situation pressed down on her. Charlie's life was in her hands, and she was trusting her friend with all she had left of her family. Her chest tightened, and her breathing shallowed. She refused to panic in front of her mother and coworkers. The fact Charlie knew about her anxiety was bad enough.

Calm down, Lizzie. She'd hidden her anxiety and depression from everyone. Her mother didn't even know that she took medication for her condition. Her therapist had told her over and over not to be ashamed. It wasn't her fault, and she hadn't done anything wrong. The chemicals in her brain needed a little help. That was all.

Any time she appeared stressed, her mom and the other bodyguards told her to pray and let God handle it. She knew deep down they were right, but He'd let her down as a child, so she doubted He would listen to her prayers now. Oh, how she wished she could turn to Him and give Him control.

With a deep breath, she faced her mother. "Mom, I want you to listen to Olivia. We have a plan to get you and Addy away from all this craziness."

Lizzie's mom wrapped her arm around Addy's shoulder and pulled her close. "We're in danger from your current assignment?"

And there it was, a highlight of her irresponsibility. Didn't her mom understand she was sending them away out of responsibility? Then again, maybe Lizzie was overreacting.

"Mrs. Tremaine," Olivia said, "we just want to be cautious." She rested a hand on Addy's head. "I'd hate for anything to happen to my honorary niece."

Addy walked over and threw her arms around Lizzie's waist. "I want to stay with you."

Lizzie knelt and looked her daughter in the eyes. "We're

sending you to your friend Kathy's. You'll stay with her until things calm down."

Addy opened her mouth to object, and Lizzie raised an eyebrow, challenging her protest.

Her daughter scowled and sighed. "Okay, Momma. I'll go."

"Good girl."

Addy patted her cheek. "I know you'll find the bad guy soon so we can come home."

Lizzie hugged her. "Thank you, sweetie. I love you. You know that, right?"

"Duh." Addy grinned. "You're the best."

She kissed her daughter on the cheek. "Go. Be good for Kathy's mom."

Addy moved to Olivia's side and grabbed her hand "Let's go so Momma can get to work."

"You've got it." Olivia nodded at Lizzie and ushered her little family out the door, taking a piece of Lizzie's heart with them.

"Addy's right, you know," Charlie said.

"Excuse me?" She dropped next to him at the table.

"You'll have this solved in no time."

"How can you be so sure?"

"I might not remember everything. But I can tell you're great at your job."

"Thanks." If only she believed it. The string of devastating consequences in her life said otherwise. But now wasn't the time to dwell on her poor choices. She straightened and pushed the past from her mind. She had a job to do—keep Charlie alive.

Mass confusion turned Charlie's gut inside out. For a moment, he thought he'd figured out his and Lizzie's relationship. The look in her eyes had confirmed it, but her reaction to Addy walking in hadn't given him warm fuzzies. In fact, just the opposite. Had he misread her interest? The one thing he did know is that he'd guessed wrong. Unlike what he'd originally thought, she wasn't interested. She'd slipped into business mode and hadn't given him another look other than that of a friend and partner. Maybe he should just risk embarrassment and ask.

He rubbed his aching head. "Lizzie..." He glanced up. The pain etched on her face ripped his heart to shreds. He'd sat here contemplating his feelings for her while she struggled with letting Addy go. What a jerk. "They'll be fine. You know that, right?"

"I was careless. It almost got you killed. And now my daughter and mom..." Lizzie inhaled. "Enough about me. We have to focus on keeping you safe and figure out who's behind all this insanity."

He stiffened. Apparently, she had no intention of talking about anything except work. So be it. He could do serious. "Before we shift to work mode, I'd like to thank you for saving my life."

She studied him for a moment. "You're welcome, Charlie. It may be my job to keep you safe, but you're also my...friend. And I don't think I'd be able to handle it if something happened to you."

Whoa. So, maybe... No. She'd called him friend. At least she cared. "I appreciate you putting yourself in danger on my account."

Lizzie's mouth opened then closed. She ran a hand through her hair. Ash drifted to the table, reminding him of how close they'd come to being burned alive.

He'd sulked enough. It was time to move on. "Let's make a plan. One that includes showers and food." He pasted on his cheesy grin.

His attempt to make her smile worked. "I like that idea. I'm thinking we call the EGA crew and meet up at Olivia's for a brainstorming session. Her and Wade's property is private and has top-of-the-line security. I'll ask Haley and Steven to run by both of our places and grab extra clothes on their way."

"Who knows, maybe Daniel will have pity on us and bring food from A Taste of Yesterday." Charlie's mouth watered at the thought. He hadn't remembered Daniel, but the restaurant —oh, yeah. But at this point even the idea of fast-food burgers had him drooling.

Lizzie texted everyone and placed her phone on the table. "Want to talk about the fire?"

"No. You?"

"Not yet. It still gives me chills to think how close we came."

Charlie had no desire to close his eyes. Flames and smoke filled his memory. He owed Lizzie for getting him out of the apartment after the Molotov cocktail came through the window. But during that moment before she'd found him on the other side of the fire...he shivered at the terrifying moment when he couldn't see to find a way out.

Lizzie's phone dinged multiple times. "Got a thumbs-up from everyone. Olivia said to grab keys from Angela. There's a rental in the parking garage waiting for us."

"Let's go." He pushed off the chair arms to stand, only to freeze mid push and lower himself carefully back into the seat. His muscles had tightened, and his injuries screamed. A hundred-year-old man had nothing on him.

"Hold on." Lizzie hurried from the room and returned a couple minutes later. "Here."

Charlie took the ibuprofen and a water bottle from her then swallowed the tablets. "Thanks." He placed his hands flat on the conference table and pushed to a standing position. So far so good this time. Now to get his legs moving. The amount of effort it took to stand and walk was ridiculous.

"Ready?" She dangled the keys.

"Let's do this." He ambled to the elevator and stepped inside. The doors closed and the car descended to the parking garage level. He rested his back on the wall and spread his arms, placing his hands on the rail. More so to hold him upright than steady himself against the movement. "Hope Olivia got us a sweet ride."

Lizzie chuckled. "We'll be lucky she didn't rent us a tank."

The door slid open, and Charlie stepped outside. The air had turned hot and sticky, making his soot-covered skin grimy. Hyperaware of his surroundings, he followed Lizzie toward the rental car. He felt exposed and targeted. A chill sent a shiver up his spine, and he slowed to scan the garage. Someone was out there. Watching.

Lizzie hit the car fob and her hand went to her weapon. "Get in the car."

"I can—"

She placed herself in a protective stance. "Please, Charlie. You can't fight this fight. Let me do it for you. Get in the car."

He eased himself into the passenger seat and closed the door.

Lizzie rounded the vehicle, eyes searching for the threat. She got in and started the engine.

"Why do I get the feeling of déjà vu?" Charlie slid his Glock from his concealed holster and held it in his lap.

"I don't like it either." She eased out of the parking spot and headed for the exit. "Anything?"

He'd done another visual sweep of the area and found nothing. "Maybe we're paranoid."

"Possible." Lizzie tapped the speed dial and called Steven.

"Lizzie, what's up?"

"I've got a hinky feeling."

"Which is never good." Charlie might not have his memory back, but for some reason he trusted her instincts without question.

"I agree. Where are you?" Steven demanded.

"Leaving the office."

"I'll send a patrol unit to follow you to Olivia's."

"Thanks, I appreciate it." She hung up and parallel parked a few yards down from the agency. "Let's wait for backup."

"I'd say we should have stayed put in the parking garage, but I'd prefer a quick getaway if needed."

"Steven will have that unit here fast. Until then, keep an eye out for an ambush. You watch right, I'll take left."

Charlie nodded. The last time he'd let his guard down, someone had tried to barbecue him and endangered those around him. He had no plans to let that happen again.

MONDAY, 6:30 P.M.

The gate opened and Lizzie pulled up to Olivia's house. She parked under the shade tree and turned off the engine, then rested her head on the steering wheel, willing her pulse to slow. Mentally, she knew they were safe and no one appeared to have followed them, but anxiety threatened to take over. The *what if* game played over and over in her mind.

Whoever had Charlie in his or her sights was not giving up. Lizzie had to step up her game. The severity of the situation pressed down, squeezing her chest like a vise. She gulped air, trying to fill her lungs.

"Lizzie?" Charlie rested his hand on her arm.

She struggled to pull in a breath and tilted her head to look at him. His concern brought tears to her eyes. "Give me a minute, okay?" she choked out.

He nodded.

A little bit later, Lizzie straightened. "Sorry about that."

"Don't ever apologize." He brushed a strand of hair from her cheek. "I just wish I knew how to help when it happens."

Lizzie caught his hand and didn't let go. "Telling you has helped more than you'd ever imagine. I don't have to hide it."

"You never should have to. Your friends and family would understand."

"If only I had your confidence. I don't want to burden anyone with my problems."

"Oh, Lizzie. You're not a burden. You're one of the strongest women I've ever known." Desire flamed in the same dark brown eyes that had melted her heart earlier.

She froze, unable to tear her gaze away. She really should keep her distance. At least until his memory returned. Lizzie drew in a deep breath and worked at getting her racing heart under control. At least this time, the fast beat wasn't due to a panic attack.

The man next to her had never been so serious, so compassionate. She'd always felt compelled to hold in her secrets, but for some reason she wanted to share with this new Charlie.

She shifted in her seat and leaned against the door. "You know how you asked about my fiancé?"

"Lizzie, you don't have to tell me. But I'm willing to listen."

The fact he was interested calmed her nerves. She wanted to tell him. Wanted to share what she hadn't shared with anyone. "There's a piece of my past I think you should know."

"Go ahead."

She bit her lip. "A few years ago, I was engaged to a great guy named Ethan. He loved Addy, and we clicked. I was happy for the first time in a long time. We both worked for Charlotte PD when we met. Six months before our wedding, he was shot and killed in a drug raid." She swallowed the lump in her throat. "I killed him—or at least was the cause of his death."

Charlie jerked like she'd slapped him. "Please, explain."

"I was the point person for the raid. I'm the one who gave the go ahead to enter."

"It's not your fault the bad guy shot him."

"But I missed something. I should have realized something was off. I shouldn't have given the order to go."

"Still not your fault." Charlie slipped his hand over hers. "Think back. Run over the plans. What could you have changed?"

She pinched the bridge of her nose. There had to have been a clue. "Nothing. I did everything right."

"Then quit beating yourself up. Things happen that we have no control over."

"But it was my job."

Charlie snorted. "You aren't God, Lizzie. You can't control everything. You have to let God be God."

And that was the problem. She didn't trust Him. He'd failed her too many times. "I begged God to let Ethan live. Just like... Never mind."

"Lizzie?"

His tenderness tugged at her heart, but she didn't want to have this conversation with him. Not yet anyway. "Come on. Let's get inside before Olivia comes searching for us."

Charlie huffed. "Sure."

She grabbed his arm. "I'm not dismissing you. I just need time to process."

He slid his hand up and cupped her cheek. "Whenever you're ready to discuss it, you know where to find me." Charlie dropped his hand and slipped from the vehicle.

Lizzie stared at him. This side of Charlie made her want to find out what kind of relationship she could have with him.

9

MONDAY, 7:00 P.M

How bad had Charlie messed up by almost kissing Lizzie at the EGA office? She'd practically jumped out of his arms, but from her response in the car, she'd recovered from his faux pas. He prayed he hadn't put a wedge in their friendship, but his brain wouldn't let go of the way she'd looked at him. Were they an item or not? He needed answers and could only trust one person to give them to him. Olivia. But should he ask and risk hearing the wrong answer?

He stood under the shower spray, pressed his hands against the tile, and rested his forehead on the wall, allowing the cold surface to ease his headache. He watched the black grime pour off him and wished the paralyzing fear would go down the drain with it. Every time he closed his eyes, he tasted smoke and felt heat prick his skin. An odd imaginary sensation. He finished his shower and turned off the water, then raked a hand through his wet hair, debating his next move.

After toweling himself dry, he changed into clean clothes

and used his fingers as a comb. The question drove him nuts. *Time to find out the truth.* Charlie plodded his way through Olivia and Wade's house on a mission to find his sister.

"Hey, bro, feel better?" Olivia poured tortilla chips onto a serving tray and placed a bowl of salsa in the middle. She dusted off her hands and gave him her full attention.

Better was relative. "Yes. It's good to not smell like Smokey Bear." Charlie grabbed Olivia's wrist in a gentle grip. "I need to talk to you." He glanced around and caught sight of Maddy and Quinn chatting with Katie and Steven just inside the living room. "In private." He tugged her to the back patio.

Olivia's brow raised. "What's so all hot fire important that we needed privacy?"

Charlie scratched at the scruff on his jaw. "Are Lizzie and I a thing?"

His sister chuckled. "Much to everyone's chagrin, no."

What did she mean by that? But now wasn't the time to dig deeper into her statement. He had a mission to discover the truth. "So only friends."

She nodded. "Does this have something to do with the way you've been making googly eyes at her lately?"

Charlie rolled his eyes at his sister. "You're not funny."

"I think I am." She grinned then turned serious. "Why do you ask? Did something happen?"

He shrugged, not wanting to admit how close he'd come to kissing Lizzie. "Just curious, that's all." Only friends. He'd blown it. Big time. No wonder she'd jumped out of his arms when the others had arrived at EGA. He owed Lizzie an apology. He'd swallow his pride and do what needed to be done to save their friendship.

Olivia patted his shoulder. "Don't worry about it. We all keep hoping, but the two of you have your reasons."

He hadn't a clue what Olivia meant beyond the emotional

responses he'd experienced. Stupid head trauma. He hated not knowing about his life. "Thanks, sis."

"Sure, no problem. I'm heading back in. Are you coming?"

"I'll be there in a little bit. I'd kind of like to get some fresh air after sucking on a smokestack." And noodle how he'd dig himself out of coming on too strong to Lizzie. His heart said he liked her, but he had to be careful until he figured out his past in full living color.

Olivia snickered. "Take your time." She slipped through the back door, leaving him alone with his thoughts.

Shoving his hands in his pockets, Charlie headed down to the lake. He inhaled the clean air then lowered his sore self onto the boat dock. The tree-filled shoreline and soft ripple of waves on the lake mesmerized him. Olivia and Wade had a nice place out here. He was happy his sister had found love, but he wished he remembered the details.

Hands behind him, he leaned backward. His ribs pulled, and his shoulders burned, but the stretch probably did him good. The sun dipped just below the tree line, easing the warm temps of the day, and the cicadas had started their evening whine. Charlie tilted his face to the sky. *God, help me remember. I hate feeling like the new kid on the block where everyone else knows all the secrets.*

The grass crunched in the distance. Lizzie. He'd recognize her gait anywhere, but as she got closer, it was her vanilla scent that gave her away.

Her shadow fell across him. "Mind if I join you?"

He turned and caught a glimpse of her uncertain expression. Of all the people here at Olivia's, Lizzie was the only one he wanted by his side. But how did he communicate that without scaring her off? "Not at all. Have a seat."

She lowered herself to the dock and swung her legs back and forth over the water. "It's nice out here."

"That it is." He would have thought the silence that lingered between them would have been awkward, but instead, he found it oddly comfortable.

Questions swirled in his brain. Did he dare ask?

"Listen—"

"Can I ask—"

They talked as one.

Lizzie tilted her head and peered at him. "You first."

He was afraid she'd say that. He blew out a breath. "You said you never date. I was curious why. Is it because of what happened with Ethan?" Okay, so he was a coward. But he did wonder why she never dated.

The internal war raging within her poured out into her facial expressions.

Charlie waited, letting her make the choice of telling or holding it in.

"In a way, but not entirely. I guess you could say it's too much pain that drives my decision."

"How so?" He leaned forward and mimicked her leg movements. "Or is this something I already know but have forgotten?"

She shook her head. "You know pieces of it, but not everything."

"Will you fill me in? What I don't remember, at least?"

For a moment, Lizzie appeared lost in thought. Finally, she inhaled and glanced at him. "My dad died of a heart attack when I was young, leaving my mom and me alone."

"That had to be tough."

"Yeah, it was. He had the flu and I was supposed to take care of him while Mom was at Bible study. But I decided to sneak out and meet a neighbor friend. I lost track of time, and when Mom came home, she found my dad having a heart attack. If I'd only stayed with him, I could have called 9-1-1. By the time they got him to the hospital, it was too late."

"Oh, Lizzie. You couldn't have known."

"Tell that to my dad." She bit her bottom lip and stared off at the trees along the lake. "I begged God to save him, but He didn't. I had to live with the consequences of my actions."

"How old were you?"

"Ten."

"That's a lot of guilt to put on a ten-year-old's shoulders."

"I was old enough to know better. And apparently old enough for God to punish."

"Lizzie. God doesn't—"

She held up a hand. "No, Charlie. Don't go there. I've heard it all."

His heart cracked at the pain in her voice. How did he get her to understand that God was in control and that little Lizzie wasn't responsible? "What about Addy's father?"

A sad smile formed on her lips. "Trevor was my high school sweetheart and my best friend. We made a few poor choices, but I'll never regret Addy."

Charlie hated to pry, but he wanted to fill the holes in his brain with memories. "Where is he now?"

Tears pooled in Lizzie's eyes. "I thought we'd grow old together, but he died in a rock-climbing accident our senior year. Another set of consequences I have to live with. Trevor and his buddies wanted one last outing before everyone headed off into their new lives. I was supposed to go with them as the lead climber since I had the most experience. But I had a doctor's appointment and never made it to the climb. One of his friends, Ryan, ran into trouble on the cliff. Trevor's inexperience got him killed trying to save his friend. It should have been me out there, but instead I was sitting in my car crying, trying to figure out how to tell my mom and Trevor that I was pregnant."

Charlie wanted to throw up at the unfairness of Lizzie's life.

"Ryan made it back, but Trevor lost his grip and for whatever reason, wasn't clipped in properly. He fell and died on impact." She swiped away the tears that had escaped. "He died never knowing about his baby girl."

"Oh, Lizzie." He scooted next to her and wrapped her in his arms. "No one should go through all that."

She buried her face in his chest. "I'm sorry."

"You have no reason to be sorry." He rubbed her back for several minutes while they sat in silence.

She inhaled and straightened. "I tend to keep all that to myself, but even though it hurts, it feels good to remember Trevor."

Charlie laced his fingers with hers. "Any time you want to talk about him, I'll listen."

Lizzie shifted to face him. "You're a good man, Charlie Lee."

He puffed out his chest as best he could with healing ribs. "What are you talking about? I'm a great man." He'd hoped to lighten her mood—and there it was.

A grin spread across Lizzie's face. "You're incorrigible."

"What?" he deadpanned. The banter between them felt good—felt right. Was that how they acted all the time together?

"I like this new Charlie who's willing to listen without turning everything into a joke." She patted his chest. "The Tin Man does have a heart."

"I'm sorry if I've ever made light of your problems." His gaze drifted to her lips. "You matter to me, Lizzie."

Her eyes dilated and she inched closer.

Charlie slid his hand behind her neck and tugged her to

him. He slipped his fingers through her hair and touched his lips to hers. At first, gentle and tentative, giving her a choice. When she didn't pull away, he deepened the kiss and all his senses spun out of control.

She was right where he wanted her to be.

He eased back and smoothed the mess he'd made of her hair. "That was nice."

"Hmm. I agree."

Lost in the sound of lapping water, the scent of seafood on the grill, the warmth of her gaze, he reeled from the depth of his emotions.

A sudden jolt of memory hit him. He pulled away.

"Charlie?" Confusion lingered on Lizzie's face.

His brain flooded with events from the past. All the holes filled except for a small moment in time. The day of his attack.

Susan's words crashed into him. *"Your job always comes first. And you take way too many chances. It's like you have something to prove. You'll never be a good husband. I can't be a cop's wife. No."* She shook her head. *"I can't be your wife."*

Deep down he'd known he shouldn't date Lizzie, and now he knew why. She'd lost her fiancé, a law enforcement officer, and she'd likely be unwilling to take a chance with another man in a dangerous career. He was a protector. And he refused to quit the profession that God had laid on his heart. And as Susan said, he took too many risks.

He'd never be the man Lizzie needed—the one she deserved. His heart ached, but he had to stuff down his desire and remember his lack of potential as a boyfriend.

And that meant no Lizzie.

Lizzie's heart thundered in her chest. She'd just kissed Charlie. Her friend and partner. And had broken every rule she'd made, both personally and professionally. Then Charlie had pushed her away.

It had hurt, but she couldn't dwell on it. She had to pull it together. Charlie's expression concerned her. "What's wrong?"

He stared off in the distance. "My memory is coming back."

"That's wonderful."

He rubbed the back of his neck. "Yeah, it is."

She narrowed her gaze. "You don't sound like it."

He pasted on a fake smile. "No, it's great. Really."

So much for their heart-to-heart talk. But she'd go with it, like she always had. She entwined her fingers with his. "How much do you remember?"

"I remember almost everything." He squeezed her hand and let go. "There are a couple of gray areas, but the only thing I can't recall at all is the day of my attack."

Lizzie knew the unknown drove him nuts. The fact that his past was no longer a mystery relieved her. But him suddenly putting on the brakes when she'd finally let go of her fear of getting too close...that stung. A lot. She shook off the rejection and focused on him. "The rest will come. Be patient."

"I'm trying. Something is nagging at me. I can't put my finger on it."

"How about we go tell everyone the good news? I'm sure Olivia will be thrilled that her brother's head is screwed on correctly now."

Charlie gave her a small shove with his shoulder and grinned. "You're a brat. You know that, right?"

"I learned it from you." She hauled herself to her feet and helped him up. "Come on, Hotshot." The temptation to continue holding his hand plagued her. But his odd responses confused her, so Lizzie dropped his hand and walked next to him. She'd confront him later, but for now, he needed their friendship.

Charlie sniffed the air. "That seafood sure smells good."

"Nothing better than Daniel's grilling skills."

"That's true. Do you remember when..." Charlie twisted to face her. "Man, that feels good."

Lizzie chuckled. "I'm sure it does."

Charlie continued toward the house then stopped in his tracks. His eyes widened.

"Now what's wrong?" The man looked as though he'd seen a ghost.

He didn't respond. His unfocused gazed worried her.

She took him by the shoulders and spun him to face her. "Charlie." Lizzie wanted to shake him but refrained due to his concussion.

"I know who attacked me." His breathy words sent shivers down her spine.

"Who?" Lizzie cupped his cheeks and studied him. "Come on, Charlie. Talk to me."

He blinked, snapping out of his trance. "The guys from the restaurant."

"The councilmen?" She grappled with confusion.

Charlie shook his head. "No. The delivery guys."

"Those men in the alley? Are you one hundred percent positive?"

He gestured toward the patio. "The cooking seafood triggered my memory. I'm sure. They grabbed me...and..." Charlie's face lost all color. "Each blow is permanently etched in my brain now." His respiration rate increased to an alarming rate.

Lizzie swallowed hard. She'd hoped he'd remember the who but not the hit by hit.

His panicked glance shifted to the patio.

She positioned her body to block the view of their friends. "Easy there, Hotshot."

"Thanks." Charlie gulped in air. "I appreciate..." He flicked his gaze to where Olivia and Wade stood next to Daniel. "Well, you know."

Panic attacks were all too familiar to her. It seemed fitting that Charlie was the only person who knew about them. "I'll keep your secret if you keep mine." She gave him a cheesy grin.

He chuckled. Color returned to his cheeks. "Deal."

After a couple of minutes, she squeezed his shoulders. "You ready?"

"Yes, ma'am." He waggled his eyebrows.

Lizzie rolled her eyes. The man had transformed from the reflective guy of the last few days to the ridiculous man she had grown accustomed to over the years. Why the switch now that he had his memory back?

"Hey, Lizzie."

"Yes?"

"About that kiss." Charlie stumbled over his words.

"What about it?"

"Never mind. Let's go." He shoved his hands in his pockets and ambled toward the house.

Kiss conversation over, apparently. Lizzie strode next to him, wishing he'd finished his thought, but chose to focus on the case. "You think you can describe those guys?"

"I think we both can."

"True. But it would be a good thing for you to work with a sketch artist."

His brow furrowed. "It's the same people, Lizzie."

"I understand. But what if you're projecting onto those delivery guys?"

He paused a moment then gave a slow nod. "I suppose it makes sense."

"Tell you what. I'll work on a picture of those two from the restaurant, and you work on the men who attacked you. If what we believe is true, they'll look the same."

"Sounds like a plan." Charlie stopped twenty feet from the patio. "Something's still nagging at me."

"What is it?"

"That's the problem. There are still things I don't remember. But before those guys found me, I had ducked out of sight. I have no clue why. All I know is that it's important."

"As in your cover was blown, or you witnessed a crime?"

"That's just it. I have no idea."

"We'll have to work on that memory. For now, we have some bad guys to investigate. We need to figure out who they are and why they tried to kill you."

"I guess that will have to do." He started walking again. "Time to tell everyone that I have most of my memory back. I think Quinn was hoping I'd forget several things. He's going to be disappointed."

Lizzie had to smile at the child-like enthusiasm.

Once at the patio, she watched Charlie waltz over to the crowd of men—Quinn, Daniel, Wade, and Grey. Lizzie's friends had found themselves some great supportive guys, and she was thrilled for her coworkers.

Charlie's voice filled the evening air. "Guess what, guys. I can now remember all the dirt on your wives and fiancée."

A round of back slaps and laughs had the dark blanket of depression weighing down on her. The old Charlie had reappeared. And as much as she enjoyed his fun side, she was sad she wouldn't have a chance to explore the new version of him she'd experienced over the past few days.

Lizzie lowered herself onto a lounger by the pool, away from the commotion. Normally, she'd be the first one joking and teasing with Charlie and the rest of her friends, but at the moment her heart was a jumbled mess. The warmth of Charlie's touch still lingered on her lips.

Confusion swirled around her. The heart-stopping kiss had awakened her desire to find a partner to share life with. Could Charlie be that man? If someone had asked her that thirty minutes ago, she would've said yes. But now that he'd transformed back into the class clown, she wasn't sure what to think.

Olivia sat on a chair beside her and motioned toward Charlie. "He looks happy to have his memory back."

"He is. I just..." She shrugged.

"What? You like the more serious Charlie? The one who doesn't feel like he has to make a joke about everything?"

Lizzie's mouth gaped open. How had Olivia read her mind? And worse yet, could she tell they'd kissed?

"It's not rocket science, Lizzie. Charlie covers his feelings. He's always been a happy, funny guy, putting others first. But Susan really did a number on him. He sank deeper into jokester mode and has never come out of it until his amnesia."

"I guess I've always known him as Mr. Funny Man." She tried to imagine a younger more serious version of him, but it seemed impossible.

"I suppose so. You all met him after Susan. Trust me, he's a different person now. And I'd like to see my old brother again." Olivia pushed from her seat. "I need to go grab Chaz from his daddy." She placed her hand on Lizzie's arm. "Don't let the mask of humor fool you. Charlie's deeper than that." Her boss gave her a knowing smile.

Had Lizzie been that transparent? She'd have to make sure to hide her feelings better in the future. She stood and inhaled, pushing the uncertainty to the back of her mind. She strode over and joined the group of men and women who were not only her coworkers and their significant others, but family. The only two missing were Steven and Haley. The newlyweds had left a little while ago, blaming jet lag.

Christina scooted behind Grey's wheelchair and placed her hands on his shoulders, making space for Lizzie. Christina had met Grey on her last assignment. While protecting Grey and his dog, Boss, she'd fallen in love with the man who'd sacrificed for his country. He'd been involved in a chemical weapons attack that left him in a wheelchair with long-term nerve damage that affected his balance and coordination.

Daniel told a story about a silly mishap in the kitchen at one of his restaurants.

Lizzie laughed at the visual of chefs and waitstaff sliding across the floor through salad dressing. "And I thought Charlie was the only one that had the gift of storytelling."

Charlie grinned, but she could tell it was forced. "Nah, Daniel has me beat in that area." He glanced at her and stepped back. "If you'll excuse me." He turned and retreated inside.

Olivia's gaze followed her brother, but no one else seemed to notice the shift in his mood.

"Hey, Lizzie. Are you ready for another lesson?" Katie asked.

She shook off Charlie's obvious avoidance then turned her attention to her friend and rubbed her hands together. "You know it."

"Uh oh, Lizzie's at it again." Quinn rolled his eyes. "How come you have to love learning new things? I can't keep up. Archaeology. Computer technology, marine biology. Too many ologies for me."

"I don't have degrees in those. I just like to dabble."

Wade shook his head. "Now what are you up to?"

Lizzie waggled her eyebrows. "Just learning how to blow things up."

"No. No. You're supposed to be learning how to disarm a bomb, not set one off." Katie pretended to scold her.

"Oh, so that's my problem."

Wade wrapped his arm around his wife's waist. "Olivia, honey, we need to talk about the company you keep."

"You're just now figuring that out?" Olivia smirked.

Lizzie's gaze drifted to the sliding glass door. Where was Charlie?

"Lizzie?"

"What?"

"You zoned there for a minute." Olivia said. "I asked how much longer before you graduate from Katie's school of explosives."

"Sorry." Lizzie returned her attention to Olivia. "I'd say another couple of months and then I can be her backup. Especially when she's out on maternity leave." Lizzie's mind shifted once more to Charlie and the kiss they'd shared and his not-so-subtle rejection. She had to keep her attention on the group and not raise suspicions.

No one could know that she was falling for Charlie.

10

TUESDAY, 8:00 A.M

With research on the menu for the day, Lizzie vowed to center her focus on Blackwell Seafood Inc. and not on her heart problems.

The bold aroma of Wade's special brew drifted down the hallway, a perk of staying with Olivia and her husband. Lizzie padded to the kitchen, poured a cup of the caffeinated beverage, and sipped the mind-clearing liquid. The warmth trailed down her throat, loosening the building stress. Hip resting against the counter, she gazed out the window at the glasslike pool surface and listened to the faint chirp of birds in the backyard. The view was serene, but it was the calm waters of the lake shimmering in the morning sun that mesmerized her, allowing a sense of tranquility to wash over her. Sleep hadn't come easy last night. The amazing kiss she'd shared with Charlie ran on replay in her brain. She took another sip and sighed. She'd act as though nothing happened between them since Charlie hadn't said a word about it. In fact, he'd been downright cold and had ignored her most of the evening.

She dug deep inside, pushing away the hurt, and let the scenery give her the peace she required for a day of delving into the newest lead in Charlie's case.

The click of a bedroom door tugged her from her musing.

Charlie, in black basketball shorts and a maroon South Carolina Gamecocks T-shirt, shuffled past her. His hair stuck out in multiple directions. With a *man on a mission* expression, he headed straight to the coffeepot.

Lizzie arched her eyebrow at her partner's appearance. "Good morning."

He held up a hand. "Coffee first, please."

She hid her grin behind her mug. Charlie was definitely not a morning person.

The glass carafe clinked on his cup then clunked on the warmer. He leaned against the counter and consumed the drink. Once finished, he retrieved the carafe, poured himself a refill, then ambled to the table and collapsed onto a chair. Both hands cradling his mug, he closed his eyes.

Lizzie shifted her stance and continued to wait. If he didn't say anything in a few minutes, she'd poke him to make sure he hadn't fallen asleep sitting up.

His eyes opened, and he sighed. "Okay, now you can talk."

"Are you sure you don't want an IV infusion?" She bit her bottom lip to stop her laughter from spilling out.

"I wish." He shifted his gaze to her. "You look tired."

"Back at ya." Lizzie settled across from him, unwilling to give away that she'd grappled most of the night with her feelings for him. "Christina is bringing the equipment later." Lizzie had talked to Christina before she'd left last night, requesting a setup of laptops and monitors for the upcoming research.

"Olivia said Quinn intended to drop by at some point this morning."

"Good to know." Charlie scratched the stubble on his jaw. "I hope he waits a while."

Lizzie studied Charlie. The man was a mess. "How do you ever make it to work on time?"

He scowled at her. "I'm usually not recovering from someone trying to kill me."

"You have a point." She'd come close to losing her partner more times than she wanted to count. *God, help me stay focused and do my job. Please, help me keep Charlie safe.* Lizzie startled at the silent prayer. Once again, desperation had driven her to reach out to God.

Before she could analyze her actions, the doorbell rang. Not a quick ding-dong but one of those fancy Westminster chimes.

Lizzie stood and waved her hand at Charlie. "Drink your coffee and become human again. I'll get it." She meandered through the living room to the front entrance. After a quick peek through the peephole, she opened the door. "Alice. How's it going?"

Alice Harper, CPD's composite artist, stood outside with her kit of drawing supplies. "Quinn called and said that you need a couple of sketches."

Lizzie motioned Alice inside. "Yes, we do. I'll set you up in the dining room and go first. Charlie's not quite ready for the day."

"Sounds good to me."

Lizzie pointed Alice to the dining room table then headed to the kitchen. "The sketch artist is here. Once I'm finished, it's your turn. Hopefully by the time you're done, Christina will have delivered the laptops and we can get started."

He lifted his mug in a salute. "I'll be ready."

His healing cuts and black bruises reminded Lizzie of how close Charlie had come to dying. Her mind tumbled to the past. All the men in her life—gone. She believed in God. She truly did. But during the times she'd desperately wanted Him to answer her prayers with a yes, He'd chosen no. When it came to the men she loved, God had turned His back on her and let her suffer the consequences of her poor choices.

With that sobering thought, Lizzie left Charlie sitting at the table and joined Alice for her witness sketch session.

Three hours later, Lizzie stared at the nearly identical composite drawings, hers and Charlie's. The two men from the delivery truck at Bobby T's stared back at her. To think they'd had Charlie's attackers within sight and let the dirtbags get away. She rubbed her temples to ward off the headache that simmered beneath the surface.

The doorbell chimed again.

"I've got it." Charlie strode to the front door. "Welcome to Grand Central Station."

"I see you're feeling better." Christina brushed past him. "Special delivery from EGA headquarters." She placed a box on the dining room table. "Here you go. With this, plus the rest of the stuff in the car, you should have enough electronics to feed your inner geeks."

Lizzie opened the box flaps and dug through the supplies while her friend retrieved the remaining equipment. Three laptops, with as many monitors and accessories, were scattered on the table. Lizzie was in electronic heaven. "Thanks, Christina."

"Anytime. Gotta run. I'm meeting Grey and Boss for brunch. Can't be late for my guys." Christina grinned and hustled out the door.

Charlie's gaze drifted from the entrance to Lizzie. "I don't think I've ever seen her quite so happy."

Lizzie positioned one of the monitors behind her laptop. "She's crazy about Grey. They make a good match. Grey's her fun, and she's his confidence."

"I'm glad. I haven't had an opportunity to really get to know Grey, but from the time I *have* spent with him, he seems like a great guy."

"He is. When Christina allowed him beneath her tough exterior, it was like she broke free of her past and is actually living now."

"I know Grey's surgery to repair his neuropathways wasn't as successful as he'd hoped so he can't ditch his wheelchair, but I'm praying the physical therapy helps him regain more of his mobility." Charlie lowered himself onto a dining room chair and booted up his laptop.

"No matter what happens, Christina will see him through." Lizzie dreamed of a life where she had a partner that supported her, one she told her deepest secrets to. But God had all but slammed that door shut. Then there was Charlie. She'd shared more with him than anyone else in her life. And there was the kiss that lingered in her mind...

Lizzie positioned another monitor on the dining room table and reached for an HDMI cable. Her arm bumped Charlie's. She jerked back. "Sorry."

His eyebrows rose. "No problem."

Great. Now he thought she was nuts. Lizzie had to get over the rejection and not let it interfere with work or their friendship. Determined to shake it off, Lizzie exhaled and retrieved the cable.

Over the next half hour, Lizzie and Charlie made quick work of creating a makeshift office, one worthy of an IT company. They settled in and searched the web for information on Blackwell Seafood Inc.

Lizzie brought up multiple screens searching for the businesses Blackwell supplied along the Carolina coast. "Says here Blackwell Seafood is headquartered out of Charleston."

"I've got multiple warehouses, but there's one about ten miles outside of Columbia." Charlie tapped a map on the monitor.

"Perfect. Now we have several locations, but keep digging. I want to know who these guys are and why they targeted you."

Wade and Quinn stood at the archway of the room.

"Wow, Quinn. You're right."

Quinn folded his arms across his chest. "I told you. Giving these two electronics is like feeding a gremlin after midnight."

"Ha. Ha. Very funny." Lizzie leaned back and stretched her arms above her head. "Whatcha got?"

Quinn turned serious. "Names."

The click of Charlie's keyboard stopped. His Adam's apple bobbed. "Who?"

"One Leroy Lambert and a Donald Petty. Both arrested for aggravated assault and a couple of possession charges. As far as I can tell, no dealing though. However, I can confirm they work for Blackwell Seafood, Inc."

Quinn handed Lizzie the file he'd brought. She opened it and shared the contents with Charlie. "Looks like the guys we met in the alley at Bobby T's."

"The same guys who..." Charlie's face took on a haunted look and he stared off into space.

The knowledge that he'd mentally relive his beating for years to come made Lizzie's stomach twist. She cleared the emotion from her throat. "Thanks, Quinn. This helps a lot."

"I—Sorry." Charlie's gaze connected with hers.

"Don't be," Lizzie whispered. The guys had settled across from her and Charlie, so she resumed her conversation with them. "I'd like to know what links Lambert and Petty to the undercover neighborhood."

The front door clicked shut and Laila waltzed in, followed by Katie and Steven. "Need some help?"

"Do lions eat meat?" Charlie stood and made room for the laptops that Laila and Katie had brought.

"Charlie, good to see you up and moving." Steven straddled a chair and sat down.

"Thanks, man. Each day is a little better."

Steven rested his arms on the top rung. "Lizzie, long time since we've chatted. What's your new endeavor?"

Katie snickered. "Trying not to get blown up."

Charlie's gaze landed on Lizzie.

Thanks a lot, Katie.

"What's she talking about?"

Might as well get it over with. "You know how I like to learn new things."

"Yes." Charlie drew out the word and narrowed his eyes.

Lizzie inhaled and straightened her spine, preparing for the backlash. "I've taken up defusing bombs. Katie's teaching me."

"You're doing what?" Charlie's voice boomed through the room.

"Remember the last few times when Katie's skills came in handy?"

Charlie didn't answer but grumbled his disapproval.

"Ignore him." Steven waved a dismissive hand toward Charlie.

She shifted to face Charlie. "I figured we could use another person familiar with explosives."

Charlie jaw twitched. "And what's next? Are you going to take lessons from Laila and become an expert in Krav Maga?"

"Hey now," Laila piped in. "There's nothing wrong with that. I've seen Lizzie's fighting technique. She'd be great at it."

"I agree," Lizzie said. "Maybe once I'm an explosives

expert, we'll talk about lessons. I've always wanted to learn Krav Maga and up my hand-to-hand combat skills."

"Sounds good to me." Laila nodded and returned her focus to the laptop in front of her.

Charlie threw up his hands in defeat. "Wade, you're the psychiatrist. Talk some sense into Lizzie."

The man chuckled. "I'm not getting in the middle of this."

Quinn shook his head. "Okay, so Lizzie plans to get herself killed. What else do we have?"

Lizzie stuck her tongue out at Quinn and caught Charlie's scowl out of the corner of her eye. He'd supported her before when she'd taken on new challenges, like when she'd learned sniper skills from Christina. And the time she'd taken flying lessons from Daniel. What had changed? "Can we please focus on the case and not my latest adventure?"

The group returned their attention to the task in front of them.

Ten minutes later, Katie leaned back and rubbed her baby bump. "I'm trying to link Charlie's undercover drug deals to Blackwell. And I've got nothing."

"If there's no connection, then why attack Charlie?" The whole case was giving Lizzie a headache.

"Unsure." Charlie's distracted response got Lizzie's attention. His fingers flew over his keyboard. "Check this out."

She leaned over. The closeness sent her senses haywire. She shifted back a bit so she could focus on the computer screen and not her swirling emotions. "Blackwell's delivery schedule?"

"Take a look. There's another delivery to the Columbia area including Bobby T's tonight."

Excitement zipped along Lizzie's spine. This could be the break they needed.

"Time for a stakeout." Charlie placed his palms on the table and leaned forward. "I'm grabbing a couple hours of shut-eye to rest my brain then we'll head out."

Lizzie grabbed his arm. "I don't think so. They'll know who you are."

Charlie's lip curved upward in a lazy smile, challenging her to disagree. "Surprise. I'll see you in a little while." He rose from his seat. After waving her off, he ambled toward his bedroom.

Lizzie rubbed her aching temples. Her gaze shifted to Quinn, Wade, and Steven. "Anyone else think this is a bad idea?"

Their matching frowns didn't require a verbal response.

After several moments of silence, Quinn slapped his knees. "I need to give the mayor a call. Be back in a few." He slipped from the room.

The rest of the group returned their focus to gathering information.

Lizzie's gaze drifted to the hall where Charlie had disappeared.

She couldn't do her job and keep him safe if he kept putting himself in danger.

The dark mahogany desk and tall office chair gave Mayor Eliza Baker an air of power, but right now she felt anything but. Her head pounded, and the new drug and gang wars in her city weighed on her. She tapped her pen on the desk pad.

Councilman Ted Reynolds sat across from her, anger flickering in his eyes. "So, what are you doing about it?" The man seethed.

"Ted, as I told you before, the gang unit is on it."

"Whoever killed those men and dumped them in Crips

territory is asking for retaliation. We can't have a gang war on our hands. We need to discover who's behind the taunt."

Eliza sighed. "I know that. And I have people on it."

"And what about the drugs? What are you doing about that? I heard you pulled the task force."

Oy. The man was like a dog with a bone. "Once again. It's being handled."

"I don't see how." Ted leaned forward. "You're dropping the ball, Mayor."

She pinched the bridge of her nose. "Calm down."

"You have to be kidding, right? People are going to die and you're sitting in your castle, refusing to do anything."

God, help me hold my tongue.

Her phone beeped. She almost laughed at the timing. She pressed the button. "What is it, Bonnie?"

"I'm sorry to interrupt ma'am, but Detective Holcombe is on line one."

"It's fine. Please tell him I'll be with him in a minute."

"Sure thing, ma'am."

Eliza turned her attention back to Ted. "Listen, I know this is personal. I'd feel the same if my child almost died from an overdose, but I can assure you, I'm not ignoring the problem." If only the man knew the lengths she'd gone to find the big fish.

"I certainly hope so. I'd hate to see you lose the next election."

She raised a brow. "Is that a threat?"

"No. Just a friendly warning that the good citizens of Columbia won't be happy if you don't clean up the streets."

"Well, thank you for your concern."

Ted stood and glared at her, then marched out the door without another word.

She collapsed back on her chair and closed her eyes. Some days she questioned her decision to become mayor.

Eliza sat forward and tapped line one. "Quinn. What a pleasant surprise."

"Thank you, Mayor. How are you doing today?"

"You're the bright spot in my day."

Quinn laughed. "That good, eh?"

She smiled. "Between a grumbling councilman and a letter from a certain brother, it's been a long day."

"Let me guess. Ted Reynolds was spouting off again about how worthless the police department is."

"Not the PD this time. He focused his ire on me and my inability to rein in the drugs and gangs in our city."

Quinn blew out a long breath. "The man doesn't have a clue."

"No, and I want to keep it that way."

"And the other?"

"Just Jacob Stone's brother asking me to use my influence to push for tougher laws against gang members."

"I don't disagree with the man."

"Neither do I, Quinn. But you and I know we're both trying to fix the problem."

"That we are."

Guilt tugged at her. She'd practically begged Charlie to go undercover, and he'd paid the price.

How lucky could he get? He positioned himself within earshot of the mayor's office and rested his back against the wall next to the water fountain. Pretending to concentrate on his cell phone, he turned his ear toward the conversation leaking from the small crack where the door hadn't latched shut.

"How is he doing?" Mayor Baker asked.

"Sore but healing," the voice on the speaker phone answered.

"Good. Good. I'm glad. Does he remember anything?"

"Most of his memories have resurfaced, but he still can't recall much about the day of the attack. Although, he can identify the two thugs who beat him up."

The mayor sighed. "So, no details about the setup?"

"Sorry, ma'am. I'll keep asking, but he's frustrated enough I'm afraid it will only make it worse."

"I understand. He's done a great job so far."

"He has. But I'd really like this one."

"Me too, Detective."

So, the man had started to remember. The losers he'd hired to eliminate the mayor's undercover snitch had better get the job done before the guy put it all together and derailed his plans.

His jaw clenched at the thought of failure in extracting justice on those who had ruined his life.

"We think we've uncovered a link to the drugs. I'll keep you posted on what we find."

"Please do." The call ended and a rustle of movement filled the conversation gap.

He pushed off the wall and meandered three offices down the hall and slipped inside.

He shot off a text to his contact. *Possible connection 2 U. Eliminate threat.*

A smile curved on his lips. The man would cease to exist—soon. And his revenge on all involved would continue to play out just as he'd designed.

Nighttime, a rental car, and plenty of coffee—ah, the life of being on a stakeout.

Charlie rolled his eyes. *Yeah, right.* He peered through the binoculars and came up empty—again. Despite the seat belt latch digging into his hip, the evening had a peaceful element to it. If only his mind would stop mulling over the kiss with Lizzie at Olivia's dock. He'd dreamed about it for years, and it hadn't disappointed. Attraction to Lizzie had never been a problem. Her hesitation and his feelings of unworthiness had safeguarded his heart from making a mistake. When his memory had blocked the reasons that he couldn't date her, he'd stepped over the line. Then his memory resurfaced and he'd all but ignored her. She'd acted normal all day, but now the silent treatment was getting to him.

Charlie shifted and leaned against the door. "You okay?"

"Yup." Lizzie kept her gaze on the warehouse.

Oh, yeah, he'd messed up. "I'm sorry, Lizzie. I had no intention of hurting you."

"Forget it."

He snagged her wrist in a loose grip. Her rapid pulse drummed against his fingers. "Lizzie, look at me."

She jerked from his touch, and her gaze met his. "What's there to say? You turned your back on me. It hurt—a lot." She inhaled deeply, tucking her irritation into the background. "But we're friends. Partners. And right now, you're my client. End of story."

He swallowed hard. He had to make her understand that she deserved more than his sorry self. "It's not that I don't want to be with you. It's that I can't."

She shook her head. "That's a cop-out. Either you do or you don't."

"It's not that simple. You deserve someone worthy of you." The next words killed him to admit. "I'm not that man."

Lizzie snorted. "Right. Whatever. It's over. Let's not talk about it and ruin the friendship that we have."

Charlie rubbed the old bullet wound on his thigh. A souvenir that reminded him of Susan's departure and how it had skewered him in the heart, leaving him floundering and hating himself. He might not have climbed out of the pit of self-destruction if Olivia hadn't intervened. Charlie thanked God for his sister every day, but the pain of Susan turning her back and spewing hateful words at him, even if they were true, still stung.

Lizzie whacked his arm, startling him out of his reverie. "Check it out."

A white delivery truck with the Blackwell Seafood Inc. logo pulled up and parked next to the loading dock.

"Well, what do you know." Charlie passed Lizzie the binoculars.

She inhaled. "Lambert and Petty."

"My favorite boys." He drummed the dashboard as anger and fear warred within. "What are they doing?"

"Loading crates of what looks like seafood."

"That makes sense, but why try to take me out for a fish delivery?" Charlie considered a host of reasons but came up lacking in the answer department.

Lizzie lowered the binoculars, scooched down in the seat, and settled in. Charlie followed her lead and rested his head on the passenger window, maintaining a full view of the delivery truck.

Neither he nor Lizzie spoke for the next thirty minutes. His annoyance intensified as he mentally crafted different scenarios in an attempt to figure out how his undercover assignment connected to these delivery guys. A buried memory plagued him. He'd forgotten something important, and the harder he tried to remember, the more frustrated he got. By the time

Charlie's assailants strode into the warehouse, his irritation had gotten the best of him. He had to get answers.

Charlie retrieved a GPS tracker from the console and shoved it into his pocket. "Come on." He grabbed the door handle and stormed from the car.

"Charlie, wait." Lizzie scrambled to catch up with him. "Slow down. Do you want to get caught?"

"No. But we have to figure out what's going on. We don't have time to sit around."

She clasped his bicep and jerked him to a stop. "Why?"

That was a great question. He had no idea why. A gut feeling told him time was running out. "I can't explain. Please, trust me. It's important."

She bit her bottom lip, appearing to mull over his request. "Okay. Let's go."

The truck sat fifty feet in front of them. He and Lizzie skirted around a few vehicles parked in the lot and stole their way to the white truck. Gravel crunched under his shoes and an owl hooted in the woods off to Charlie's right. He slipped behind the box truck and pulled the back door open a few feet. The metal rattled, sending his heart racing. He froze. "Please, God, don't let them hear us."

"I second that," Lizzie whispered and rolled under the open door into the cargo area.

After a quick scan of the surrounding area, Charlie joined her. He stood and allowed his eyes to adjust to the dim light. "We really shouldn't be here."

"You should have thought about that before you jumped out of the car and marched over."

"There is that." Charlie lifted a crate lid. "Fish."

"What did you expect? It *is* a seafood supply company." Lizzie checked another wooden box. It too was full of ice and fish.

The odor of fish and stale air churned Charlie's stomach. He'd never look at a seafood dinner the same way again. They explored the majority of the crates until Lizzy brushed her hands together. "I was so sure we'd find drugs."

Charlie pivoted, examining the enclosed space. "I don't want to say it, but what about under the ice and fish?"

"That would definitely help cover the evidence." She sighed, lifted a lid, and gestured into one of the boxes. "Undercover drug dealers first."

"Cute." He moved a couple of swordfish aside and plunged his arm into the ice. The freezing cold hit his skin, and he bit back a groan. He swirled his hand around the bottom of the crate and hit something hard inside plastic. He fought his numbing fingers to grab it and yanked it from the ice. A clear bag holding an Uzi dangled from his grip. "I think we found their secret."

Voices carried on the night air.

"We have to get out of here," Lizzie mouthed.

Charlie shoved the gun to the bottom of the container and rearranged the swordfish. He lowered the lid and jerked his head toward the door.

Lizzie slipped out and ran to the trees.

With her safe, Charlie dropped to the ground. He lowered the door and gave the latch a quick flick. The metal clanked.

"What was that?" Footsteps shuffled in Charlie's direction.

He dropped and rolled under the truck.

"See anything?"

Charlie slid the back-up Beretta from his ankle holster and pointed it toward the bumper.

Black boots stood at the rear of the truck. "Nothing."

"Then let's get these deliveries done."

Charlie held his breath. His gaze never wavered from the feet of the man threatening to discover his hiding place.

The boots paced back and forth then stopped. "All right, I'm coming."

Charlie released the air from his lungs. He slipped his hand in his pocket and retrieved the tracker. He placed the magnet side to the undercarriage of the truck and scrambled to the woods.

The truck rumbled to life and eased from the parking lot.

He lay on his back, arms out, gun in hand, staring at the canopy of trees. *Whoa, that was close.*

Fingers gripped the neck of his shirt. "Don't ever do that again!" Lizzie whispered through gritted teeth. "I thought I'd lost you to those maniacs."

Charlie fought the urge to laugh at her mom scold. If he wanted to live, he'd keep his comment to himself. "At least I got the tracker in place."

"Really? That's what you're worried about?" She released her grip and plopped beside him.

He clasped her wrist. Her pulse thumped at an unbelievable rate. "Lizzie?"

She shook her head. Her shoulders rose and fell while she focused on the tree in front of her.

The close call had consumed his thoughts. He hadn't considered how she'd react. *Way to go, man.* "Lizzie, I'm sorry. When I heard him coming, I dove under the truck to place the tracker. I shouldn't have taken the chance."

"You scared me." Her voice steadied. "We're partners and right now I'm responsible for your safety. I don't want anything to happen to you."

Charlie pulled to a seated position and grimaced. His actions had aggravated his injuries. When this was over, he planned to sleep for a week. He re-holstered his weapon and wrapped his arms around his bent knees, praying the sudden dizziness wouldn't last long.

Lizzie stood and dusted off the seat of her pants then extended her hand. "Come on, Hotshot. Let's go find the bad guys."

He accepted her help and rose to his feet.

She laid her hand on his arm. "I'm sorry I overreacted. I'll do better next time." Without another word, she headed to the car.

Charlie scanned the area one more time and noticed the distance between where the truck had parked and the tree line. His breath hitched. Only by the grace of God had either one of them escaped without being seen.

11

TUESDAY, 10:30 P.M

Lizzie gripped the steering wheel and tried to keep an emotional distance from the whole Charlie thing, but whether she wanted to admit it or not, her heart had jumped off the cliff without her permission.

The tires hummed over the pavement, the only sound disturbing the deafening silence inside the vehicle. She'd come close to losing it all because her emotions had gotten the best of her. How she would "decouple" herself from Charlie and continue to maintain a close friendship, she had no idea.

Sweat slicked her palms, making the hard plastic sticky under her fingers, enhancing the difference between this vehicle and the comfort and safety of her BMW. Lizzie aimed the rental car down the county highway, following the flashing dot on Charlie's GPS.

She glanced in the rearview mirror and wanted to scream.

Charlie straightened in his seat. "SUV. On your six."

"Yup, I see him." She refocused on the road ahead and considered her options. "Distance?"

"Five car lengths."

She scanned the area. The late hour had cleared traffic from the two-lane road, leaving no witnesses. The perfect place for an ambush. Just what they needed.

Charlie shoved his phone in his pocket and shifted for a better view. "Three lengths. He's speeding up."

"Hang on." She stomped the accelerator and the car lurched forward, forcing her back against the seat. Charlie grunted on the passenger side.

"He's still gaining." Charlie braced his hand on the door handle.

With a burst of speed, the SUV rammed the rear of the vehicle, propelling her forward. She yanked the steering wheel but failed to keep the vehicle straight. A second hit sent them spinning across the pavement and careening into the ditch.

Lizzie struggled to maintain control against the long grass and uneven ground. She swerved to miss a fence and struck a rut, sending the car airborne, and they flipped upside down. She screamed just before the hood crashed into the ground and glass shattered around her. The jolt forced her body forward, the seat belt stopping her forward motion and whipping her back against the seat. The vehicle teetered and creaked and came to rest at an odd upside-down angle.

The seat belt cut into her shoulder, and her arms dangled from her inverted position. Blood whooshed in her ears. She blinked and then blinked again while her mind scrambled to put the pieces together.

The hiss of the engine pulled her from the depths of confusion. An accident. The tail she'd picked up at the warehouse. Oh, no—Charlie.

A groan escaped her lips as she twisted to look at him.

Blood trickled from a gash on his forehead. Or was it the same cut from before that had reopened? The man had more bruises than Lizzie dared to count and added more every day. She stretched over and searched for a pulse. The strong thump against her fingers sent a wave of relief coursing through her.

What if the person decided to make sure he'd succeeded in killing her and Charlie?

She had to get him out of here.

Fingers wrapped around the seat belt strap, she pushed the release and tightened her grip in an attempt to slow her fall. Her body landed on the roof of the sedan with a thud. Fire shot down her arm. Her fingers tingled and momentarily went numb. She rubbed her shoulder and shifted to sit on the ceiling of the car and took inventory of her injuries. The bruise across her body from the seat belt ached, and her knee was sore, most likely from hitting it under the steering column. Why the airbags hadn't deployed was a mystery, but she was grateful since she didn't have a broken nose to go with the rest of her bruises.

She sagged against the car and wiped at the wetness on her cheek. Blood painted her finger. Great. She had a cut on her face to go with her other injuries.

"Charlie." Lizzie shook his shoulder. "Charlie, can you hear me?"

He shifted and cried out. His eyes fluttered open. Pain tormented his gaze. "Lizzie?"

"Take it easy." She analyzed the situation. "I'm going to release the latch and help you down."

He gritted his teeth. "Guess I don't have a choice."

"Not really, Hotshot. I'm worried the bad guys will circle back. We have to get out of here and find a place to hide." One hand and her sore shoulder braced Charlie, the other hand pushed the release. Charlie fell onto her. She wobbled and groaned, but maintained her balance and eased him down.

He hissed in a breath.

"All good?" she asked.

"Sure. Let's go with that." With significant effort, Charlie moved to a seated position. "Lizzie, can I admit that my body is killing me?"

She grinned for the first time all night. "I promise I won't tell, if you won't."

"Deal." Charlie froze. "Do you smell that?"

A hint of smoke filled the air.

What more could happen in one night? Scratch that. She didn't want to know. "Turn around."

"What?"

"Turn around. Get away from the windshield."

He spun and pressed his legs into the roof and his back into the seat, angling toward the front window.

Lizzie pulled her knees to her chest then smashed her boots into the safety glass. Two attempts later, the shattered window dropped to the ground.

"I'll go first. When I say, crawl out. And hurry. I don't like this." Lizzie pointed her gaze at him. "Got it?"

He nodded. "Go."

She wriggled out on her hands and knees. The windshield crunched beneath her palms, pricking her skin but not cutting it. When she found grass, she ducked under the car frame. "Okay. Your turn."

"Coming."

Lizzie slid her Glock from her waist holster and held it low and to her side. Her gaze roamed the surrounding area. She couldn't see the SUV from her position but maintained her diligence, just in case, until Charlie freed himself from the wreck.

"Please, tell me you have a plan." Blood and sweat stained his bruised face. "My head hurts too much to think straight."

She took in the terrain and jutted her chin toward the tree line. "Over there. Let's take cover behind those trees." A gray cloud drifted from the engine, and the odor grew more intense.

"I'm not liking the smoke." Charlie's voice was more tense than she'd ever heard it. She'd be surprised if the man didn't have flashbacks from the apartment fire.

Gun aimed at the road, Lizzie stood. If the bad guys had stuck around, she refused to give them a clear shot of Charlie. "Stay beside me." She helped him to his feet and wrapped her free arm around his waist. "Let's go."

They hurried to the woods. Once behind the trees, Charlie collapsed to the ground and rested his forehead on his bent knees. "I'm getting a little tired of this."

With no sign of the SUV, Lizzie crouched beside him and brushed chunks of glass from his hair. She'd failed him—again. "I promise. I'll protect you."

He caught her hand. "I've never doubted that. And we'll protect each other, okay?"

"Agreed. I just..."

"Trust me, Lizzie. I don't want anyone else to have my back."

"Are you sure?" Her words came out breathier than she'd intended.

"Positive." His gaze intensified.

An engine revved.

They both pulled away.

Had the person who had run them off the road returned to finish the job? She had to get her act together and stay focused, or it would cost Charlie his life.

"Stay here." Gun in hand, she eased from the trees for a better view.

"Hello? Anyone down there?" An older man stood at the road, squinting at the wreckage.

With a quick decision to trust him, Lizzie stepped from the wooded area. "Hello."

"Well, hello, young lady. It looks as though you need some help."

"Yes, sir, we do."

"What can I do for you? I've called the sheriff's office about the accident, but not an ambulance."

She took a few steps up the small bank, cringing at her own injuries from the crash, and studied the man before making a request for a lift. "That's okay, I don't think we need one. We could use a ride though."

"Sure thing."

"Hold on." She hurried to Charlie. "Think you can get up?"

"Once again, what choice do I have?" He pushed to his feet. "You sure we can trust this guy?"

"No. But we have to get out of here, and he appears to be the safest route at the moment."

Charlie nodded and followed her out of their hiding place among the trees.

The older man gave Charlie a once over. "You sure about that ambulance?"

Lizzie chuckled. "He's a sight, isn't he?" She ignored Charlie's glare. "I'll take him to the doctor later."

Charlie stumbled to the road and straightened. "Thank you for helping." He stuck out his hand.

The man shook it. "No problem. Name's Henry."

"Nice to meet you, Henry. I'm Lizzie and this is Charlie. We really appreciate this." Lizzie placed a hand on Charlie's back, more for her comfort than his, and followed Henry to his truck.

"Go ahead and jump in." Henry climbed behind the wheel.

Lizzie glanced at the mangled rental car. Smoke continued to snake from the engine but hadn't caught fire. How had they survived? And having a Good Samaritan come along? She had to give credit where credit was due. *Thank you, Lord.* "Henry, you're a godsend."

The man belly laughed. "I don't think anyone's ever called me that before, darlin'. But I'll take it." He cranked the engine and shifted to face them. "Where to?"

The hospital or EGA should be her response, but she glanced at Charlie. "Have a preference?"

He retracted his cell phone from his pocket and exhaled. "Downtown near Bobby T's Seafood would be great."

"You've got it, young man." Henry accelerated down the county highway. He chattered nonstop with Charlie, giving Lizzie an opportunity to text Olivia.

Lizzie: *Crashed car.*

Olivia: *Where?*

Lizzie gave her the location.

Olivia: *U OK?*

Lizzie: *Mostly. Discovered guns. No drugs.*

Lizzie watched the three dots wave up and stop, then start again. Apparently, Olivia was having issues getting her brain wrapped around what they'd found.

Finally, the text came through.

Olivia: *Any ideas?*

Lizzie: *Not a clue. Heading to Bobby T's.*

Olivia: *Got it. I'll take care of the sheriff.*

Lizzie: *Thx.*

Olivia: *Watch your back.*

Lizzie lowered her phone and glanced out the window. Checked the mirrors twice and decided no one was following them. How had she missed the tail, and what was up with the guns? Did they have something to do with the new influx of drugs that Charlie had been hired to stop? Or was something else unrelated going on?

She glanced at Charlie. Inadequacy wrapped around her. She'd tried to do it alone, and failed. Only one choice remained.

God, I've done a terrible job so far. Please, help me keep Charlie safe.

All common sense had exited Charlie's brain. He wanted to wrap his arms around Lizzie and plant a kiss on her that she'd never forget. But he'd hate himself tomorrow if he played with her emotions. He really needed to stop with the wishy washy. He needed to be either on or off the relationship ride. Charlie sighed and tuned back in to Henry's chatter.

Henry droned on about the local farmer's market. "I told my wife, Vera, that Jeremy should enter his tomatoes in the county fair, but do think that boy will listen to his granddad? Of course not."

Lizzie's leg pressed against Charlie, sending a zip of electricity through him. He attempted to tamp down his attraction, but the close quarters made it difficult.

"How old is your grandson?" Lizzie asked.

"He had his thirtieth birthday a few months ago. The whole family got together for a spring picnic. We had a ball." Henry lifted his cap and wiped his brow.

"Sounds like you have a close family." Lizzie shifted, leaning closer into Charlie.

He stiffened but failed to recover before she noticed.

She shot him a confused glance.

"Yes, little lady, we do. The missus and I are blessed to have three amazing grown children. They all married wonderful spouses and have given us a passel of grands."

"How long have you been married?" Charlie had no idea where that question had come from. Apparently, his mouth and head had lost their connection. The last thing he wanted to talk about was marriage and what he couldn't have.

"Fifty-five years next month. Best years of my life."

Charlie longed for what Henry had, a long happy marriage. He glanced at Lizzie. Strands of her brown hair had slipped from her ponytail and hung around her face. He took in her beauty. What would it be like to wake up next to her every morning for the rest of his life? He shook off the thought once again.

Henry adjusted the air conditioner in the truck. "You two are a cute couple. Just what people said about me and Vera. When are you planning to tie the knot?"

Charlie's jaw drop. "We...I..."

"Sorry. The missus always tells me I don't know when to shut my trap."

Lizzie gave Charlie a cheesy grin and patted his knee. "We haven't set a date yet, have we, sweetie?"

She had to be kidding. He glanced at her and saw the twinkle in her eyes, daring him. Little brat. Two could play at this game. He grasped her hand and brought her knuckles to his lips. "Not yet, but I plan to remedy that situation—soon."

Her pupils dilated and her muscles tightened.

Gotcha.

Henry chuckled. "Yes sirree, just like me and the missus."

Lizzie narrowed her gaze and tugged her hand from his, and Charlie bit his lip to suppress a smile. "Henry," Lizzie said. "I can't thank you enough for giving us a lift."

"No trouble at all." The older man turned onto Main Street and headed toward the restaurant.

Charlie pointed to a small parking lot a block from Bobby T's. "Right over there will be great."

Henry turned into the lot and pulled to a stop. "You sure you want to be dropped off here?"

Charlie opened the door. "This is perfect. Thanks again for the ride."

"Glad to be of assistance."

Charlie slid from the passenger seat and bit off a groan. His muscles had stiffened like an over-starched shirt. Every injury on his body decided to protest at that moment, but he grasped the top of the truck bed and hobbled out of Lizzie's way.

She scooted across the bench seat and stepped down. "Take care, Henry."

"You too, young lady. And try to talk that man of yours into seeing a doctor."

"I'll try, but he's a stubborn one." She winked at Henry, and the man chuckled.

"I'm right here," Charlie muttered under his breath.

Lizzie snickered.

He took a step back. "Thanks, Henry."

Lizzie latched the door closed and waved.

The older man lifted his hand in response and drove off.

"Can you move?" she asked him.

"That's the question of the day." Charlie jutted his chin toward Bobby T's. "That's a long way down there."

Lizzie bit her lower lip, and her eyes sparkled with amusement.

"All right, let's do this." Charlie took a step and hissed at the arch of pain that swept over him. "Stupid car accident." Lizzie wrapped her arm around his waist to support him, but he waved her off. He knew she was dealing with her own aches and pains. "I'm good. Just stiff and sore. Any updates on the car?"

Lizzie rubbed her shoulder where the seat belt had been. "Olivia texted back a few minutes ago. She talked with the sheriff's department. They're having the car towed in for evidence and investigating the scene. I'm sure they'll want our statements."

"No problem. A dark SUV rammed us and caused us to crash. Done."

"I have a feeling they'll want a few more details than that." Lizzie stopped at the crosswalk and waited on the light to change to Walk.

Charlie glanced down at the curb. The six inches from the sidewalk to the street seemed like a forty-foot drop. He wanted to plop down and throw a temper tantrum like a two-year-old who needed a nap. But he had to figure out what those delivery guys were up to before they tried to kill him —again.

The light flashed Walk and Lizzie stepped from the curb and came to a sudden halt when he hadn't followed.

He clenched his jaw and prayed his legs didn't give out. "I'm coming."

"Hang in there, Hotshot. It's only a little farther."

"Not close enough." The smell of cooked fish wafted in the air, making Charlie's stomach rumble. He hadn't thought he'd ever want to eat fish again, but the fried aromas stated otherwise. Wonderful. Now he was hurt *and* hungry.

Lizzie pointed to a late-night coffee shop. "Let me get you settled and check out where our boys are."

The argument that landed on the tip of his tongue disintegrated. He'd hit his limit and they both knew it. The accident had set a whole new wave of agony rolling through his head.

Once he was seated at a corner window table with a decaf coffee, Lizzie patted his shoulder. "I'm going to find our friends. Stay out of sight."

Charlie arched a brow. "Where am I going to go? I can barely move."

"Good point. I'll be right back."

He'd never forgive himself if she got hurt. No matter how much his head screamed at him, he couldn't let her go it alone. "Lizzie, hold up. Give me a minute and I'll join you. I don't want you going alone."

"Nope. You're my client. I'm not putting you in danger." She slipped out the door before he could respond, and jogged across the street. Her ponytail bounced with each stride.

His gaze followed her path and watched the shadows swallow her up.

Charlie tugged his cell phone from his jeans pocket. Finger on the speed dial button for his sister, Olivia, he fought the urge to call for backup. He had to trust Lizzie's training. But he cared about her—way too much—to let her do this by herself.

Forget his injuries. He should have pressed harder for her to wait. Charlie rolled his neck and stretched his muscles then headed out the door.

12

TUESDAY, 11:30 P.M

Lizzie had to compartmentalize her emotions before she got Charlie killed. His battered face and struggle to make it to the coffee shop had her wanting to take him to Olivia's and lock him away so no one could hurt him ever again. But that was her mom side talking. Not that she saw him like her child. Far from it. Her heart ached to give in and love the man. But she'd never forgive herself when he died because she'd chosen to love him. Yes, she realized how stupid that sounded. She couldn't love someone to death, so to speak. But with her history and God's silence to her prayers, it was a little hard to convince herself otherwise.

She shook her head, dislodging the horrible reminder, and quickened her pace. Lizzie hunched down behind a parked car and scanned the area.

A light glowed from the rear of the restaurant, and three men exited the back entrance. The restaurant manager, Councilman Reynolds, and Mayor Pro Tem Stone chatted for a minute, then shook hands and went their separate ways.

Lizzie's mind scrambled to make sense of the scene that had played out in front of her. What were those men up to at this time of night? Too bad she wasn't close enough to hear the conversation.

She made a mental note to ask Steven to dig deeper into the three then continued her search for the truck. A moment later, she spied the truck she'd been looking for.

The vehicle had stopped at the back of the alley, and the two men stood, shoulders propped against the side of the vehicle. The red glow of two cigarettes brightened and dulled. The low conversation was indistinguishable.

Trees dotted the edge of the parking lot, giving her cover to get closer. She stayed hidden and hurried from one car to the next then crept behind the nearest tree. The voices carried through the air, and Lizzie strained to listen.

"He better not be late. I've got plans," the nearest man said. She recognized him as Donald Petty.

Leroy Lambert flicked his ashes, sending them floating to the ground, and took another draw on his cigarette. "You tell him that. I'm keeping my mouth shut."

The two men continued to grumble back and forth.

So, they planned to meet another person. No doubt to hand off the guns. Lizzie focused on the distant conversation in hopes of picking up any other juicy tidbits of information.

Someone stepped up beside her and pushed against her arm. She bit back a scream.

"It's just me, Lizzie," Charlie whispered, his breath tickling her cheek.

"Don't ever do that again," she hissed through gritted teeth. "Why aren't you at the coffee shop?"

He pulled away and gave her an *Are you kidding me?* look. "You think I'd leave you out here alone?"

"You're in no condition for this. You're playing the client, and I'm playing the bodyguard. Remember?" Lizzie wanted to pull a Jethro Gibbs move and pop Charlie in the back of the head. It would serve him right.

"Stop nagging and pay attention." He pointed to the gun delivery twins. "What have they said?"

"Nothing important so far except they're meeting someone tonight."

Charlie braced his hand on the tree. "I wish Mr. Unknown would hurry up and make an appearance."

"You could have watched the whole thing from a comfortable chair inside." Lizzie still wasn't happy with him for coming out into the open. He had to realize that his actions made protecting him that much harder. "Sit down before you fall down."

"No can do."

She flicked a look at him. "Why on earth not?"

"Cause I won't be able to get back up."

Lizzie chuckled under her breath. "Well, there is that. Next time—"

The throaty muffler of a car rumbled in the distance, and Lizzie peeked around the tree trunk. A sleek black sports car with chrome side pipes whipped into the parking lot and pulled to a stop near the white box truck. The door opened, and a scruffy-looking man emerged from the driver's side. He rested his hand on the top edge of the window and scrutinized the area. Once he appeared satisfied, he slammed the door and sauntered to the truck.

The fine hairs on her neck spiked. Lucas, the drug dealer she'd run into while playing Rod's girlfriend, moved toward the two men. "What's he doing here?" She kept her tone hushed.

Charlie peeked over her shoulder. "Not a clue. From what I do remember, he doesn't deal weapons, only drugs."

Leroy and Donald straightened, dropped the cigarettes, and snuffed them out. Leroy stepped forward. "Hey, Lucas."

Lucas scowled at the ground where the cigarette butts lay then lifted his gaze to the two men. "Are they all there?"

"Of course." Leroy patted the metal side of the truck.

"Good. Get them delivered." The drug dealer handed over two envelopes. "Half now and half when I'm satisfied you've finished the job."

Donald flipped through what Lizzie assumed were dollar bills. "Whoa, wait a minute. This isn't half. Where's the rest?"

Had Donald seriously just questioned his drug boss? Lizzie had a bad feeling about what was coming but refused to blow her and Charlie's cover. Her job centered on Charlie's safety, not protecting the idiot that helped sell drugs to kids—or in this case, guns.

"After you messed up and let yourselves be followed, you expect more? You're fortunate that I'm paying you at all. Boyd had to clean up your mess and run them off the road. He doesn't come cheap." Lucas rested his hand on his hip.

"I don't like this," Charlie whispered in her ear.

Lizzie agreed, but what choice did she have? She couldn't use her phone to text or dial for help because the light might give away their location. She focused on Charlie. "Not much we can do."

A gunshot rang out.

Charlie shoved her against the tree and let out a grunt.

Lizzie shook off the sting of bark digging into her sore shoulder and slid her Glock from her holster, then eased from Charlie and peeked around the corner. Donald lay on the ground, blood pooling beneath him. A straight shot to the heart. She itched to call it in and run to assist, but Charlie came first—and there was nothing she could do for Donald at this point.

"Are you going to argue too?" Lucas snarled.

"No. I'm happy with my pay." Leroy's words quivered.

Lucas slipped his gun into his waistband. "That's what I thought. Now, clean up this mess and get the merchandise delivered."

"Yes, sir."

Without another word, Lucas returned to his car and sped from the parking lot.

Lizzie drew in several long breaths to calm her racing heart. They had to stay quiet and set up a rendezvous with Olivia. "Let's get out of here before Leroy spots us."

Charlie nodded but didn't move, continuing to cling to the tree.

"Are you okay?" Had he done more damage when he'd pushed her against the tree?

"Yeah, yeah."

She watched him ease to an upright position and took inventory of his visible injuries. The man required down time to heal. After getting away from the alley, she'd try to convince him to lie low for a few days.

Once in the clear, she steered him toward the coffee shop and the same seat he'd occupied before at the side of the window. Lizzie placed a call to Olivia, requesting PD for Donald's body, and asked for someone to pick them up, and then another call to Steven about the three men meeting at Bobby T's. With a promise he'd look into it, she hung up and ordered coffee for her and Charlie.

Hands cradling the warm mug, Charlie's gaze met hers. "This has to stop."

"I agree, but what can we do? Quinn and Steven are compiling information. We just have to be patient."

Charlie sighed. "I'm going back undercover to finish my assignment. I have to figure out where those guns are going."

What? Had the man hit his head again? "No way!"

"I'm sorry, Lizzie. I can't sit here and let more people die." He rested against his chair. "Besides, I can't hide for the rest of my life."

"I don't expect you to. Just until you can move without cringing."

He eyed her and jutted his chin.

Her heart dropped. She knew that determined expression. There wasn't going to be any talking him out of it.

Fear took over and she reached out to God again. *What am I going to do if I lose him too?*

WEDNESDAY, 1:00 A.M.

There wasn't a place on his body that didn't hurt, but someone had to put these drug dealers out of business, not to mention figure out what was up with those guns—and it looked like it was going to have to be him.

Charlie remembered talking to Jimmy, but whether or not he'd set up the sting continued to elude him. He rubbed his temples. Had Jimmy said something about guns in their conversation as well? Charlie just didn't know. And what about Lucas?

"I don't like this, Charlie," Olivia said. "You still can't remember everything. What if you slip up?" She sat on the couch with her arms crossed over her chest, challenging him to disagree.

Charlie melted into the recliner, thanking God that Olivia had come to their rescue and brought them to her place. But at one o'clock in the morning, after a harrowing evening, his patience and energy level had dropped to subzero levels and he just wanted to go to bed. Arguing with his sister was not on the top of his to-do list. Charlie's head hurt and he'd had enough of not knowing what was going on.

"We need that information. Jimmy is a huge piece of the drug scene. If Quinn can take Jimmy down and broker a deal, then we might catch the person responsible for the increased drug traffic in Columbia and the surrounding areas. Plus, those guns bother me. I thought Lucas was a small fish. But he seems to be a bigger player than we originally thought. When did Lucas venture into weapons?"

Olivia glared at him. "And that's the other thing. Those guns change the scope of your undercover assignment."

Charlie couldn't deny that point. He sent a pleading look to Olivia. "I have to try to at least take down Jimmy. Then we can regroup before we target Lucas."

"Listen." Wade settled on the couch, wrapped his arm around Olivia, and rubbed her shoulder. "I'm not encouraging nor discouraging this. But, are you sure you have the stamina?" He directed his question to Charlie.

Charlie couldn't hide his grimace. "A few ibuprofens and a good night's sleep and I'll be ready for action."

Lizzie grunted. "Right. Like all those injuries are going to disappear." She stood at the window and gazed into the backyard, hugging herself with her back to him.

"I know what I'm doing," he said. "I'm not a rookie here. I'll find out what I can about Lucas and the guns, set up the drug deal, and get out."

Lizzie spun to face him. "And what if you've already set up the deal? What then? He'll know something's up. You look terrible—"

"Why, thank you. I appreciate the compliment."

"I'm not joking." Lizzie's muscles tensed.

Charlie pushed from his chair and struggled to hold back a groan.

She raised an eyebrow.

He ignored her unspoken dare and stepped to her side. "What's up with you? You've never had a problem with me pushing my limits before."

"I've never..." Her voice trailed off.

"Come on, Lizzie, talk to me." The desire to wrap his arms around her almost won out. But he kept his distance.

Tears pooled on her lashes. "You'll go and won't come back. You'll leave me, and you'll get killed, and it'll be my fault."

He ran a hand down her arm. "I'm not going to die."

"They came close to succeeding the first time, and now that I... Trust me, it'll happen." She choked back a sob.

A throat cleared behind Charlie. He'd forgotten all about Olivia and Wade. Apparently, Lizzie had too.

"We'll give you two a minute." Wade escorted Olivia from the room.

Charlie ambled over and lowered himself onto the couch. He patted the cushion next to him. "Come here, Lizzie."

She looked as though she might argue but finally joined him.

"Please, tell me what's wrong," he said. "This is so unlike you. Giving me grief, yes. Telling me I'm going to die and tears? Not so much."

Lizzie shook her head.

"We've been friends and partners a long time. If I could, I'd beg for the opportunity to be more, but you deserve more than what I can give." Charlie tucked a strand of stray hair from her ponytail behind her ear. "What's going on?"

After a few minutes, she shifted and cupped his cheek. "I can't lose you too."

He covered her hand with his. "Why do you think that?"

"You just don't get it." She sniffed.

"I'm trying, but I need you to clarify. In English. In basic terms that I can understand."

She pulled away and stood. Her back rigid, she paced the room.

"Lizzie?"

"Remember how I told you about my dad, Addy's father, and my fiancé?"

"Sure. I'm sorry about what happened to them, but what does that have to do with me?"

A crease marred her forehead and a tear trickled down her face. "I loved them all so much. My dad of course because he was my dad. Trevor was my high school sweetheart. I thought we'd have a lifetime together raising our daughter. After he died, I never thought I'd find someone else, especially since I had a baby, but then Ethan came along. We were six months from our wedding when he was killed. I thought my life was over." She swiped at the wetness on her cheeks. "Don't you see?"

No. He didn't. Charlie grappled with her words and how they related to him. "Lizzie, your life hasn't been easy. And I don't blame you for being cautious, but I'm still not connecting the dots."

She spun to face him. Eyes wide, her chest rose and fell at an alarming rate. "Every man I love dies! God's turned his back on me, and I don't know... It's like He's punishing me or something by taking the men I love. I don't want to lose you too!"

Whoa. He sat, staring at her, stunned, unable to speak. Had she just admitted to being in love with him? Surely she just meant she loved him as a friend. A partner. Right? *Lord, you really know how to throw my emotions into chaos. How do I handle this?*

Charlie grasped her hand and tugged her onto the couch. "Lizzie. Calm down before you hyperventilate." He'd come back around to her declaration later, after he had time to process what she'd said. Right now, he'd do anything to alleviate her worries. "I can't sit by and allow these guys to hand out drugs like candy. And the guns create another layer of worry. Yes, I'm hurting and exhausted, and I'm not insensitive to your pleas. But if I can stop the influx of drugs and discover where those guns are going, I have to do it. It's not only my job, but who I am." He smoothed his hand over her hair. "I *am* going back undercover, but what can I do to help you deal with that fact?"

Body trembling, she peered up at him. "Wear a wire. Let me be prepared to step in if things go sideways."

A wire might prove dangerous, but if it eased Lizzie's worries, Charlie would take that risk. "Okay. Done. I'll wear the wire."

Relief shone in her eyes. "Thank you."

Lizzie rested her cheek against his chest and held him as if he'd vanish if she let go.

"I'm going to be fine," he said. "You'll see." He placed his finger under her chin and lifted. "And, Lizzie, you need to start trusting God again. He is listening to your prayers, I promise."

13

WEDNESDAY, 1:00 P.M

Of all the ridiculous moves, Charlie slipping back undercover topped them all. Heart racing and palms sweating, Lizzie was terrified her request of a wire had signed his death certificate. She wanted to give up control to God, and she had reached out to Him in the past couple of days, but the little girl in her couldn't let go of the fear that He'd ignore her pleas—again.

With a white-knuckle grip on the steering wheel, Lizzie maneuvered the rental car through the thinning morning traffic and pulled into a parking spot a few blocks from the targeted neighborhood. Not ideal if he got into trouble, but far enough away that no one should notice her. She inspected the area. Apartments and stores lined the street. The buildings were a step up from the run-down residences and businesses where Charlie's undercover apartment was.

Convinced it was safe to let Charlie out, she shifted in the driver's seat. His bruises and healing gash on his forehead had her irritation bubbling beneath the surface. "Don't do anything stupid and get yourself killed." She clamped her mouth shut. Snapping at him wouldn't help the situation, but at the moment, her mouth and brain functioned on different wavelengths.

Charlie fiddled with the rolled cuff of his button-down casual shirt. "Who, me?" He glanced up and gave her a lopsided grin. "I'll be fine. Assuming I can get this shirt to cooperate."

"Here, let me." She leaned over, adjusted the cuffs and collar, and left the top two buttons undone. She lifted the dragon medallion with the listening device that she insisted he wear from his chest and confirmed it faced the correct direction. Her gaze drifted to his face, and she cupped his cheek. He hadn't shaved, and the stubble felt rough against her hand. He'd mussed his hair to match his bad boy image. One she found extremely attractive. She pulled in a steadying breath. "There ya go."

"Thanks, Mom."

She rolled her eyes. "You really are a dork."

"I know."

The smug expression on his face made her laugh. Leave it to Charlie to break the tension. "Just be careful."

He placed his hand over hers. "Please don't worry, Lizzie. I'll be fine."

So he thought. If only she'd kept her feelings for him stuffed away where they belonged, she'd have more confidence in the outcome of his plans. She retracted her hand, immediately missing the warmth of his skin. "You remember the code word?"

"Watermelon."

She shook her head. "I have no idea how you'll incorporate that into a natural conversation, but knowing you, you'll do it with ease." She forced the taut muscles across her shoulders and neck to relax. Charlie didn't need the pressure of her worry.

He waved a hand like swatting a fly. "Sleep last night did me a world of good. I've got this."

Lizzie inhaled a shaky breath and tucked the earpiece into place. "Okay, Hotshot. It's showtime."

Hand on the door handle, Charlie paused. "Pray for me."

Tears filled her eyes, and she blinked them back. She'd do it for him, even if the outcome scared her to death. She nodded.

"Thank you." He opened the passenger door and exited the car. She should've tried harder to stop him, but even as the thought entered her mind, she knew the effort would've been pointless.

God, I haven't trusted You with my prayers in a long time, but I promised Charlie. Please don't let this go south. Give him the wisdom to know what to say and do. I'm counting on You.

Charlie strolled to the corner and pivoted to face her. "Comm check." His voice came through loud and clear.

She gave him a thumbs-up, wishing, not for the first time, that it was a two-way communication device. But they couldn't risk someone spotting an earpiece.

His shoulders rose and fell, then he straightened, added a swagger to his step, and crossed the street. He continued down the block, acting as if he owned the neighborhood.

Lizzie smiled. For the first time since Charlie had insisted that he go back undercover, her fears lessened. His cocky demeanor, whether forced or natural, assured her that he was up for the job.

Her cell phone rang and she slapped it to her ear. "Tremaine."

"Hey, Lizzie, it's Steven."

"Steven." Worry crawled up her spine. "You just missed Charlie."

"That's okay. I don't have anything that will help. I'm just checking in. Quinn and I are ready to move in if Charlie needs us."

Lizzie closed her eyes and let the relief wash over her. Charlie had backup beyond her.

"Yo, Rod. How's it going, man? You look rough." A gruff voice filtered over the earpiece.

"Hang on, Steven." She listened for the code word. After a short conversation, Charlie bid the unknown man goodbye. Air rushed from her lungs. "Sorry about that."

"No problem."

"Charlie headed out a little while ago. I'm monitoring the situation several blocks away."

"He's good at his job, Lizzie. He'll be okay." Silence lingered on the line. "Are you dressed for the part in case you have to intervene?"

"Yes. One *arm candy getup* on and ready for action. And thanks for the assurance. I'm not used to sitting back waiting. I'm feeling a bit helpless. My partner—and client—is out there without me."

Steven chuckled. "You and the other ladies have to be in on the action. That's what makes you all great at your job."

Lizzie appreciated the compliment, but left it hanging. "What if he messes up? What if he says something that tips Jimmy off?"

"You'll deal with it. We want Jimmy and the guy at the top of the new influx of drugs, but Charlie's safety comes first. So don't hesitate if you think he's in trouble."

The churn of her stomach settled at Steven's words. No more second-guessing her priority. Her focus remained on Charlie's well-being, not on the worry of blowing his cover.

"Thanks, Steven. I needed that."

"Anytime." A puff of air filtered over the line. "Although, I have to admit, that new development of guns worries me."

"Me too. I wish I knew how those fit into all of this."

"We'll figure it out."

"Any news on our businessmen?"

"Not yet, but we're working on it."

Lizzie rubbed her forehead. "Ever feel like you're being pulled in too many directions?"

Steven chuckled. "Every day. Listen, I have to go, but we're here if you need us. Keep me posted on Charlie."

"Thanks. Will do." She hung up and stared down the block, again wishing she'd protested harder.

Charlie's mic picked up a rhythmic whoosh and thump. His even breaths accompanied by the medallion brushing against his shirt and bouncing against his chest comforted her.

"Here we go," Charlie whispered.

Lizzie sat up straight in the driver's seat and checked her instinct to go for her weapon.

"Jimmy, my man. What's up?"

"How's it going, bro? What happened to you? You cheat on that woman of yours and she beat you up?" Jimmy chuckled.

"I'm not stupid. Who'd cheat on that?"

That? When she got her hands on him... Lizzie paused then smiled. Charlie would never say that to her. He knew what he was doing and how to talk to Jimmy.

"Gotta point. Haven't seen ya 'round."

"Just checking out my other business ventures for a while. Anything new around here?"

"Nah, man. Same ole, same ole."

A long pause twisted a knot in Lizzie's gut.

"We good to go?" Charlie's nonchalant words started her breathing again.

"Yup." A smack echoed through the earpiece.

The scuff of shoes on concrete and short, uneven breaths filled her ear. Her hand flew to the door handle, and she flung the door open. She was too far away, and he needed her. How had Charlie talked her into this? She bolted from the car and stopped at the crosswalk. *Get a grip, Lizzie.* Even if under duress, Charlie would have uttered the code word.

People flowed around her as she stood at the curb. If she barged in and he didn't need help, she'd blow his cover. She bit her lip as her mind spun with uncertainty.

"Don't move, man."

"What's up with you, Jimmy? Put the knife down."

Lizzie raced down the sidewalk and slipped around the corner. She skidded to a halt. Jimmy's arm wrapped around Charlie, and the glint of a blade lay against his throat.

"It was you, wasn't it?" Jimmy snarled.

"I have no idea what you're talking about."

Go or wait? She fought the instinct to pull her concealed weapon. She inched closer and took up position fifty feet away, ducking behind a building. Charlie still hadn't used the code word. She willed her racing pulse to slow but didn't have much luck. *Trust him, Lizzie.*

"The bust at the drug house on Friday night. You're the one who snitched." Jimmy pressed the knife harder onto Charlie's throat, piercing the skin.

Blood dripped from Charlie's neck. "Nah, man. Wasn't me. I got jumped and was in the hospital."

"That's what your mess of a face is about?"

"Yeah. Go ahead. Call the hospital and ask."

Come on, Jimmy. Let him go. Lizzie would give it another thirty seconds. If the situation didn't change, she'd intervene. Her hand slipped to the small of her back. The cold metal of her gun eased her frayed nerves. She'd sniper trained with

Christina and could make the shot if needed. Although, a handgun at this distance added a layer of uncertainty.

Jimmy released Charlie and shoved him away.

Charlie stumbled and righted himself. His hand swiped where the knife had cut and he glanced at the blood on his fingers. "What are you trying to pull? Not a great way to do business. I'm rethinking my offer."

"Sorry, man, but there's a mole on the streets. And since I hadn't seen you in days, I assumed it was you."

Charlie shook his head. "Are we done here?"

Jimmy nodded. "Same plan as before?"

"I guess. But don't pull that garbage again." Charlie scowled at the drug dealer.

"See ya, soon." Jimmy held out his fist, and Charlie bumped it with his.

Lizzie collapsed against the brick wall. Charlie's life had flashed before her eyes. She'd come close to barging in and taking Jimmy down.

Relief flowed through her at the sight of Charlie heading her way. She planned to give him a piece of her mind. How dare he not call for backup when Jimmy had pulled the knife.

She narrowed her gaze, and her heart sank to her toes as he approached. His pallor and labored breathing scared her.

He fell into step beside her.

"Charlie?"

He shook his head.

They made it to the car and she hurried to the passenger door and opened it. He stumbled the last few feet, and Lizzie grabbed his arm to prevent him from faceplanting on the pavement. When he lowered himself onto the seat, she knelt beside him and retrieved the first aid kit from the glove box. She peeled open a package of gauze and held it to his neck. "What's wrong?"

His chest and shoulders rose and fell in a jerky motion. "Skull...meeting...tight chest...can't breathe."

She clutched his wrist and timed his pulse rate. Way too fast. The man might stroke out or have a heart attack if he didn't calm down.

Charlie felt like a fool, and there wasn't a thing he could do about it. He'd come close to saying the wrong thing. When his gaze had drifted to the skull tattoo with flaming eyes, his memory of setting up the drug deal returned. Just in time. The bust was still intact. Then Jimmy had pulled the knife on him. Charlie had thought for sure he was a dead man.

Thank you, God, for the nudge of memory and saving my life. But I'd really appreciate it if You'd help me breathe.

Streaks of white lights in his vision mixed with a collapsing gray tunnel. He knew he was seconds from passing out.

"Slow down. You're hyperventilating." Lizzie eased his face to look at her. Her wide brown eyes filled with worry. "Breathe with me."

He mimicked her breathing pattern, and the lightheadedness slowly faded. The world came back into focus.

"Sorry." Charlie covered his face with his hands.

She took his hand and placed it over the gauze then reached across him for the water bottle resting in the cup holder and twisted off the cap. "Here. Drink."

He took the offered bottle and drained half of it before directing his attention to Lizzie. "Thanks."

She nodded.

"When I saw Jimmy's tat, the memories flooded my brain. The drug deal setup, date, and time came tumbling back. The next thing I knew, I had a knife to my throat. I thought..."

Nope, he refused to go there. "Anyway, once I turned to leave, the flashback came hard and fast. I hate that feeling of helplessness. How do you live with panic attacks?"

Lizzie shrugged. "I've learned coping techniques. That along with medication balances the chemicals in my brain."

Until he'd worked with her twenty-four seven, he'd never known about her depression and anxiety. Now, he admired her strength. He wiped the sweat that beaded on his forehead with the bottom of his shirt.

"Well, whatever it is, I'm impressed."

She snorted. "I'll remind you of that next time I drive you crazy." She turned serious. "Are you okay if I go ahead and turn on the car so you don't overheat and add to your misery?"

"Please." He moved his legs and she shut the passenger door.

Once in the car, she cranked the engine and adjusted the air vents in his direction.

He dabbed his neck and found the bleeding had stopped then leaned back on the headrest and closed his eyes. "Let's go to my house."

Without a word, Lizzie put the car into drive and pulled from the parking lot.

His head pounded from the fading adrenaline, and his body ached from the fight to catch his breath. The hum of the tires on the street lulled him to sleep.

A hand shook his shoulder. "Charlie. We're here."

He lifted one eyelid and discovered they'd arrived at his house. Charlie straightened in the seat and ran a hand over his face. "I must be more tired than I thought."

"You needed the rest." Concern continued to linger in Lizzie's eyes. "Think you can move?"

Now *that* was a good question. Charlie opened the door and swung his legs from the car. He pushed himself to a standing position, then ambled up the sidewalk to the two-bedroom bungalow he'd purchased after moving home to Columbia.

The noontime sun beat down, adding to his misery.

Lizzie held out her hand. He chose not to argue and handed her the keys. She unlocked the door and peered inside. Charlie stepped around her, headed for the living room, and collapsed on the overstuffed couch.

"Come on over." He patted the cushion beside him.

Lizzie didn't join him but paced along the front window. The muscles in her clenched jaw twitched.

Charlie struggled to keep his eyes open, but the calm partner who'd helped him home had vanished and he needed to find out why. "What's going on?"

She continued to wear a path in his carpet.

He tilted his head and studied her. "Lizzie?"

She came to an abrupt halt. "You could have died because of me."

"Wait. You?" What was she talking about? His scrambled brain tried to sift through the events of the past week. "I don't understand."

"You just don't get it." She huffed and threw her hands in the air. "I need to call Olivia and hand off your protection to someone else before I get you killed."

"You are *not* calling Olivia."

She spun and glared at him.

His shoulders sagged. "Lizzie, sit. You're making my head hurt." *Please, talk to me.*

Mouth twisted to the side, she marched over and plopped down. "Fine."

"Would you stop with the attitude for a minute and tell me what's going on?"

She stared at the ceiling then inhaled.

Good. She'd relaxed enough that a conversation was possible, and he'd pry because that's what partners did. "You mind telling me why you're so upset?"

"I don't want you to die," she whispered.

The words were like a punch to the gut. Of course. He wanted to smack his forehead. All the men in her life had died, and he'd had a close call today.

He interlaced his fingers with hers. "Lizzie. I'm not your father, or Trevor, or Ethan."

She focused on the far wall, refusing to look at him. "You'll leave me too."

He was fairly intelligent, at least he'd always thought so, but following a woman's thought process wasn't his strong suit. This whole situation confused him. His partner exuded strength when they worked together. Which he'd discovered was a wall she'd built to mask her internal turmoil. He squeezed her hand. "Why are you so scared? Please, tell me the truth and not some made-up excuse."

When she faced him, fire lit behind the torture in her brown eyes. "Because I love you, you idiot!"

He blinked. She loved him? Liked, sure. Attracted to, yes. But loved?

"I'm sorry. I shouldn't have said that." She started to stand.

He gently wrapped his fingers around her wrist, holding her in place. "You love me?"

She bit her lip and nodded.

Before his head caught up with his heart, he pressed his lips to hers. She stiffened then encircled her arms around him and deepened the kiss. For the first time in years, his chaotic world settled. He never wanted to let her go.

Charlie eventually ended the kiss. He rested his forehead against hers and worked at settling his racing pulse. "That could get addictive."

She smiled. "Oh, yeah."

As much as Charlie tried to regret his actions, he couldn't. He loved this woman—had for a long time. She thought her love was a curse and would no doubt struggle with his professional risks. She faced the same dangers, but her fears would dictate her needs, not common sense. And he couldn't—wouldn't—leave a job he considered a calling. Not for her—or anyone. Unless God asked him to shift careers, he'd remain a bodyguard and protect those who needed him for as long as he was physically able.

And then there was what had happened while he'd lay there recovering from his bullet wound. Susan's painful words echoed in his head—that he'd never be a good husband and father. But Lizzie made him want to try.

However, she deserved honesty—not only about his career choices, but about his past—before he had any right to say the words back to her.

God, please don't let me hurt Lizzie. She's my partner, my best friend. Give me the courage to tell her the truth.

14

WEDNESDAY, 4:00 P.M

Warmth flooded Lizzie. She touched her lips. Charlie had kissed her—actually kissed her after she'd all but yelled at him that she loved him. Not the best declaration of love, but it had apparently worked.

She released a satisfied sigh and met his gaze. The desire that filled his eyes had dulled. Her nerves coiled, ready to burst if he told her that they shouldn't have kissed. "Don't you dare say it."

"Lizzie."

Tears welled at his pleading gaze. "No way. You'll never convince me." She lifted a trembling hand and pinched the bridge of her nose. She'd handed him her heart, and he intended to stomp on it. When would she learn to let her feelings go?

"It's not fair to you if I'm not honest." Charlie clutched her fingers and kissed the tips.

"You know my secrets. All of them." Tears spilled over her

lashes. "Even my most private one about my depression and anxiety."

He nodded. "And I'm honored you shared them with me."

"Then tell me why." The man sat there pretending to fall on his sword with his refusal to love her. But there was nothing honorable in his rejection. He'd better have a good reason for ignoring the feelings flowing between them or she'd consider flattening him—injured or not.

He pursed his lips. She saw him struggle to choose his words carefully.

His concern touched her, but knowing the truth became important, for his sake and hers. She softened her tone. "Charlie. We've been friends and partners for the past few years. You've never had more than a casual date. And many at that."

He scooted back and scowled. "Are you calling me a player?"

"If the shoe fits." She forced a grin that faded as fast as it formed. "But no, you're not a player. I'm just stating a fact. I know you better than most of the Guardians. I've seen your kind heart when you do things behind the scenes for the rest of our coworkers, our friends. You put everyone else first. It's like your happiness doesn't matter to you." She paused and gripped his hand. "Why haven't you moved on since Susan?"

His eyes widened.

She'd surprised him with her assessment. Good. Someone needed to shake up Mr. Cool once in a while. "Well?"

"I..." He closed his eyes for a moment before he turned his full attention to her. "Lizzie, you're special to me. If that kiss didn't convey that, then I did something wrong."

Her face heated at the memory. Oh, it communicated a lot. That's why his dismissal stung. "The message was loud and clear."

He smiled, a bit too smug for his own good, then blew out a breath. "I can't leave EGA."

What? Why did he think he'd have to leave? Because of them working together? "You know Olivia wouldn't require one of us to quit."

He shook his head. "No, Lizzie, that's not what I mean. I will always have a job in protection. Whether as a bodyguard or going back into law enforcement. I won't put aside the career God meant for me. For you or anyone."

Her mind whirled, trying to sort out his words. The meaning behind his statement hit her like a right hook. She flinched. "You think I'd ask you to quit?"

"Yes." He reached up and smoothed her hair. "You said yourself that you feel like you're cursed and any man you love will die. I have a dangerous job. You'll never relax. And I can't walk away from who I am. I'm not inclined to risk my heart and have a replay of Susan's departure."

The truth of his words stung. She wanted to refute his assessment of the situation but couldn't. "I don't know what to say." He was right. Lizzie wanted to deny his statement, wanted to scream at the unfairness, but she held her emotions in check.

His shoulders drooped and the sadness in his eyes ripped a hole in her heart. "As much as I want to jump in and explore a relationship with you, I can't. We'd both get hurt. Susan was right—I'm not husband material."

Lizzie's spine straightened. "What are you talking about? What did that woman say to you?"

"Sheath your claws." He laced his fingers with hers and rubbed her thumb.

She shook her head. How dare that woman bad-mouth him. "No. I want to know what she said."

"Susan said my job always came first. And that I take way

too many chances, like I have something to prove." He shrugged. "Which I guess all of those things are true."

"No. I disagree. You might take risks, but you're never careless." She'd known the man three years. He might take chances, but he wasn't reckless.

"Thank you, Lizzie." He lifted her hand and kissed her knuckles. "There are two things you can count on. I will always be your friend. And if you can ever give your fears over to God and can handle the uncertainty of the danger, and I can put my demons to rest, I will gladly explore whatever this is between us."

That did it. Tears spilled over her cheeks. Charlie had proved once again to be the kind of man she wanted in her life. *God, can I do it? Can I trust You with the man I love?*

"Just so you know, I plan to work on trusting God so I can get another one of those Charlie kisses." The kind that curled her toes and made her head spin. But she refused to tell him that. His ego did *not* need encouraging.

"I'm looking forward to it." He nestled deeper into the couch and tugged her close.

She rested her head on his chest and listened to his heartbeat. Strange. The rhythm calmed her and melted the tension away.

The sun that had once streamed through the window had moved in the sky, leaving a perfect view of his front yard. She absorbed the beauty of the landscape. The roses peeked through the bottom of the glass and a weeping cherry tree filled the lawn with color. She let herself drift in the moment. They sat in each other's arms and time stood still. She never wanted to leave this cocoon of contentment.

Lizzie eventually accepted reality. "We should call Quinn, Steven, and the team, and let them know about the drug sting."

Charlie sighed. "Yeah, we should." He seemed reluctant to release her. The feeling was mutual, but they had work to do.

Lizzie eased away, instantly missing his touch.

Charlie stood, appearing to give his muscles a moment to adjust then strolled down the hall. He returned a few minutes later with his laptop. After booting it up, he logged into the scheduled video chat. Boxes filled with friendly faces dotted the screen. Her coworkers—extended family, really—greeted her and Charlie.

"Glad to see you safe and sound." Olivia smiled.

"Me too, sis." Charlie rubbed his thigh, something Lizzie caught him doing when stressed.

After a round of greetings and expressions of relief, Lizzie dove in. "I know y'all want to hear about the trip down undercover lane. I'm pleased to say that Charlie's brain decided to engage."

A few snickers and a glare from Charlie made Lizzie smile.

"Thanks a lot." Charlie rolled his eyes.

"What do you have for us?" Quinn asked, moving them along.

"I didn't get anywhere with the guns because it got, shall we say, a little intense, but I remember the date and time for the sting." Charlie shifted and grimaced.

Mental note to self, get him some pain relievers when the video call ended. Lizzie handed him a throw pillow and he stuffed it behind his back.

He muttered his thanks and continued. "The deal is set for two days from now at 8:00 p.m. at the abandoned warehouse on Two Notch Road. It's the day after the mayor's birthday party, so it gives you plenty of time to set it up, Quinn." Charlie paused, opened his mouth then closed it.

"Charlie, what is it?" Maddy prodded.

Lizzie nudged him but he didn't respond. Her gut twisted.

She prepared to slam the laptop closed if he had a flashback. No need for the team to witness that. She waited to see if he snapped out of it.

Olivia's expression turned from relief to worry. "Lizzie, what's going on?"

She shrugged and mouthed, *I don't know.* Lizzie clasped his hand and squeezed. *Come on, Hotshot. Talk to us.*

He blinked. "Oh, sorry."

"Mind telling us what just happened?" Katie added her concern.

Charlie ran a hand over his hair. His eyes darted back and forth like he was searching the files in his brain for an answer. "Something about the mayor. There's a memory in there." He tapped his head. "But I can't dig it out."

The group talked on top of each other, throwing out ideas. But Lizzie focused her attention on Charlie's reaction. The more he fought to regain the information, the more pain crossed his features.

Steven cleared his throat, and everyone stopped talking. "Charlie." Lizzie welcomed Steven's normal, calm tone. "Is there a threat against her? Think about your impressions. Don't focus on specifics."

Quiet descended throughout the team as they waited for Charlie's response.

He rubbed his forehead. She could see the wheels turning, seeking the answer.

"Talk it out," Lizzie whispered.

He peered over at her and exhaled. "I overheard something, and I remember dread pooling in the pit of my stomach. For the life of me, the *what* eludes me. All I know is that it had something to do with the mayor, and I was desperate to call Quinn."

"I don't like it," Quinn growled.

"Normally, I'd tell my husband to stow the bear, but this time I agree with him," Maddy said.

Charlie clenched his fist. "I'm sorry, guys. I just can't recall why it bothered me."

Steven leaned in. "It's okay. You'll figure it out."

Charlie dropped his head on the back of the couch and closed his eyes. "Before it's not too late, I hope."

"You've remembered the drug sting. That'll take a lot of new drugs out of play in Columbia," Olivia reminded him. "It'll come to you, bro. Don't force it."

Charlie stared straight ahead and didn't respond.

Olivia turned the conversation in another direction. "Anyone come up with information on the guns Lizzie and Charlie discovered?"

Charlie readjusted his position on the couch and shook his head. "That was a bust on my end. Jimmy didn't even hint at another business, and I wasn't in a position to probe."

"My CI doesn't have anything either. It was news to him." Quinn rubbed his jaw. "There's something about this that feels off."

"I'm right there with you," Steven said. "I've used my contacts as well. No one knows of anything big going down."

Laila straightened. "This screams gangs. I'm going to do a deep dive and see if I can unearth something on that front."

"Do it," Olivia agreed. "I talked with Mayor Baker, and she has nothing new on that front. Just the normal grumbling between gangs. But she seemed concerned with those two bodies left in Crips territory. It makes me wonder what's going on."

"I second that." Quinn crossed his arms. "I'll put some more feelers out with our gang task force."

"Be careful not to alert them to our special drug assignment," Charlie warned.

Quinn scowled. "Really?"

"Now, boys, play nicely in the sandbox," Maddy scolded the two of them.

Lizzie bit her lip to keep from laughing.

"What about the men Lizzie saw at Bobby T's?" Olivia asked

Steven rocked a pen back and forth between his fingers. "Nothing yet. I'm considering just flat out asking the manager."

Lizzie glanced at Charlie and frowned. She could feel the fatigue rolling off him. It was time to put an end to the conference call and make this man get some sleep. "It's been a long day, y'all. I'm going to convince Hotshot here to get some rest."

The corner of Charlie's mouth quirked upward into a lopsided smile.

He knew her plan, and that was okay with her. Someone needed to put him first once in a while.

"Sounds good." Olivia took charge. She reminded everyone about the mayor's birthday party and updated them on the Mental Health Awareness rally. After confirming assignments, one by one the team clicked off.

Lizzie took the laptop, closed it, and set it on the coffee table.

Charlie released a long stream of air. "Thank you."

She patted his leg and stood. "Let me get you some food and some ibuprofen. Once you're done eating then you can head to bed." The fact he didn't protest going to sleep before seven in the evening slightly worried her. But she had no intention of leaving him and would be around to keep an eye on him. Tonight, after he was tucked away in his bedroom, she'd crack open the laptop and dig into the local gangs, the trio at Bobby T's, and Blackwell delivery. Her head hurt just thinking about the work ahead.

Lizzie fixed Charlie a plate and grabbed the bottle of ibuprofen. "Here ya go."

Charlie accepted the sandwich and ate in silence. Once finished, he swallowed the offered tablets then hauled himself to his feet. "I appreciate all you've done." He paused. "And I know that look. No need to bunk on the sofa. Take my extra bedroom." Not waiting for her response, he trudged down the hall and disappeared through a doorway.

Lizzie plopped down on the couch and laid her head back. *God, he's hurting. In more ways than one. I feel helpless. What can I do to ease his pain? I lo...* She stumbled on her next words, not wanting to say them again. Panic and peace warred within her brain. God was in control whether she liked it or not. But what if she didn't like His answer? She just hoped it didn't involve Charlie losing his life.

Over the next few hours, she called Addy to check in, ate dinner, and did background checks on anyone and everyone she could think of from Larry Lambert, the mayor's administrative assistant, the Mayor Pro Tem Jacob Stone, all the way to Mayor Baker herself. She scribbled notes to investigate later.

Her phone buzzed. "Tremaine."

"Hey, Lizzie."

"Quinn. What's up?"

"Checking in on our boy. He looked a little rough around the edges earlier today."

"Asleep. He crashed about..." She glanced at her phone for the time. 11:00 p.m. "About four hours ago."

"He needs the rest."

"He does." Lizzie glanced at her notepad. "Quinn?"

"Yes."

"I've been doing an info dump on all the players that might have knowledge or overheard about Charlie's undercover gig."

"I'm listening." Was it her imagination, or had Quinn's demeanor changed in those two words?

"Not a lot there in regards to the drugs, but I did run across something interesting." She doodled a bubble around Jacob Stone's name. "The mayor pro tem's nephew was killed in a drive-by shooting."

"I'd heard that."

"Did you hear that no one was convicted?"

Quinn remained silent.

Lizzie propped her stocking feet on the edge of the coffee table. "And his sister-in-law committed suicide last year."

"That's why he's creating the new community program on mental health awareness. What are you getting at?"

"Don't you find the connections odd?"

"Yeah, maybe. I'll take a closer look." A baby cried in the background. "Got to go. Little Miss Stacy is making her presence known and it's my turn." Quinn didn't sound at all upset about his duty. In fact, his grizzly bear had turned into a teddy bear at the mere mention of his daughter's name.

"Have fun, Quinn."

"Thanks, Lizzie." He disconnected the call.

Lizzie tapped her phone to her chin, mulling over her conversation with Quinn. She blinked when she realized her thoughts were spinning in circles. Her brain mush, she shut the laptop and decided to get some sleep before tackling the puzzle again.

After confirming all the doors and windows were locked, she ambled to the guest room and fell face down on the bed, in no hurry to move.

Charlie's earlier words about God listening to her prayers swirled in her mind. Was it finally time to give Him another chance? She bit her lower lip, debating her next words. It was time to put up or shut up. Maybe. But she couldn't quite go all in. *God, please help Charlie heal. I'm trying to trust You with his life. But it's hard since I don't know what Your answer will be.* Pressure built behind her eyes. *I can't lose him. I just can't.*

Oh, the things he discovered by simply listening.

The floor of City Hall that held the mayor's office was a wealth of information. He'd kept a low profile while getting a cup of coffee and said a quick good morning to the receptionist before heading to his—for lack of a better word—meeting.

Eavesdropping on private conversations was a gold mine.

In the short time span, he'd learned the mayor had formed a small task force to stop the drugs coming into Columbia. And Jimmy had fallen into her web of deceit.

Well, good for her. It was about time someone did something about the drugs. His lip curved upward. Poor Jimmy. The man had served his purpose, and if he went down for dealing drugs, so be it.

And Lucas had the distribution of guns well in hand. A few guns to the Crips, a few to the Bloods with a nicely placed rumor, and then let nature take its course. He smiled.

He had no worries about Lucas identifying him. He'd played the part well, and Lucas would send them on a wild goose chase if the cops pried information from him. All he cared about was making those that hurt him and his family pay.

And pay they would.

He sent a text to the man he'd hired to eliminate Rod. *I hear you failed again and he's asking questions.*

I don't know how he's still alive.

I suggest you end him before he remembers me.

He'll die soon.

This is your last chance. It's either him or you. What the punk didn't realize was that his own days were numbered.

He glanced around, making sure he stayed under the radar and shot off another text to another one of his minions. *Everything a go?*

Yes.

Short and simple. He knew this guy wouldn't fail him. Once the job was done, he'd have his revenge. His jaw clenched at the thought of how his life had turned upside down. He tucked his phone in his pocket and strolled down the hallway.

He took a deep breath, settling his anger, and pushed the door open.

"Good morning."

He wanted to reach across and strangle the cheerful person in front of him but decided against it. Avenging the wrongs would be worth the wait.

THURSDAY, 5:00 P.M.

Charlie had slept for close to twelve hours before waking for a quick meal and going back to bed. The rest had held a healing that he'd craved since the whole fiasco started. Even though his injuries lingered, the intensity had dulled.

He'd pulled himself from bed around noon and joined Lizzie in the kitchen for lunch. She'd filled him in on the latest happenings while they ate. The afternoon consisted of phone calls and video chats regarding which direction to focus on next. The drug stings were going as planned, but the lingering question about the guns he and Lizzie had found continued to stump them. The gang task force had heard rumblings of a showdown, but nothing concrete. Lots of possibilities on all fronts, but no answers.

At four o'clock, they'd stopped working and prepared for the mayor's party.

Now, Charlie stood in slacks, dress shirt, and tie in the middle of the mayor's birthday bash at the hotel, mingling and enjoying himself. Well, enjoying all but the tie. He ran a finger under his collar. Stupid monkey suit. He rubbed his clean-shaven jaw and sighed. It felt good to look human again and not like drug dealing scum.

He eyed Lizzie's mom and Addy, who had come out of hiding for the party after a long battle with Lizzie to let them attend. Mayor Baker promised full security by SLED so the Elite Guardians and their families could have the night off and relax.

Charlie scanned the room and spotted several agents sprinkled around the perimeter. The people in the banquet room were well protected. His gaze shifted to his right near the refreshment table.

Lizzie bent down to hear Addy, then threw her head back in a laugh. He'd never seen Lizzie so happy. He didn't blame her. Addy was a special young lady. But Lizzie seemed different. Content, maybe.

Unable to stay away, Charlie sauntered to her side. "Hello, ladies."

"Hey, Uncle Charlie." Addy practically bounced with excitement.

"You look beautiful, Ads."

"Thank you." She spun, giving him a full view of her yellow dress with butterflies dotting the skirt.

He knelt beside her. "Sorry that I can't pick you up and twirl you around yet, but I'd sure like a hug."

Addy wrapped her arms around his neck and squeezed.

He clenched his teeth but didn't let go. Her hugs were better than any prescription a doctor gave.

"Easy, Addy." Lizzie placed a hand on her daughter's shoulder. She shot him an apologetic smile.

"I missed you, kiddo." Emotion clogged his throat. He blinked away the moisture and stood. "You look pleased," he whispered to Lizzie.

She flashed him a smile that melted his heart. "I am."

It was more than having Addy here. "Want to share?"

"Let's just say, I'm trying."

His knees almost buckled. Those were the sweetest two words he'd heard in a long time. If she fully trusted God with her fears, she'd conquer the first mountain keeping them apart. Then there was his own chasm he needed to jump, but he was working on it too.

He slipped his hand into hers and held tight before releasing his grip. "I'm glad."

"Me too." She ran her hand down his arm. "I'm not there yet, but a huge weight has lifted."

"I'll take it." The desire to pull her into a kiss about overpowered his common sense. "I…um…" Man, he had to get away from her before he did something stupid.

Her eyes twinkled, knowing exactly what her touch had done to him. "Problem, Hotshot?"

He narrowed his gaze. "Brat."

"I do my best." The smile that graced her face flashed with delight.

Charlie laughed. "Excuse me while I go find Quinn or Steven. Their ugly mugs should get you out of my head."

Lizzie swatted his arm. "Go."

After working the room in his best Charlie fashion, he grabbed a water bottle and found Olivia and Wade in their own little world away from the crowd.

Wade wrapped her in his arms and whispered in her ear. She smiled and kissed him.

The joy that consumed Charlie made his heart ready to burst. His sister was content and happy with her life. Something he never thought would happen.

He smirked and strolled over. As her brother, he had a certain annoyance factor he had to maintain. And breaking up her and Wade's canoodle time worked. "Hey, sis."

"Charlie." She huffed then kissed him on the cheek. "Having a good time?"

"When don't I?"

The scowl that graced her face made him chuckle.

"Seriously, I'm good." And he was. Mostly. If he ever wanted a future with Lizzie, he had to find the courage to confront his past.

Olivia studied him then nodded. "Glad to hear it. Heard from Mom and Dad?"

He groaned. "Mom's fussin', wanting me to come home so she can hover. And Dad's Dad. Acting as if nothing ever happened. I'm not sure which I prefer." That was a lie. He wanted acknowledgement from his dad that he was worthy to care about.

His sister patted his arm. "You'll survive."

"I doubt it." Charlie loved his family. Even when his mother smothered him and his father stayed at arm's reach. But sometimes the combination was a bit much.

"May I have your attention?" Mayor Baker stood at the podium on the small stage at the front of the banquet hall and tapped the microphone. She waited for the voices to quiet and smiled at the crowd. "I know tonight is about me getting older." The people around the room chuckled. "But before we cut into that cake in the middle of the room, I want to thank everyone for joining me tonight. I appreciate your support and friendship. Please enjoy your evening. Dessert will be served soon." The mayor concluded the announcement.

Once the mayor stepped away from the microphone, the din in the room increased. People turned to continue previous conversations.

"When would you like to cut the cake?" The mic picked up a voice in the background.

The hairs on the back of Charlie's neck stood. He knew that voice, but from where?

The figure attached to the voice slipped behind the curtain.

Charlie made his way through the crowd and disappeared backstage. He spun in a circle. No one was there. But he couldn't shake the feeling of impending doom.

Frustrated at his Swiss cheese memory and paranoia, he weaved through attendees and scanned the ballroom, searching for a clue as to why his senses were on overload.

A man looked over his shoulder and slipped outside.

Unable to put his finger on why it bothered him, Charlie aimed for the exit at the far glass door and hurried into the night. He blinked, allowing his vision to adjust to the dim lighting. Charlie scanned the courtyard and found nothing. Where had the man gone?

Maybe he was paranoid and seeing danger where there was none. He had to get his head on straight.

Charlie inhaled the night air and lifted his face to the sky. *God, I could really use Your help right now. I can't think clearly. And what am I going to do about Lizzie? I'm afraid Susan was right and I'm not husband material. Lizzie deserves more than what I can give.* His thoughts trailed to her and how he'd told her to trust God with her fears. But was he?

Lights twinkled along a wandering path around a three-tiered water fountain in the middle of the hotel garden, and the floral scent of roses and lilies that filled the night air soothed his nerves. He followed the meandering trail to a bench on the far side of the oasis. Exhaustion hovered over him, threatening to take him under. He dropped onto the cement bench, rested his forearms on his knees, and hung his head. Pond scum rated higher than him. He'd practically railed Lizzie for not trusting God with her future and had his words thrown back into his face. Hypocrite. That's what he was. Plain and simple.

He hadn't given his pain about his dad over to God. He'd held onto it and let it fester. Susan was right. He did take risks to solve cases and get the job done, hoping his father would treat him like he wasn't a big disappointment. *What do I do, God?* He'd laugh if it wasn't such a stupid question. The answer had dangled in front of him since the day he'd let his father's action dictate how he lived his life on the edge. *Scratch that. I know what to do. But, God, it's hard to put aside my pride.*

He inhaled a deep breath and pushed from the bench. He strolled to the fountain, taking in the incredible night sky and amazing garden around him. Water bubbled from the top tier and fell into the pool at the bottom. He paused and ran his fingertips through the water.

"Charlie." Lizzie hurried toward the fountain, her heels clicking on the stone walkway.

"Hi, Lizzie."

"I saw you rush out of the ballroom. Is everything all right?"

"It's fine."

"Want to tell me why I had to leave my daughter to come find you?"

"You didn't have to leave."

Her eyebrow rose. "Really?" She waggled her finger between them. "Bodyguard. Client."

Yeah, he hadn't thought about needing protection. "I thought I recognized someone, or something triggered a memory."

"What was it?"

"I'm not sure. It was more of a familiarity."

"I'll get the team on it if you can give me anything specific."

"If I figure it out, I'll let you know."

"Good. Now, let's get you back inside." She grabbed his arm and tugged him to follow her.

"Ladies and gentlemen, may we have your attention again?" The muted announcement wafted through the open banquet room door. "The waitstaff are passing around champagne and sparkling cider. Please take one for our toast to the mayor."

Charlie froze, causing Lizzie to stumble.

"Charlie?"

That voice—the missing piece of the puzzle.

15

THURSDAY, 8:00 P.M

With the threat still active, Lizzie hated leaving her daughter and mother alone, but she had a job to do. And Charlie's current state worried her.

The outside speaker crackled to life again. "Ladies and gentlemen, please join me in singing 'Happy Birthday' to Mayor Eliza Baker."

A far-off stare clouded Charlie's eyes, and then his face lost all color. He grabbed her hand and broke into a sprint, pulling her with him.

"What is it?" She struggled against her high heels, but the trust of partnership had her running alongside him.

"The hit is on the mayor. A bomb. Here. Tonight."

His words registered, causing her stomach to plummet. *Oh no. Addy.* She regained her balance and kept pace with him step for step. She had to get her daughter and mother out of there.

A deafening boom erupted from the banquet room.

The wall of windows exploded outward. She jerked Charlie to the ground and covered his body with hers. Glass peppered the bare skin on her back where her dress dipped below her shoulders.

The concussive blast had scrambled her brain and left her ears ringing. Charlie stirred beneath her, and she shifted. Shards pierced her palms.

Addy! Mom! She had to get to her family and friends. Lizzie lifted off Charlie. Tears streamed down her face, stinging the cuts on her cheeks. Staggering to her feet, she wobbled, and the world swirled once more. A kaleidoscope of colors wavered in her vision. The blast must have messed with her inner ear. By sheer willpower, she remained standing.

She lifted her gaze and her heart dropped. Smoke billowed from the opening where the wall of windows had been. Her pulse raced and panic threatened to take her under, but she fought against it. "We have to get in there!"

Charlie grabbed her wrist. "Lizzie, wait."

She slapped his hand away. "No! Addy's in there! Now. Come on." Lizzie had abandoned Addy to search for Charlie, and her choice might have cost her daughter her life. Why had she let Addy come tonight?

Without another word, Charlie followed her. She stepped over debris and caught her heel. Charlie snagged her arm, steadying her. If only she could remove her shoes, but she'd take a twisted ankle over making hamburger of her feet from all the glass and metal. Lizzie stepped through the shattered window. Her gaze traveled over the destruction. Bodies lay on the floor covered in rubble. A few people slowly stood and scanned the room in a dazed state. Lizzie squinted and found Steven lifting a table and shoving it to the side.

Where was her daughter?

Regret smothered Charlie. If only he'd remembered five, ten minutes earlier, all these people would've had a chance to escape the blast.

Thick smoke and dust filled the air, clogging Charlie's throat. The room wasn't on fire, but the smoke lingered. He coughed and noticed Lizzie doing the same. He yanked off his dress shirt, buttons flying, and handed it to her.

The crease in her forehead deepened then her eyes widened in understanding. She rolled the shirt a few times then tied it around her head, covering her nose and mouth.

Charlie tugged the neck of his undershirt up and used it as a mask. He stepped over a chair and turned to help Lizzie across the rubble. Her dress had done a great job capturing his attention earlier this evening when she'd entered the banquet room, but now the tattered garment hindered her movements. And she was going to break an ankle in those heels. However, she wasn't letting it stop her. She soldiered on.

The room had an eerie silence to it. No one was screaming. Sobs and the clunk of debris being moved, along with a soft hum of voices working together, were the only sounds. He'd worked disasters before, and the shock of a trauma caused unusual reactions.

A body lay motionless under a piece of table. Charlie knelt and hoisted the section of wood from the victim. Blank eyes of a waitstaff member stared up at him. Eyes of the dead. He checked for a pulse anyway, confirming his suspicions. He glanced at Lizzie and shook his head. Swallowing hard, Charlie lowered the man's eyelids and sat back on his haunches. Funny, the guy almost looked asleep. He pushed off his knees and stood.

Lizzie grabbed his hand and tugged him along. "Come on.

We have to find Addy." Her voice wavered between fear and determination.

"Slow down, honey. We don't want to miss her by moving too fast." He could tell that she struggled to keep the panic at bay, but years in law enforcement had given her the ability to compartmentalize. And right now, she was trying hard to keep the boxes of mother and first responder separate. He'd seen the shift in her when they'd entered the building. Her training had kicked in, but fear laced her features.

He and Lizzie found two more dead in close proximity to the first. One had a missing hand, and a ceramic plate had sliced the other man's stomach open. Charlie had experienced worse while at Atlanta PD, but tonight...he swallowed the bile pooling in his throat. *Man up, dude.* He took a step forward. His foot slipped and Lizzie grabbed his elbow, stopping him from skating across the floor. He scanned the area where the bodies lay and ran his gaze over the ground. The slick substance had splattered everywhere. Cake icing.

Charlie pointed to the blast pattern. The explosion that ripped through the room had originated on or under the center table that held the birthday cake. "The bomb was near the cake. Look at the directionality of the cake guts."

Lizzie cringed, and tears pooled on her lashes.

Okay, so maybe with their current situation, he should have chosen a different word. "Sorry."

She sighed and shook her head. "Placed for maximum damage." Her eyes drifted to where her mom and Addy had stood before he and Lizzie had left the ballroom.

"Let's keep going."

She powered through and continued with the search in a methodical fashion. He knew she wanted to run in screaming for her family, but she held it together.

Movement to his left snagged his attention. A man helped a woman to her feet then brushed dust and debris from her hair.

Charlie's lungs froze. Quinn and Maddy. They were alive. "Quinn!"

His friend searched, found him, and waved. "Charlie."

"You okay?"

"I've been better." Quinn coughed and created face coverings similar to his and Lizzie's.

Charlie and Lizzie trudged through the carnage, careful where they stepped, and joined Quinn and Maddy.

The two women hugged.

"Have you seen Addy and my mom?" Lizzie's voice quivered.

Maddy rested a hand on Lizzie's shoulder. "We'll find them."

Tears rolled down Lizzie's cheeks, and Charlie tugged her close and held her while she sobbed silently against his chest. "Hang in there. Everything will be okay." The horrible thoughts racing through her mind had to be unbearable. He'd move every piece of debris by himself if it would help uncover Addy.

Lizzie eased back. Panic filled her wide eyes. "I have to find her."

"We will, honey." Charlie kissed her forehead.

Voices and the *thunk* of shifting debris hummed throughout the room. People popped up from behind overturned tables and other pieces of wreckage, reminding him of the game Whac-a-Mole. Reality had sent his brain into defense mode. *Whatever works to get you through the ugly.* That's what he and his ex-fellow law enforcement officers had always said. The gallows humor ran rampant during his years on the force. The coping mechanism worked well for him even if people thought of him as the class clown.

He had to get Lizzie refocused on the rescue and off her fears. Charlie shifted to Maddy and Quinn. "How do you want to do this?"

"Let's split up and work systematically through the rubble." Quinn pointed to a section several feet away. "Start there and work our way out in separate directions."

"Sounds like a plan." Charlie motioned for Lizzie to go ahead of him.

The four worked, removing debris and searching for survivors. The longer time passed, the more worried Charlie became. The situation had taken its toll on Lizzie. Her desperation fueled his own. His sister along with the other Elite Guardians were still missing.

"I need some help here." Lizzie tugged on a piece of ceiling. "Oh, please be Addy." The hope in her voice broke Charlie's heart. He helped lift the rubble and a hand shot out and grabbed his forearm. A scene from a horror film flashed through his mind. He checked his instinct to jerk away and clapped his hand over the one holding his arm. He knew those fingers. Olivia.

"Hold on, sis!" He patted her hand and let go.

Lizzie's eyes widened and she dug faster.

His heart thundered. Olivia, his only remaining sister, needed him to keep it together and get her out. Charlie steeled his worry and got busy helping Lizzie.

A couple minutes later, Olivia wriggled her upper body from the hole where the blast had buried her. "Thanks," she wheezed. "Wade? The others?"

"We haven't found him yet. Quinn and Maddy are working in the other direction."

"Then help me up and let's get to it."

Charlie offered his hand and helped his sister to a standing position. He winced at the cut on her leg and the red welt on her face. But that was better than dead.

She gave Lizzie a quick hug then smacked him on the shoulder. "Come on, bro."

The three of them continued the search for Lizzie's family, their friends, and other victims on one side as Quinn and Maddy covered the other. They quickly found Wade who joined in the search. Over the next half an hour, Daniel and Katie, and Steven and Haley joined them as they dug through the rubble. The fire department and ambulances had arrived along with additional help from SLED. It was nice to know that special agents were in this mess helping out. They'd look out for evidence without being told.

Lizzie dropped her chin to her chest, the expression of defeat more than Charlie could handle.

He wrapped an arm around her and kissed the top of her head. "They're here somewhere."

Violent sobs shook her shoulders.

"Ah, honey. Come here." He pulled her in tight, wrapping her in both arms, and rested his cheek on the top of her head. His heart shattered at her guttural cries. He closed his eyes. *Lord, now would be a great time to show us where to find Addy and Lizzie's mom.*

Olivia and Wade stopped searching. Tears dripped from Olivia's chin. His sister no doubt ached for her friend.

No words could come close to easing Lizzie's distress, so he opted to stay silent and simply hold her until her sobs subsided.

"Over here!" Daniel shouted from fifty feet away.

The EGA team and spouses hurried to Daniel as he pulled Lizzie's mother, Helen, to a seated position.

"Mom!" Lizzie brushed past the group and assisted Daniel in helping her mom to her feet. "Where's Addy?"

"The explosion ripped her from my hand and threw me

backward. I'm so sorry, Lizzie." Helen swiped at the blood trickling down her temple and winced. She spun to the group. "Please, find my granddaughter."

The group combed through the debris with a renewed sense of urgency.

Charlie slid his hand under a piece of steel and received a slice across his palm for his efforts. He tossed the metal sheet aside then pulled the tie from his pocket and wrapped it around the fresh wound. Great, another injury to add to his growing list. He glanced down at the red splats on the rubble, and his gaze drifted to a splotch of yellow. Addy had worn yellow. Could it be her?

"Quinn, Daniel, give me a hand." Charlie gripped a ten-foot tabletop that had broken in half. Quinn and Daniel each grabbed a section. They lifted and moved it aside.

He froze at Lizzie's harsh intake of air.

They'd found Addy.

The young girl's limp body and ashen color made Charlie's stomach roil. He swallowed past the lump taking up residence in his throat. *Please, let her be alive.*

Lizzie scrambled to her daughter and dropped to her knees. "Addy!" She dug through the remaining debris, her fingers slick with blood from her efforts. Once Addy was free of the rubble, Lizzie brushed the blood-matted hair from the girl's forehead. "Please, don't die on me."

The Elite Guardians stood silent around the mother and daughter. Wade tucked Olivia under his arm, closed his eyes, and whispered into Olivia's ear.

The others did the same, hopefully silently praying for the precocious girl who had stolen everyone's heart.

Charlie squatted next to Lizzie and placed his fingers on Addy's wrist. A pulse thumped against his fingers. But was it his or hers? He took a deep breath and adjusted his grip to reassess.

The rhythmic throb of Addy's pulse dropped him to his knees. "She has a heartbeat," he whispered.

Lizzie jerked her gaze to him. The terror in her eyes struck him to the depths of his soul. "She's alive?"

He nodded, afraid to say more for fear of losing his composure—which, at the moment, hung on by a thread.

"We need paramedics over here!" Quinn's harsh command barely registered.

Charlie stared at the girl he'd come to love like a daughter and prayed.

Lizzie cupped Addy's cheek and tears poured down her face.

Addy's eyes fluttered open. "Momma?"

A strangled cry escaped Lizzie's lips. "Oh, honey."

"It hurts."

"What hurts, Ads?" Charlie clutched Addy's hand.

"My head. Feels like when I fell out of the tree, only worse."

He wanted to laugh at her comparison. Determined to climb the giant oak in his backyard, she'd climbed to the first limb, stood, and reached for the next when she lost her balance and fell. She'd received four stitches on her forehead for her efforts. And in Addy-like fashion, she wore her bandage like a badge of honor for the next week. "Looks about the same, maybe a bit worse."

The crunch of boots came from Charlie's right. He glanced up to find the paramedics climbing over the debris, coming their way with a backboard. Air whooshed from his lungs in relief.

"Looks like you'll get to ride in an ambulance this time." He squeezed the girl's hand.

A slight tilt of her lips settled his racing pulse. "Cool."

Lizzie's silence and the dark cloud in her gaze bothered him. Depression settled in. Now, aware of her condition, he could read her expressions.

"Lizzie. Why don't you and your mom go with Addy? Helen needs to see a doctor and Addy needs you."

She nodded.

Please, honey. Say something. Her lack of response sent a new wave of concern rippling through him.

"Well, hello there, young lady." One of the medics knelt next to Addy.

"Hi."

"My name's Trent, and this is my partner, Greg. We're going to take good care of you."

Addy's hand tightened on Charlie's. "It's okay, Ads."

"Mom?" Addy's fear tore at Charlie.

Lizzie straightened and seemed to pull herself together. "I'm not going anywhere, sweetie. Let these guys check you over, and we'll get you out of here as soon as possible." Lizzie brushed a kiss on Addy's cheek, then with trembling hands she gripped Charlie's and scooted back to let the medics work.

He tucked Lizzie to his chest and rubbed circles on her back. "She's going to be fine. Addy's a tough little cookie."

"I know, but it still hurts to see her like this. I should have been here."

He got it. He really did. His heart had refused to beat when he'd spotted Addy beneath the rubble. Only now that the medics tended to her had it found its normal rhythm.

A few minutes later, the paramedics strapped Addy to the backboard and hauled her out of the warlike scene.

He peered into the depths of Lizzie's brown eyes, wishing he could take away her grief. "Go, honey. I'll find you later. I need to stay and help."

She straightened and wrapped her arms around her middle. Jaw clenched, she simply nodded and followed her daughter to the ambulance waiting outside.

He felt Lizzie emotionally distancing herself from him. Her indifference to his concern hurt. But it was his fault that the bomb went off, and his fault that Lizzie hadn't stayed by her daughter's side.

He refused to dwell on his love life or, due to his actions, the lack thereof. Others were still trapped and needed medical attention, so he shifted his attention elsewhere. "People need our help. Let's get to it."

The group dispersed and joined in the search for more victims.

Charlie's gaze drifted to the door.

Lord, I want a future with them, but I'm afraid I already blew it. Please don't let this cause Lizzie's fear to become an insurmountable stumbling block.

There was one thing he had to do first before jumping into the search and rescue.

Charlie turned to his friend. "Hey, Quinn. We need to talk. Pretty sure I know who did this. We need to get eyes on the mayor pro tem. I think he issued a hit on Mayor Baker."

16

FRIDAY, 5:00 A.M

What had Lizzie been thinking? She'd left her child to chase after a man.

Early morning light peeked through the hospital blinds, signaling a new day. Lizzie paced the small area in Addy's room, the rubber soles of her combat boots quiet against the tile floor. Thankfully, Katie had dropped off Lizzie's go bag with a pair of jeans and a T-shirt soon after she'd arrived at the emergency room with her daughter. Her dress and heels hadn't survived the night and were currently balled up in the trash.

The night had started so well. When her mother and Addy had appeared at the party, Lizzie had thrown her arms around her daughter and hadn't let go until Addy complained about being smothered. Then Lizzie had run after Charlie and things had blown up in her face—literally.

Lizzie stopped beside the bed and rubbed Addy's forehead, careful not to touch her recently bandaged cut. Common sense told her that she'd had no idea that a bomb would go off. And if she'd stayed by Addy's side, she might not be sitting next to her daughter right now. But reality didn't relieve the guilt.

"Oh, Addy. I'm sorry you got caught in the middle of this." Whatever *this* was. Lizzie straightened the blanket and tucked it under Addy's chin. The doctor had tended to Addy's wounds and given her pain meds to dull the aches and help her sleep. For that, Lizzie was grateful.

Long lashes rested on Addy's cheeks, a trait she'd received from her father. Lizzie had been jealous of Trevor's gorgeous lashes and told him so on multiple occasions. He'd smile and bat them at her, making her laugh.

The memory struck hard. She'd never worried about Addy or her mother. God had only taken the men in her life. Was she doomed to lose others too due to her careless choices? Lizzie dropped into the easy chair and scooted it closer to her daughter. She slipped her hand under the covers and gripped Addy's fingers.

God, I can't bear to lose Addy too.

She rested her head on the edge of the hospital bed and allowed sobs to rack her body.

"Lizzie?" Charlie's voice tugged at her.

She lifted her head and peered at him through her swollen, watery eyes.

In two long strides he knelt and hooked a finger on a strand of hair matted to her cheek from her tears then tucked it behind her ear. "How's she doing?"

"Addy's fine. Cuts and bruises, but nothing serious. They wanted to watch her overnight since she hit her head and lost consciousness." The pressure from Lizzie's stuffy nose and burning eyes mixed with her pounding headache. "I should have been with her."

"Lizzie. You couldn't have stopped the explosion."

"I know that. But I feel guilty for leaving my daughter.

Instead of taking care of my family, I chased after you." Tears trailed down her cheeks. She thought she was cried out. Apparently not.

"I didn't think about you following. I only wanted to find out who the man was."

"That's the problem. You didn't think." Her voice rose with each word. "You left the ballroom without backup, taking a huge risk."

Charlie jerked back as if she'd slapped him. "I'm truly sorry. I don't know what to say."

She glanced at Addy and exhaled. "Say you'll stop taking chances with your life." Ah, she wanted to shake the man.

"I...uh..." The stunned expression on Charlie's face had Lizzie reeling in her frustration.

She shook her head. "Never mind. Just tell me why this guy was so important you couldn't take the time to let me know you needed to follow him."

Charlie stood and moved away from her. "I heard a voice by the stage that sounded familiar, and the man acted sketchy. When I saw him leave, I hurried after him. But I couldn't figure out why it bothered me so much. Then I heard the mayor pro tem speak and remembered the bomb."

Okay, so he had a decent reason, but still, he'd left without saying a word. If he wanted to take risks, she refused to be more than friends. "I was your bodyguard. You put me in a tough position. I had to choose between my daughter and you. That choice almost cost my daughter her life."

"Lizzie. You don't know that." Charlie moved closer and clutched her hand.

She pulled out of his grasp. "No, Charlie. I can't. Not right now."

He ducked his head. "All right. I understand. I won't bother you again."

"That's not what I meant." Lizzie pinched the bridge of her nose. "I'm not firing you as my friend. I'm just not sure I can be more than that."

"I get it." His shoulders slumped. "I'll go hang out in the waiting room until the team meeting." He pushed open the door and disappeared into the hall.

Lizzie hadn't meant to hurt his feelings, but she had to consider her future—one in which she could control the outcome by making the right decisions.

"Lisbeth Tremaine, what did you say to Charlie? He looks like someone kicked his dog." Lizzie's mom stood in the doorway, her arms crossed and a scowl on her face.

Oh great, the full name. "Nothing, Mom." Lizzie didn't have it in her to argue.

Her mom strolled into the room. "I've stayed silent long enough."

"What are you talking about?"

"I've watched you hold men at a distance."

"Mom—"

"No. I'm not going to let you miss out on a future with a great guy because you can't let go of your fears."

"This has nothing to do with fear." Okay, so maybe it did—just a little. "It has to do with people suffering due to my poor choices."

Her mother's eyes went wide. "Is this about your father?"

"And Trevor. And Ethan. I left Dad alone, and he had a heart attack. Then I wasn't there when Trevor tried to save Ryan. I'm the one who should have done it. I was the better climber. Instead, I was trying to figure out how to deal with a teenage pregnancy." Her pulse raced. She couldn't get the words out fast enough. "Let's not forget that I was in command of the drug raid and gave the order to breach, and Ethan got killed."

"You really think you control life and death?" Her mother shook her head.

Lizzie opened her mouth, but her mom held up her palm.

"Oh, my girl, God is the one in control, not you. Yes, it's tragic that the men you loved died, but God isn't the enemy. Don't you see?" She tucked a strand of hair behind Lizzie's ear. "He's given you so much. A beautiful daughter. Wonderful friends. He's prepared you for the job you do. Who else can empathize with clients that are experiencing the worst moments of their lives, and who else has a protective streak a mile wide?"

She let her mother's words sink in. Lizzie hadn't trusted God—she'd tried to take control and failed miserably on multiple occasions.

"I love you, honey. It hurts to see you turn your back on God."

"But He was the one who turned—"

Her mother pierced her with a look.

Okay, so maybe *she* was the one who'd walked away and not God. Lizzie fiddled with the edge of Addy's blanket. She'd already told Charlie she'd try harder to trust God. Now her mom had hit her with the hard truth.

Could she release control and give her worries to God? "I'll think about it."

"Do that. I don't like seeing my daughter hurting."

Her mother's words upended everything Lizzie believed. She and God had a long conversation coming, but at the moment, she owed Charlie an apology. By no means was she ready to commit to a relationship, but he was her friend no matter what did or didn't happen between them.

"How's my granddaughter?"

Lizzie shook off her train of thought and squeezed Addy's

hand. "She's okay. They gave her something to help her sleep. I'm guessing she'll be out for another couple of hours."

"That's a good thing. She needs her rest." Mom stood next to Addy. Her eyes filled and she blinked. "I'm glad her injuries are minor compared to what could have happened."

"You and me both. It still bothers me I wasn't there for her."

"Honey."

"I know, Mom." Lizzie glanced at the door. The team would gather soon. Should she stay with Addy, or should she join her coworkers and help figure out who did this?

"Go."

She narrowed her gaze at her mother. "What about Addy?"

"I'll stay with her and text or call if she needs anything. Besides, Katie's coming to stand guard while you take care of business."

God, here's our first conversation. She inhaled. *What should I do? Stay or go?* A voice didn't boom through the room nor did a hand push her through the doorway, but a sense of peace filled her.

"Okay. I'll go. But please tell me if Addy needs me."

"I promise, darling."

Lizzie strolled to the door and placed her hand on the frame. She glanced over her shoulder and prayed she had made the right choice to leave her daughter.

The florescent light buzzed overhead, and the *thunk* of the vending machine caused Charlie to jolt with each purchase. Bad dreams would visit him in the coming nights with the memory of the explosion never far from his mind. The added trauma sparked more flashbacks and moments of anxiety. His nerves felt like they were constantly zapped with electricity. The TV droned in the background, running the news story of the previous evening's events. He had no desire to relive that particular moment in time.

Charlie rested his elbows on his knees and dropped his face into his hands. He'd chased after a man he thought acted suspicious, trying to end the craziness, and where did it get him? In the doghouse with Lizzie and back to no hope of a future with her. He'd really messed things up. When would he learn not to take chances?

"Hey."

He lifted his head and met Lizzie's tentative gaze.

"Look, I'm sorry. I had no right to rail on you like that."

He shrugged. "Well, I'm not so sure."

"Mom kinda let me have it." She closed the distance between them. "I owe you an apology."

"Not necessary."

"I think it is."

Charlie motioned for her to take the seat next to him.

Lizzie exhaled. "Listen. I'm not sure I can do the relationship thing. That's still up in the air, but we are partners—friends. That won't change."

Just to hear her say he hadn't lost her friendship helped. He couldn't deny he wanted more now, but if that's all she was able to give, he'd take it. "Thanks for that." Charlie slouched in his chair and kicked his legs out in front of him and crossed his ankles. He chose not to fill the silence that lingered between them.

She sniffed and wiped a finger under her eye.

Charlie grabbed the tissues from the magazine table and held them out.

"Thanks." Lizzie plucked several from the box and dabbed her cheeks. "While we have a minute before the others arrive, can you tell me what you remembered about the mayor? And what all that was about right before the bomb went off?"

He clasped his hands on his stomach. "I told Quinn last night, and he's looking into it, but I'm pretty sure the mayor pro tem planted a bomb meant for Mayor Baker." He paused and frowned. "At least I think it's him. The voice is so close to his, I can't imagine who else it would be." Charlie's knee bounced. "He hired someone else to do it. I heard their plan the day those goons tried to kill me."

"But why?"

"I don't have any idea. I wish I did." That part was a mystery. One he promised himself he'd solve.

The quiet shattered when the Elite Guardians team, minus Katie, strode into the waiting room and greeted them. Each woman hugged Lizzie and asked how Addy was doing, then the group circled the chairs and took a seat.

"Steven called," Haley said. "What's the deal with the mayor pro tem?"

The reason for the get-together smacked into Charlie again. He straightened. "Who has eyes on the mayor?"

"She was brought to the hospital. Quinn is checking on her status and security right now," Laila said.

"Tell him to be careful who he trusts." Charlie didn't know how deep the plot to kill the mayor went, and that bothered him more than he cared to admit.

"On it." Laila slipped from the group and placed a call.

Daniel and Steven strode in and dragged chairs over.

Lizzie squeezed Charlie's hand. He appreciated her encouragement and support.

"So, here's the deal. The night those thugs almost beat me to death I overheard a conversation. It's nagged at me, but until moments before the explosion, I hadn't remembered. When I heard the mayor pro tem's voice, it came rushing back."

Olivia leaned forward and clasped her hands between her knees. "What did he say?"

"Assuming it *was* him, he told someone to take out the mayor. That he didn't care how, just to get it done."

"Do you know who he was talking to?"

Charlie shook his head. "No. But the man responded saying he'd take care of it, and the mayor would end up in a million pieces. Now we know the reference was to a bomb." Charlie met each team member's gaze. "Who do we know that likes to play with explosives?"

"I'm not sure, but one of the kitchen staff saw someone messing with the cake table. He didn't think anything of it at the time," Steven said.

"Do we have security footage?"

Steven nodded. "I'll forward it to everyone." He tapped his phone several times. "Done."

Everyone's cell phones pinged.

Charlie opened the video and shared the screen with Lizzie. "I suggest we get Katie's opinion. She's the ATF expert."

The group nodded in agreement.

Olivia shot off a text message to have Katie view the video.

A few minutes later, Olivia received an answer. "Katie says to look at a Vincent Copeland."

"Hold on a second. Let me ask my lieutenant to do a search on Copeland." Steven sent a message.

While they waited for the response, each person reviewed the video again.

"Got it."

In unison, the group turned to Steven.

"Well?" Haley practically growled at her husband.

"The department received a notice that dishonorably discharged ex-military explosives expert Vincent Copeland turned hitman-for-hire was last seen in the Charleston area. Not much of a leap that he made his way to Columbia."

"Sounds like a good possibility. Does his signature match?" Charlie asked.

"Uncertain. According to the latest I heard, the techs are still recovering pieces. It'll be a while before we know the makeup of the bomb. However, we know whoever set the explosive used C-4. And before you ask, yes, Copeland is known for using that particular element in his bombs."

Christina tapped the arm of her chair. "Lizzie, you've been training with Katie. Any input?"

Lizzie pursed her lips and shook her head. "Not really. I've studied a few C-4 configurations, but I don't have the background Katie does."

Charlie shivered at the thought of Lizzie defusing bombs. Why on earth did that girl insist on learning hard things? *Because she gets bored.* He smiled at his answer. Same reason she'd studied archaeology when they'd first met. At least digging in the dirt was tame...well, Katie and Daniel might disagree after Daniel's niece had found herself neck deep in trouble during her archaeology internship. Charlie guessed nothing was one hundred percent safe, but seriously—defusing bombs?

"Charlie?" Laila called his name, breaking him from his musing.

"Sorry. Lost in thought." He scanned the group. "What did you say?"

Laila tapped her phone on her palm. "I said, Quinn's on his way. He confirmed the mayor was admitted to the hospital for observation and is safe for now."

"Good. Good." Charlie exhaled.

Quinn rushed into the room a few minutes later. "We

searched the hospital. No signs of the mayor pro tem. I've put a BOLO out on the man."

A *be on the lookout* would alert the local police, and Charlie appreciated the effort but doubted it would help. Jacob Stone had proved a slippery one. "Any idea where he'd go?"

"Not a clue." Quinn scowled.

Daniel rubbed his jaw. "He has a plane at the municipal airport."

Charlie's jaw dropped. "Excuse me?"

"He's a pilot, but also has a crew if he doesn't want to fly himself. I've seen him in passing at the airport."

Olivia held up a hand. "Wait. I thought you had your own private airstrip in your neighborhood."

"I do. But on occasion, I meet my flying buddies for coffee. There's a great little shop at the municipal airport called Jitters. Stone has hangar space there. I've noticed him on multiple occasions."

Charlie bolted from his seat. "Then let's go. That man is not getting away." He'd move heaven and earth to make the man pay for hurting little Addy.

"I'll go with you." Daniel stood. "I know the area and I'm armed." He turned to Olivia. "You said you wanted me on the payroll for contract jobs."

Olivia nodded.

"Consider this my first job." Daniel jerked his head toward the exit. "Ready?" The man had transformed from loving husband and restaurant owner to a larger-than-life, capable ex-Marine. Correction, there were no ex-Marines. According to Daniel, *once a Marine, always a Marine.*

Charlie halted. He was doing it again, rushing into danger. He spun to face Lizzie and lifted a brow in question.

"Go ahead. I'm good." Lizzie gave him the sweetest lopsided smile.

"Never know, I might've just acquired a new partner." Charlie smirked.

Lizzie swatted his arm and stuck her tongue out at him. "Find your bad guy, Hotshot."

He relaxed a smidge. He'd elicited the response he'd hoped for.

"And, Daniel?"

"Yes, ma'am?" The man wiped his hand over his mouth but couldn't hide his smile.

"Keep an eye on him. He tends to get into trouble."

Charlie gave her an exaggerated eye roll. "I do not."

"Come on, *Hotshot*. We have a dirty mayor pro tem to find." Daniel tugged him toward the exit by the shirt sleeve.

Once out of eyeshot, Daniel released him. "Nice job, getting Lizzie's mind off of things."

Daniel had no idea how close to a bull's-eye he'd hit. "Yeah, she needs a little lightness right now. And you didn't do too bad yourself." Charlie huffed. "Hotshot? Really? You had to go there?"

Daniel chuckled and pushed through the hospital door to the parking garage. "You think we'll find him?"

"We have to." Charlie refused to allow a guilty man to go free if he could help it. "I'm not giving up until the man is behind bars."

Daniel gave him a sideways glance. "And if that doesn't happen?"

Good question. Charlie sighed as the possibility took root. "We'll deal with it."

But he hoped it wouldn't come to that.

17

FRIDAY, 9:00 A.M

Lizzie wiped her sweaty palms on her jeans and took several deep breaths. Charlie had headed out to catch a killer, and Lizzie prayed he'd return unharmed. But he'd given her the gift of normalcy before he left with his teasing jab.

She massaged her temples. "Now what?"

"I'll head to Bobby T's. Seems like the hot place to be," Quinn said.

Haley's eyebrow raised. "Meaning?"

"Besides the connection with Larry and Donald, or Lucas showing up when the guns arrived?" Quinn sighed and toned down his sarcasm. "I just got word that the security footage also shows suspicious activity from one of the waitstaff. Since Bobby T's catered the party, I want to go ask some questions. And I think it's time to quit trying to be stealth and ask the manager why he was meeting with Reynolds and Stone after hours."

"Agreed." Steven stood. "I'm going to go check on the

mayor and see if she's up for a chat. I want to see if she has any insight on the attack last night."

"Go. I had Angela deliver a few laptops. We'll start digging into Mayor Pro Tem Stone." Olivia pulled a messenger bag onto her lap and extracted three computers.

"Keep us posted." Quinn strode for the door with Steven on his heels.

"All right, ladies. Let's divide and conquer." Olivia handed out the laptops. "Lizzie, you and Christina take Stone's past, see what you can find. Laila and Haley, you two dig into Bobby T's. Things seem to happen around that place. And Maddy and I will see what we can find on Vincent Copeland. If he's the one behind the bombing, I want to know everything about him."

Each pair took the offered laptop and buddied up. The room grew quiet, except for soft conversations and the click of computer keys.

Thirty minutes and several trips to check on Addy later, Lizzie's breath caught. She glanced at Christina for confirmation. Her friend nodded.

"Guys. I think we found something." Lizzie waited until the group focused their attention on her. "Remember when Stone started the Mental Health Awareness campaign? We knew his sister had committed suicide due to the loss of her son. Stone made no secret of that. He even talked about how it drove his brother, Parker, to start drinking. The brother's a mess and stays out of the public eye. But what Jacob didn't say was that his nephew died in what the police think was a gang initiation kill. The police arrested two gang members, but the prosecution didn't have enough evidence to convict, so they let the suspects go free. Want to guess who the prosecutor was?"

"Six years ago?" Olivia bit her lip then her eyes widened. "Mayor Baker?"

Lizzie tapped her nose. "You got it."

Laila scooted forward to the edge of her seat. "So, this is all about revenge and not the drugs or guns?"

"I don't know about the drugs and guns part. Maybe, maybe not. But I think we found the motive for the hired hit on the mayor."

Haley nudged Laila and pointed to the screen. "And the plot thickens. Guess who owns Bobby T's?"

"Scott Smith. Why?" Maddy asked.

Hayley shook her head. "Scott Smith doesn't exist. Well, at least this Scott Smith."

Lizzie narrowed her gaze. "Who is it?"

"Stone Inc." Hayley sighed. "It's buried in the documents. You have to deep dive for it, but it's not impossible to find."

"So, Stone Inc. is the owner of Bobby T's where the pen in the alley led to the delivery guys, Larry and Donald. Charlie makes a deal with Jimmy for the drug sting. But it's not Jimmy who ends up at Bobby T's, but his competition, Lucas, that shows up, shoots Donald, who's delivering guns—not drugs—in the alley behind the restaurant. Meanwhile, Stone hires Copeland to take out Mayor Baker. He hears that Charlie remembers what happened and has decided to disappear before it all goes sideways for him. Does that sound right?"

Everyone nodded, but Christina slouched in her chair. "Still seems like we're missing something."

Lizzie swallowed past the huge lump in her throat. "We are. Think about it. If you want revenge, are you going to settle for the prosecutor or are you going to go after the guys who killed your nephew and ultimately your sister? And are you just going to up and leave before you complete your mission?"

"No." Maddy ran a hand over her face. "He's going to finish it. All of it. The guns. What better way than to get guns in the hands of a rival gang than a drug dealer?"

"Lucas has the guns," Olivia said. "And he plans to hand them over to the Crips and Bloods. Automatic war. In the crossfire, Bloods gang members will die, and the death of Stone's family is vindicated. We have to warn Quinn and Steven about a possible gang shoot-out."

"I'm on it." Maddy yanked her cell phone from her pocket, excused herself, and dialed.

Something continued to niggle at the base of Lizzie's neck. She filtered through the information they'd uncovered, but no matter what she did, the thought wouldn't coalesce. "What about Mayor Baker? You just said Stone is not going to walk away without completing the job."

"Vincent Copeland." Olivia sighed. "Stone paid him to finish the job. From what we discovered, Copeland doesn't leave evidence behind or a job unfinished."

"In other words, he's cleaning up his mess. The mayor is under protection here at the hospital and not accessible." Lizzie flinched. "Funny things were going on at the restaurant and Quinn's there. What if Copeland plans to blow up the place to eliminate any evidence? I'm going down there. If they find a bomb, maybe I can help. But I need to check on Addy first."

She stood and Olivia grabbed her arm. "Lizzie. I'm not going to stop you from going to the restaurant, but please be careful. I'll call Quinn and send backup. The rest of us will hit the ground running with the information we have." Olivia handed her a set of keys. "Take my car."

Lizzie nodded, appreciating her boss and friend. "Thanks." She made her way to Addy's room and eased the door open. "How's she doing?" she whispered.

Katie now sat in a chair on the other side of Addy with full view of the doorway, protecting Lizzie's child. Lizzie owed Katie big-time.

Her mother came to greet her with a hug. "Sound asleep."

The realization of what she was about to do tore at Lizzie. She'd left Addy before and look what had happened. *What do I do, God?*

"Lizzie, what's wrong?" her mom asked.

She hesitated. Lizzie didn't normally air her concerns with her mom. Her mother had already considered her a burden years ago after her father passed away. "I'm not sure what to do." Go or stay with her daughter and let someone else take care of things? She explained the situation to her mom and Katie.

Katie shifted in her seat. "I understand your dilemma, but Addy's fine."

Lizzie shook her head. Going to a meeting down the hall was one thing. But if she left the building, she was leaving her responsibilities to others. Her heart began to race. Anxiety inched its way in and she struggled to breathe.

"Lizzie." Her mom rested a hand on her shoulder.

She closed her eyes, and breathed deep, forcing her reaction down.

"I know you're worried, honey, but you are amazing at your job. Go. They need you. I'll stay with Addy."

Her eyes flew open. Her mother thought she was amazing? "But I don't want to burden you."

"Lisbeth Tremaine. You have never been—nor will ever be—a burden."

For a moment, Lizzie couldn't speak. *Never a burden?* "But...but..."

"But what?"

"What about after Dad died? I heard you tell one of the ladies from church what a burden it was since Dad was gone." Lizzie refused to let the tears fall.

"Heard wh—? Ohh...oh no. Oh, honey, I never thought of you as..." Her mom exhaled and closed her eyes. "Oh, Lizzie. I wasn't referring to you." She opened her eyes and gazed into Lizzie's. "I hadn't had days off in weeks and you deserved more. I was talking about the bills, and the weight of the world was pressing down on me. I had a little girl who needed my attention, and I so desperately wanted to give it to you." Her mom opened her arms. "Come here."

Lizzie fell into her mother's hug.

"I'm sorry you believed that all this time."

She peered up at her mom like she had years ago. "You really think I'm good at my job? You don't resent having to take care of Addy all the time?"

"Oh, baby girl. I'm so proud of you and what you do." Her mom smoothed her hair. "Don't you ever forget that."

Lizzie's heart burst with relief, love, and acceptance.

"Now. Go. Katie and I have this. Go be what God designed you to be."

She kissed her mother's cheek. "Thank you."

After slipping her phone into her boot—opposite her ankle holster that held her weapon, to keep it from falling out of her back pocket—she sprinted down the hall and took the stairs to the exit. Lizzie slammed her palm against the crash bar on the door and entered the parking garage. She scanned the area for Olivia's car, but her gaze landed on a Blackwell Seafood delivery truck. "What in the world?"

She changed course and examined the vehicle. Where was the driver? And better yet, why *was* the truck here?

A cloth clamped over her nose and mouth. Lizzie tried to scream even as an arm tightened around her. She kicked at the person's shins then aimed for the face, claws bared. But she knew it was a futile attempt. Already the drug was doing its job. Before she reached her target, her arm went limp, and darkness dragged her under.

Awareness came slowly. Lizzie battled against the weights

on her eyelids. The last thing she remembered was the delivery truck and…the cloth. She concentrated on the memory and anything that might help. Her mind whirled, sending her stomach on a roller-coaster ride.

Think, Lizzie. Think.

A sweet odor before the world's light turned off…chloroform. No wonder her head ached. She struggled to open her eyes, but failed and fell into the black abyss.

Where had the man escaped to? Each passing moment that Charlie and Daniel sat in the car ratcheted Charlie's nerves.

He held up the binoculars and scanned the airport but found no sign of Jacob Stone. "Are you sure about this, Daniel?"

"Positive." Daniel pointed across the parking lot to the open hangar that stored several aircraft. "His Embraer Phenom 100 is outside hangar four."

"Where?" Charlie shifted the binoculars to the direction Daniel referenced and searched for the four-seater plane.

"See that sleek white metal thing that looks like a small jet?"

Charlie glanced at him and shook his head. "Funny. Not funny. I think you need to leave the comedy act to me."

"Sure thing, *Hotshot*."

Of course the man had latched on to Lizzie's nickname for him. Charlie rolled his eyes and returned his attention to the plane. "You're killing me here."

Daniel chuckled then sobered. "I've got nothing over by the office. Do you see anyone at the hangars?"

"Nothing. Maybe we're wrong." He bounced his knee. All the sitting and uncertainty made him antsy.

"Could be, but I'll give up my firstborn if I'm wrong." Daniel pinned him with a glare. "And don't you dare tell Katie that."

Charlie pretended to lock his mouth with a key and throw it away, then grinned at him. "Your secret's safe with me."

"Yeah, right." Daniel released a stream of air. "Maybe we did get it wrong."

"I'll call Lizzie and check in before we abandon this idea." Charlie slipped the cell phone from his pocket and dialed her. No answer. He jabbed the END button and tried Katie.

She picked up on the second ring. "Matthews."

"Hey, Katie. I'm still not used to the name change." Charlie smiled. He was glad his friend and coworker had found happiness with the man sitting next to him.

"What's up?"

"Is Lizzie with you?"

"No. I haven't seen her since the last time she came in, kissed Addy, and flew out of here."

"Any idea where she went? I called, and she didn't answer."

"She went to warn Quinn about a possible bomb at the restaurant. But I haven't heard from her since, and that was about forty minutes ago."

He closed his eyes. Another bomb. And Lizzie in the midst. "Okay. I'll try again. If that doesn't work, I'll check with Quinn."

"Let me know if I can help."

"Thanks, Katie." Charlie hung up. Under normal circumstance he'd hand Daniel the phone to say hi, but his Spidey sense hummed. He hit the speed dial again. "Come on, Lizzie. Pick up."

"Charlie?" She slurred his name.

"Oh, thank heavens you're okay."

"Umm, not exactly."

He sat up straight in the passenger seat. "What are you talking about?"

"When I got to the parking garage, someone put a cloth with chloroform over my face. I just woke up. I'm inside a box truck. I have no idea where I am or how long I was out. The brain fog is terrible." He heard the underlying quiver in her voice. "Not gonna lie, Charlie, I'm scared. But I'll find a way out. Knowing you'll send out a search party for me helps."

"Are you tied up? Can you move?"

Daniel turned and stared at him.

Charlie punched the speaker button. The phone shook from the slight tremor in his hand.

"No and yes." A scuffing noise filtered over the line. "I'm up. Hold on. The world needs to stop spinning."

"Take your time, Lizzie." The car closed in on him. He resisted the urge to escape outside where he could breathe.

After a moment, she spoke. "I'm good. Let me turn on my phone flashlight and see what I can find out."

A stifled gasp reached him.

"Lizzie!" The silence that followed almost stopped his heart.

"We have a problem." She paused. "Jacob Stone is dead."

"What?" His gaze flew to Daniel.

"GSW to the forehead. Probably died before he hit the ground." Her law enforcement training had taken over. She simply reported her findings.

"Are you sure he didn't commit suicide?"

"Not unless the gun got up and walked away. It's not by the body."

"That doesn't make any sense if he's the one targeting the mayor." Charlie glanced at Daniel, whirled his finger, and took his phone off speaker.

Daniel nodded and placed a call. "Olivia. Lizzie found Stone. He's dead."

Aware of the conversation in the background, Charlie focused on Lizzie. "I don't like this, Lizzie. You need to figure out where you are ASAP so we can find you. Is your phone location tracker on?"

"Yeah, should be. Give me a minute. I want to look around."

Charlie heard the echo of her footsteps inside the truck. The harsh hiss of an intake of breath sent a shiver racing down his spine. "Lizzie, talk to me."

"There's a bomb in here," she whispered.

A bomb? Charlie's pulse shot to an alarming rate. "Lizzie, you have to get out."

"No can do, Hotshot. I'm running the light around the interior. The whole thing is wired to blow if the doors are opened."

"Do you have any idea where you are?"

"Not a clue. But if Mayor Baker is still the target, it only makes sense the truck never moved and is in the hospital parking garage."

Charlie drummed his fingers on his thigh. "Listen, since the mayor pro tem isn't coming to the airport, we're heading back to the hospital."

"Hang on, I'm going to get a closer look."

"Charlie, take a look." Daniel gestured toward a blue sedan pulling up to the hangar. "That's Stone's car. But who's in it?"

"I don't care. We have to help Lizzie."

"Hey, Hotshot."

Charlie returned his attention to the phone. "Yes."

"Stay where you are. There's a timer. Five minutes and counting down. You'll never make it. I have to call Katie. I have no choice but to defuse it."

Maybe God had urged her to take up the new hobby. If so,

he owed Him a huge thanks. "It's a good thing you're learning about explosives."

"You know it. Now, go after the mystery man, but you better promise you'll come back to me."

She couldn't be serious. "You're the one dismantling a bomb."

A small chuckle reached his ears. "There is that. And Charlie."

"Yeah?"

"I love you."

She had to choose right now to say that? The woman had rotten timing. "Right back at ya, honey." The phone went dead. "God, please give her wisdom and a steady hand. I really want to see her again."

"Amen."

Startled, his gaze went to Daniel. Had he said the prayer out loud?

As if reading his mind, Daniel nodded. "What do you say we stop the guy in Stone's car and ask him a few questions?" He turned off the engine and exited the vehicle.

Charlie tucked his phone away and slid from the passenger seat. He checked his weapon and followed Daniel to the edge of the office building, staying out of sight from the hangars.

He checked his watch. Three minutes remained. His heart kicked up a notch. Sweat beaded on his forehead. His knee bounced in time with each second that ticked by. He was going to lose her. Stomach churning, he did the only thing he could do—pray.

God, I need Your help down here. I have to focus on the situation in front of me, so I'm trusting You with Lizzie.

18

FRIDAY, 12:00 P.M

Insanity described Lizzie's current situation. She'd laugh at the madness of it all if she had time. She'd called Katie immediately after hanging up with Charlie since this was well above her skill level.

Phone propped on a block of C-4 to free her hands, a red wire, green wire, and blue wire lay draped across Lizzie's palm, and her other hand held a small multi-function pocketknife she carried in the tiny front pocket of her jeans. Her brain spun in multiple directions. The bomb in front of her, Charlie approaching an unknown subject, and her daughter lying in the hospital. Maybe the person who'd abducted her had moved the truck. Probably not. And with the amount of C-4 in the truck, if she didn't stop the explosive from detonating, the hospital would cease to exist along with a lot of people in it. Including Addy and her mom. Her heart threatened to beat out of her chest at her runaway thoughts.

The things Lizzie knew for sure? She had to trust that

Charlie would come back to her—and she had to keep her focus or the rest wouldn't matter.

"Lizzie?" Katie brought her attention back to the immediate problem.

"Sorry."

"Stay focused." A harshness to Katie's voice shocked her. "What do you see?"

The fog hovering from the chloroform clouded her thoughts, allowing her brain to wander—and that was deadly. She struggled to push the fears from her mind. No longer a mom or partner, she didn't have that luxury. Lizzie inhaled and forced her mind to stay on task. "That's part of the problem. I have to use my cell phone flashlight and deal with the bomb at the same time." She adjusted the angle of the phone and prayed it stayed in place. "Okay, I think I have it."

"Trace the wires just like I taught you."

Lizzie ran a finger over each wire to its origin. The heat inside the truck pressed down on her, adding to her misery. Sweat trickled between her shoulder blades and down her temples. She sucked in a breath and wanted to cry. "We may have an issue."

"What's that?"

"The blue wire and red wire disappear into the device. I can't figure out which one to cut."

"Hold on," Katie demanded.

Was she kidding? Lizzie glanced at the time. Two minutes. She closed her eyes. *Lord, is this how it's going to end?*

"Lizzie!"

She blinked. The voice hadn't come from her phone, but outside the truck.

"Lizzie, it's Steven. Can you hear me?"

"Steven, get out of here!" The last thing she needed was to worry about another person. She had her hands full—literally.

"No can do."

"Why on earth not?"

"Because you were right. The truck is in the hospital parking garage."

She laid her head on her forearm. This couldn't be happening. "There's enough C-4 in here to take out an entire city block."

"Well, that doesn't sound good."

Leave it to Steven to be the master of understatements.

"Lizzie, what can I do?" he asked.

Save my daughter. Get me out of here. Tell Charlie I'm sorry. But she had to face reality. "Tell Katie to come up with a solution."

"I heard that," Katie piped in. "I think I have it. I scanned Vincent Copeland's MO."

"And?" Lizzie glanced at the time. The red numbers continued counting down, getting closer to zero. One minute. Sixty seconds before she and everyone within the blast zone met their Maker. Correction. Fifty-five seconds. Fifty-four. If she didn't get this right, her daughter would die. She wanted to scream at the unfairness of it all.

"Cut the blue wire."

Lizzie placed the blue wire inside the small scissors. Her fingers trembled. Unable to squeeze the blades closed to snip the wire, she leaned down and wiped the sweat from her brow with her arm. What if Katie was wrong? "Are you sure?"

"No. But it's my best guess."

The numbers on the timer glowed with an eeriness that sent a shiver up Lizzie's spine. She traced the lines again. She needed a solid answer, not a guess—and came to the same conclusion. Her friend was right. Only an educated guess would get her out of here alive—or end it all, taking more lives with her.

"God, if we're wrong, say so now."

"I second that request," Katie whispered.

The timer continued ticking down.

Twenty-five seconds.

It was now or never. Literally. A sense of peace washed over her. Was it because she'd see God face-to-face as soon as she clipped the wire? Or because the blue wire was the right decision?

Time had run out to debate the choice.

At ten seconds, Lizzie slid the blue wire into the tiny scissors, closed her eyes, and made the cut. She stilled. Frozen. Had she blown up?

"Lizzie, you okay in there?"

She opened her eyes at Steven's question. A laugh bubbled from her. She was alive.

Katie joined her with a giggle of her own.

"What is so funny, you two?" Steven's exasperation was evident in his tone.

Lizzie stifled another giggle. Stress did funny things to a person, and her weird reaction had always manifested as laughter. "Nothing. Where's the bomb squad? I want them to take a look at the outside of the truck before we open the door."

"Shawn Garrison just walked up."

"Hey, Lizzie. How's it going?" The bomb tech's nonchalant attitude almost sent her into another fit of laughter.

"Oh, just hanging out with a bunch of explosives and getting a little closer to God."

"Sounds fun."

She rolled her eyes at Shawn's response. She had a new respect for the calm way the bomb squad handled these situations. "Think you can clear the truck so I can get out of this thing?"

"No problem. Give me a few minutes."

"Katie, you still there?" Lizzie asked.

"You know it."

"Thanks, friend. You saved my bacon today."

"Don't mention it. And I sincerely mean that."

"I hear ya." Lizzie slid to the wooden floor of the truck, pulled her knees up, and rested her head on her knees. "How's Addy and my mom?"

"Oblivious. I stepped outside the room when you called."

"Good. Let's keep it that way for now, please?"

"Will do."

Lizzie hesitated before hitting the END button and disconnecting her lifeline. She didn't need it anymore, but that didn't keep her from delaying the action. Her trembling fingers ended the call, and she turned her attention to the man outside the truck. "Hey, Steven. Call the ME's office. Tell Francisco he has a body."

"Already did. He's on the way."

The crash of adrenaline took over. Her body shook uncontrollably, and she didn't fight the reaction. When her brain reengaged, she and God would have that long conversation, but for now, she sent up a simple thanks.

The back door swung open, and Shawn's face peered at her through a spaceman-like face shield. Lizzie blinked at the light flooding the interior of the truck.

He smiled. "Well, what are you waiting for? An invitation?"

"Maybe." She struggled to stand and wobbled once she got upright.

Steven hopped in and steadied her. "Whoa, there. Take a second and get your bearings."

She tightened her grip on his arms and took several deep breaths. At least her anxiety stayed at bay and she only had to deal with fading adrenaline.

"Someone get a water bottle!" Steven yelled over his shoulder.

"I'm okay." She hated the fuss, but accepted that she required help until her body recovered.

"Sure you are. And I plan to keep it that way." An officer handed Steven a bottle. "Drink."

"Bossy much?" She accepted the water and tipped back the bottle. The cool liquid eased her nerves and coated her dry throat.

"I've been called worse." A lopsided grin graced his face.

Steven? Quinn, yes. They'd all lived through his sour attitudes, but Steven was one of the calmest, gentlest guys she knew. Who on earth would think anything bad of Steven? Whoa. She'd crashed harder than she thought if her mind traveled to analyzing Steven and Quinn.

"Looking better."

She scowled at him. "I didn't look that bad."

"Only like you'd fall over in a slight breeze." He held up his hands in mock surrender. "Adrenaline fades are the worst. Couple that with disarming your first bomb. You're allowed."

"Thanks. I think." She rubbed her forehead. Her headache had dulled and her muscles had stopped quivering, but, man, she was tired.

He chuckled. "Come on. I don't care if Shawn says it's safe. This C-4 is making me nervous."

Lizzie dropped from the truck. Her knees almost buckled, but she managed to stay upright. She felt like she'd run a marathon. With confirmation that Addy and her mom were safe and unaware of the situation, she turned her attention back to work. "Did Charlie and Daniel catch the guy in Stone's car?"

Steven stayed silent.

"Steven?"

His set jaw sent a shiver up her spine. "Not yet."

She no longer cared about the truck bomb or the dead Jacob Stone. Her adrenaline surged once more. "Get me out there."

"Lizzie."

She pinned him with a glare. "Now, Steven. Take me, or I'll find my own way."

He released an exasperated sigh and jerked his head toward his car. "Come on."

They climbed in his department vehicle and shot out of the parking garage.

"There's a protein bar in the console. Eat it." Steven maneuvered through town, his attention never wavering from the road. But his command came out loud and clear.

Lizzie stopped her sarcastic response and followed his directions. Steven was right. She needed the food to reverse the effects of the stress-induced fatigue. A nap sounded good too, but that luxury had to wait.

Charlie was in trouble—she felt it deep in her bones.

God, I'd appreciate it if You'd keep him safe from whoever's behind all this.

Ultimately though, she had to trust God. His ways weren't always hers, and she had to accept that.

Parker Stone's grip tightened on the steering wheel of his brother's sedan. He hadn't intended to kill him. But Jacob had given him no choice. His brother, Mr. Mayor Pro Tem, wanted to honor Parker's wife with some stupid awareness thing. Hadn't Jacob realized that avenging Adam's death and making the responsible pay was the only way to ease the pain of loss? But no, Jacob had threatened to call the cops and gave him no choice but to shoot his own brother.

He smacked his hand on the dashboard. Stupid. Stupid.

Stupid. Parker gritted his teeth hard enough his molars might crack. Not that he was terribly sad his brother was gone, just that he'd forced Parker's hand in being the one to end his life. Whatever. He'd left the mayor's demise in the hands of Vincent Copeland. The man wouldn't let him down like the other punks he'd hired. Vincent was a professional and never left a job unfinished.

The sparse airport traffic gave Parker a boost of relief. He drove toward the plane that sat outside at the far end of the hangar and called the pilot. "Is it ready for takeoff?"

"Yes, sir. Will Mr. Stone be joining us today?"

"No. He's dead after all the excitement last night and needs a long nap." A smile pulled at Parker's lips. Long nap indeed. "I'm parking now. I'll be there in a few minutes."

True to his word, Parker climbed the stairs to the aircraft three minutes later. He inspected the interior of the plane. His brother had made upgrades since the last time Parker traveled with him.

Nice digs, bro. Too bad you aren't around to enjoy it.

"Ready, sir?" the pilot asked.

"Yes. Let's get moving. I'd like to take off as soon as possible."

The pilot nodded and tucked into the cockpit.

Parker took a seat and ran a hand over the soft leather arm rest. At least he'd travel in comfort while the gang world in Columbia exploded with activity.

He glanced at his watch and smiled. The gun delivery was moments away and with that, his revenge would be complete.

Confusion wrapped around Charlie's brain.

"Say that again, Olivia." He ducked behind an SUV with Daniel on his six.

"I said. It's Jacob Stone's brother, Parker."

"I think you'd better explain and fast."

"The company Stone Inc. that owns Bobby T's is Parker, not Jacob. From everything we've found, Jacob was on the up-and-up. He wanted to help the community with a mental health awareness program. We missed it. Parker's the one who's bent on revenge. Gangs killed his son, and his wife committed suicide. He blames Mayor Baker for letting the men responsible go free. Since he's rarely seen in public, no one connected the dots. I'll fill you in later on the rest. Just be careful."

"Got it. Olivia, call for backup and EMS. We have a plane to stop." Charlie hung up and relayed the information to Daniel. He motioned to the hangar. "Let's go."

The plane's engines roared to life.

Not yet. Charlie refused to let Parker get away. He sprinted toward the open door.

"Charlie, wait!" Daniel yelled from behind.

He ignored his friend and jumped the small set of stairs. Rolling inside, he slammed into the far side of the plane. Air whooshed from his lungs.

"Go!" Parker yelled to the pilot and dove for Charlie.

Charlie raised an arm to deflect a blow and returned the favor, connecting with Parker's jaw.

Seriously, God. Another street fight?

The plane steered to the runway and picked up speed, knocking him and Parker to the floor. He scrambled toward the pilot. Charlie had to keep the plane on the ground. The outside door remained opened. Fumes from the engine seeped inside. He swallowed back the taste of jet fuel.

Charlie didn't know much about flying but surely the pilot

wouldn't or couldn't take off without closing it. Although, he wouldn't put it past the guy to try.

Parker grabbed Charlie's ankle and yanked him down.

His chin hit the armrest of a seat with a sickening thud. Stars exploded behind his eyes.

Their speed increased. Charlie shook off the daze and bolted to his feet, ignoring the pain once again racing through his body. But he couldn't focus on the pain. He was in a fight for his life.

The glint of a gun flashed before him. He lunged for Parker's wrist and held on, his body protesting, his grip weakening, but he refused to let go.

Parker twisted, aiming the gun closer and closer to Charlie's head.

In one quick motion, Charlie slammed Parker's hand against a wooden table between the seats.

The gun went off.

Charlie slapped his hands over his ringing ears.

The plane veered to the left, throwing him off balance. He fell onto the edge of a seat. Pain seared his torso. He gulped in air, forcing down the agony.

Parker stumbled toward the cockpit.

It was then that Charlie realized the stray bullet had hit the pilot. Hands on the seats, steadying himself, he peered out the front windshield. His breath hitched. A fuel tank loomed ahead. No time to turn the plane, Charlie yelled at Parker. "Get out!" Not waiting for a response, Charlie dove from the plane.

The explosion rocked the world, and Charlie tumbled across the pavement. A wave of heat and flames rolled toward him.

Lord, don't let Lizzie hide away from life when I'm gone.

19

FRIDAY, 12:30 P.M

A fireball and plume of smoke sent ice through Lizzie's veins. Charlie!

While Steven sped toward the airport, she willed the vehicle to move faster.

Daniel had relayed the scene to her and Steven on the drive from the hospital. She knew Charlie was on that plane. Not far from Daniel's car, Lizzie's stomach lurched. "Stop the car!"

Steven hit the brakes.

She flung the door open, fell to her knees, and retched. Another man she loved—gone. *God, why? Why can't I have someone to love? Are Your plans for me to stay single the rest of my life?*

"Take this."

A napkin wavered in her vision. She took it and wiped her mouth, but no amount of tissue would dry her eyes. Tears poured off her chin. She swallowed hard and peered up into Steven's tortured gaze.

"He was in there, wasn't he?" she squeaked out.

Daniel jogged over, knelt beside her, and rubbed her back. "Yes. But the door was open. He might have gotten out. The fire department promised to look."

She choked back a sob. "Why did he do it? It wasn't worth his life."

"He refused to allow Parker to destroy any more lives. And if the worst is true, he accomplished his mission."

"Don't." She slapped at the wetness on her cheeks. "I don't care about some altruistic mission. I just want Charlie back."

"Lizzie."

"Steven, stop. I don't need you trying to convince me, too." She knew the guys were only trying to help, but she didn't need their meaningless words.

"No, Lizzie." He tapped her shoulder and pointed. "Look."

A man walked toward them, and a backdrop of smoke and flames shadowed the figure. But Lizzie knew the build of the person and the way he moved. "Charlie?"

At Charlie's name, Daniel spun to see what she and Steven stared at.

"Charlie!" Lizzie sprinted toward him, passing the firefighters who'd run toward the flames, and flung herself at him.

He gave a pained grunt, but caught her, stumbled, then wrapped his arms around her.

"I thought you were dead!"

"Me too, honey. Me too." Charlie gave her a squeeze, then put distance between them.

"You're really here? You didn't die?" Tears flowed down her cheeks as she peered at his soot-stained face and tattered clothes.

"No...I..." He shook his head then laced his fingers with hers and walked toward the ambulance parked at the perimeter of the scene. He chose not to speak as they walked away from the devastation.

Not knowing what caused his reaction, she remained quiet. Maybe shock had consumed him and he required time to process. Or his injuries were worse than they appeared. It took everything in her not to press him for details.

Without a word, he climbed into the waiting ambulance and sat on the gurney. Lizzie joined him and took a seat on the bench beside him. The haunted look in his eyes ripped at her heart. But until he spoke, she'd honor his need for silence.

The paramedics got to work, cleaning Charlie's wounds and assessing the damage done by the explosion and who knew what else that had happened inside the plane.

Charlie cringed when the medic touched a burn on his arm, but never uttered a sound.

She didn't like the muted response. But all she could do was sit and watch as the man she loved closed in on himself. A vise clamped onto her heart and squeezed. She hadn't lost him in the plane crash, but she felt like she was losing him all the same. And yet, he left his fingers curled around hers.

Daniel stood at the door of the ambulance. His gaze met hers and he shook his head.

"Let's get you to the hospital and have the docs take a look." The paramedic adjusted an oxygen mask on Charlie.

Charlie simply rested his head back against the elevated gurney and closed his eyes.

Tears pooled on her lashes. She wanted to shake the man. Tell him to snap out of it, but a quiet voice inside her told her to wait.

Daniel leaned in and patted her knee. "I'll meet you there."

Lizzie nodded and tightened her grip. Charlie squeezed back, but continued to remain silent. *Charlie, what is going on? Why are you shutting everyone out?*

Fifteen minutes later, and no reaction from Charlie beyond holding her hand, the paramedics wheeled him through the double doors of the emergency room.

She had to release his hand, but followed his gurney around the corner and stopped at the hallway leading to the treatment bays. A lump formed in her throat and the darkness of depression swirled around her, but she refused to let the emotion take over. She spun on her heel, gave the unit clerk at the desk Charlie's name, and asked to be notified when the doctor finished.

The doors whooshed open, and Daniel strode in. "How is he?"

"To be honest, I'm not sure." Lizzie ran a hand over her face. "He's clammed up. He never spoke. I'm worried about him."

Daniel gestured toward the waiting room and guided her in that direction. "I called Olivia. The team's on the way."

"I can't believe it's happening again."

"At least this time we know he's going to be okay."

Lizzie stopped and stared at her friend. "Is he? This is different, Daniel. He's mentally checked out." She sighed and took a seat and settled in to endure the wait.

Fingernails digging into the edge of the chair, Lizzie glanced at the wall clock. Fifteen long minutes had passed. The doctor was taking too long.

"Lizzie." Olivia rushed over and gave her a hug.

The team, minus Katie and Christina, trailed behind Charlie's sister.

Lizzie made a mental note to thank Katie in a special way for staying at Addy's and her mom's sides.

Olivia sat next to her, leaned forward, and rested her elbows on her knees. "Daniel and Steven gave us the CliffsNotes version, but I want to know more."

"There's not much to say." Lizzie sorted her thoughts. "He emerged from the plane explosion like the hero in an action movie. But instead of reacting like Charlie, he barely responded."

"Did he say anything?"

"I told him I thought he was dead, and the only words he's spoken were 'Me too, honey. Me too.' Then he went silent." A tear dripped from her chin and she swiped it away.

Grey wheeled in and skidded to a stop next to the group. Christina wasn't far behind him. "I was at physical therapy when I heard about Charlie. Is he okay?"

"I wish I knew." Lizzie's chin dropped to her chest.

Grey scooted closer and placed a hand on her arm, his leather fingerless gloves rough against her skin. "Are you okay? Do you need anything?"

She narrowed her gaze and studied him. Her heartrate shot up. He knew about her depression and anxiety. She read it in his eyes. "How do you know?"

He gave her an *Are you kidding me?* look and pointed to his wheelchair. "Really?"

Oh. She hadn't considered Grey's struggle with depression. "I guess you do know."

"Yes." He softened his voice. "And I think it's time to reveal your secret."

"Grey, I can't." He asked too much of her. She'd buried this secret for so long... Could she tell her friends?

"Yes, you can." He squeezed her arm. "Trust me."

Christina's gaze bounced between her and Grey. "Someone mind telling me what you two are talking about?"

Lizzie scanned the group. Curious eyes stared at her. She patted Grey's hand and sucked in a deep breath. She could do this. They were friends. They wouldn't judge. At least she hoped not. "I...um..." She sent a pleading look at Grey. Poor guy had only known her for a few months and here she begged him for help.

Grey didn't skip a beat. He launched into the words that would help her tell her story. "Lizzie and I have something in common. Although, I'm sure for different reasons." He gave her a smile. "We both suffer from depression."

The group gaped at her.

"How did we not know this?" Laila asked with a stunned look on her face.

Lizzie stopped Grey from continuing. He'd broken the proverbial ice and for that she was grateful. "I was diagnosed with depression and anxiety eight years ago. I've learned to cope with it. My therapist gave me a few techniques to curb the severest of reactions, but I take medication to rebalance the chemicals in my brain."

"And from what I've seen, you're doing an amazing job," Grey said.

His words were a balm to her battered soul. The man understood. His praise meant a lot. "Thanks."

Olivia clasped Lizzie's hand. "Is there anything we can do for you?"

"No. Just don't let it change how you treat me. I'm the same ol' Lizzie."

"Of course not. I just meant dealing with everything." Olivia waved a hand around the room. "It can't be easy."

"It's not, but I'm coping. And I'm worried Charlie's traveling down a very dark path."

"If you're worried about a repeat performance of four years ago, I can assure you he's stronger than that. But he needs to make peace with Dad, and soon."

Lizzie's jaw dropped. Olivia knew about the struggle Charlie had with his dad?

Olivia huffed. "If my brother thinks he can hide things from me, he's sadly mistaken."

Lizzie chuckled and nodded.

Her boss gave her a knowing smile.

A doctor in a white lab coat and stethoscope around his neck entered the waiting room. "Is the family of Charlie Lee here?"

Olivia jumped up. "Over here. I'm his sister."

The man shook Olivia's hand. "Nice to meet you."

"How is he?"

"No worse for wear. He has a few burns, but most are no more than a bad sunburn. His ribs could use some extra TLC, add to that several more bruises, but overall doing well."

"What room are you sending him to?" Olivia asked.

The doctor snorted. "Are you sure you're his sister?"

Olivia waved him off. "Stupid question."

"I have the nurse working on his release papers."

"Thank you."

"Glad I could help." The doctor turned and strode from the room.

"Olivia, do you mind if I go with you?" Lizzie needed to see for herself that Charlie was okay. She prayed he'd worked through whatever had sent him inward and was ready to talk.

"You go first. I'll wait." Olivia hugged her then shooed her toward Charlie's room.

She strode down the hall, uncertainty gripping her with every step. What if he didn't want her? Lizzie shook off the thought and threw her shoulders back. This wasn't about her. It was about Charlie and how to help him.

"Knock, knock." She drew back the curtain and found Charlie pulling his scorched and tattered shirt on over his head. His torso looked like a rainbow of purple, blue, green, and yellow. So many bruises in different stages of healing. She wanted him to stay in the hospital overnight but decided to save her breath. "Can I drive you home?"

He hesitated then shook his head. Charlie returned his focus to the task of dressing. He scooped up the truck keys and his wallet from the roller table and jammed them in his pockets then picked up his cell phone and swiped the screen.

"Charlie, please, talk to me." Tears burned the back of her eyes.

He looked up and met her gaze then took two long strides and stood before her. He gripped her shoulders and gazed into her eyes, then placed a kiss on her cheek. "I'm sorry, Lizzie, but I have something I have to do, and I need to do it alone."

Lizzie froze. She hiccupped a sob.

Everything in her screamed that she'd lost another man she loved—but this time, it wasn't by death.

Charlie's body ached and his burns stung, but his heart had shattered when he walked out on Lizzie. He'd wanted to explain, but had been afraid if he'd said anything more, he'd break down. And he couldn't do that without taking care of what God had impressed upon him to do.

So, he walked on, fighting the urge to run—well, limp—back to her. But if he ever intended to be the man she deserved, he had to deal with his past. His near-death experience had taught him that.

"Charlie." Olivia hurried toward him and wrapped her arms around him.

He stood in her embrace, unable to give his sister the assurance she needed.

She pulled back and narrowed her gaze. "Charlie?"

His eyes burned, but he couldn't respond. One more word and the dam of tears would break. He swallowed against the boulder that occupied his throat. But Olivia needed his reassurance.

Charlie sucked in a breath. "I love you, sis." With a pat on her cheek, he strode through the exit and out into the parking lot.

He blinked, letting his eyes adjust to the afternoon sun. After finding his truck where'd he left it hours ago when he'd arrived at the hospital to check on Addy, he crawled in the driver's seat. Thankful he'd refused narcotics for pain meds, he cranked the engine then lowered his head to the steering wheel. *God, help me.* Words refused to come. He had no idea what he needed, just that life seemed beyond his capabilities to deal with at the moment.

When he raised his head, he spotted Olivia and Lizzie near the hospital doorway, tears streaming down their faces.

"I'm sorry," he whispered.

He pulled out his cell phone and texted the two women. *Please forgive me. I just need time.*

Charlie shoved the phone in the cup holder then shifted the truck into drive and pulled from the parking lot, leaving his sister and the woman he loved in the rearview mirror. He was being a jerk, and he knew it, but he needed time alone to sort through his jumbled thoughts—and he didn't know how to make them understand that. They'd want him to talk about it and let them try to help. And they couldn't. This was between him and God.

Twenty minutes later, he pulled into his driveway. Charlie dragged his aching body from the vehicle and into his house. He silenced his phone, laid it on the kitchen counter, and tossed his keys and wallet next to it. The stench of smoke wafting from his clothes turned his stomach. He'd come so close to death he'd tasted it. And he hadn't liked the vision of his life that had passed before his eyes.

The bed called to him, but first he needed a shower and clean clothes.

He ambled to the bathroom, turned on the shower, then stripped off his ruined shirt and jeans and stuffed them in the trash. After adjusting the temperature, he stepped under the water, rested his forehead on the tile wall, and let the warm spray target his strained muscles. He groaned as the pulse of the shower thumped against his bruises.

Finally clean and in non-scorched clothes, Charlie collapsed—carefully—on his bed. He rolled onto his back and stared at the ceiling.

God, we need to talk. Charlie threw his arm over his eyes and huffed. *I admit it, I'm a coward. I need to face my father, but I'm scared he'll reject me all over again.*

Mind spinning, Charlie fell into a deep slumber. Five hours later, he stumbled to the bathroom then headed to the kitchen and scrounged for food. Once he'd curbed his hunger, he crawled back into bed. When he woke in the morning, he rubbed his eyes. Grogginess and pain battled for his attention. He swung his legs over the side of the bed and hung his head.

Coffee or ibuprofen? Both.

He ambled to the kitchen, popped a pod into his Keurig, and hit the button. While the life juice brewed, he rummaged through the cabinet and found the medicine. He dumped a prescription dosage of four little orange tablets into his palm, tossed them in his mouth, and swallowed the pills dry. Charlie grimaced at the bitter taste. The coffeepot gurgled to a stop, and he removed the mug. He clutched the cup, inhaled the mind-clearing liquid, and took a sip. Eyes closed, he leaned his hip on the counter and basked in the moment. A moment without fear, without doubt, just the here and now.

He pushed off the counter, ambled to the living room, and dropped his battered body into the recliner. Once he drained the mug, he set it on the end table. His gaze landed on the Bible he'd left there before he'd gone undercover. A gift from his parents years ago.

He traced the lettering. Drawn to the book, he lifted it, placed it in his lap, and flipped it open. It landed on Ephesians 4:31–32, and he began to read. *Get rid of all bitterness, rage and anger, brawling and slander, along with every form of malice. Be kind and compassionate to one another, forgiving each other, just as in Christ God forgave you.*

Ouch. That hurt.

The words haunted him. He knew the right thing to do, but his insecurities held him back. He closed the Bible, laid it on the end table where he'd found it, and leaned his head back against the cushion. With his eyes closed, he ran multiple scenarios through his mind. They all ended with his father being disappointed in him. But holding it in only made the hurt fester. He'd lived with it long enough. The right thing to do was to confront his dad and discover what he'd done to cause his father to keep him at arm's length all this time.

Charlie pulled in a deep breath, pushed from the chair, and ran a hand through his hair. The ibuprofen had kicked in, and his body didn't protest like it had earlier.

He knew he looked like death warmed over, but he didn't care. He had business to take care of. After throwing a change of clothes in a duffel bag, he went to the kitchen and shoved his wallet in his back pocket. Then Charlie scooped up his phone and snatched the keys from the counter and strode to his truck with more confidence than he possessed.

He wove his way through town. His heartrate increased with each building he passed. How did he approach his father? Laura and Gordan Lee were great parents overall. Charlie hadn't dealt with abuse of any kind or neglect. But the invisible wall between him and his dad had left Charlie aching for his dad's approval. He searched his memories for something he'd done wrong and came up empty. The only link was to the summer he'd gotten hit by the car. That didn't make sense either. The hit and run hadn't been his fault. But for whatever reason, they'd all but forgotten about him after he'd healed.

The street leading to his parents' upscale neighborhood loomed ahead. His heart screamed for him to turn around and go home, but his head told him it was time to put the past where it belonged—in the past. With a tight grip on the steering wheel, he continued on with his mission to get answers.

Five minutes later, he turned into his parents' driveway and parked behind the house where his truck wasn't visible from the street. He wasn't hiding, exactly, he just needed the time alone with his mom and dad.

He peered through the windshield at the two-story craftsman home he'd grown up in. His parents had discussed downsizing, but the memories of Shana were too strong. They couldn't bring themselves to sell.

Part of Charlie was relieved, the other part...well, sometimes the memories haunted him. *Shana, I wish you were here. You always stood beside me. Always made me feel special.*

He rolled his neck, easing the tension, and slipped from the truck. He'd leave his duffel bag, in case things didn't go well and he needed a quick escape.

The lavender-lined walkway coaxed him to come forward. Mind made up, he strode to the door and knocked. He hadn't visited his parents since the Sunday dinner right before they'd left on their trip. When they'd returned, he'd told them to stay away, that the danger was too great. He hadn't lied about the danger, but he'd left out that he wasn't ready to see them.

The door opened and his mother peered through the

screen. "Charlie!" The screen door flew open, and Mom threw her arms around him, knocking him off balance. He reached for the door to steady himself then wrapped her in a hug. The woman was squeezing the life out of him, but he had to admit, it felt good to be in his mother's embrace.

She pulled back and brushed her hands down his arms. "Sorry. It's just so good to see you."

"Thanks, Mom." He swallowed against the lump in his throat. "Can I come in?"

"Of course." Laura motioned him through the doorway. "Can I get you something to eat or drink?"

"Water would be nice, but I can get it." Charlie headed toward the cupboard.

"Nonsense. Sit. You look a little tired." She steered him toward the table then grabbed a glass and started filling it.

He chuckled at her understatement. "It's okay, Mom. I've looked in a mirror."

She grinned. "Well, in that case. What truck did you get dragged behind?"

"Mom."

"I couldn't resist." She patted his back and placed a glass in front of him then yelled over the top of his head. "Honey, Charlie's here."

"Be right there," his father's voice boomed from the other room.

Charlie grabbed the water. The glass shook in his hand, sloshing the liquid over his fingers. He abandoned the drink and tucked his hands in his lap, away from his mother's scrutinizing gaze.

Gordan Lee waltzed into the kitchen and eyed Charlie up and down. "You don't look so hot."

The man's comment rubbed him the wrong way and Charlie's mouth took over. "Well, that's what almost getting blown up does to a person."

A cup shattered on the floor and his mother's gasp filled the room.

Charlie hung his head. He hadn't meant to blurt it out, but his dad's criticizing tone irked him. He scooted his chair back and skirted around his mom, who had frozen in her spot. "Don't move, Mom. Let me get this cleaned up."

He glanced at his father. The man stood still, his clenched jaw twitching. Wonderful. At least this time he knew what he'd done wrong.

After he'd swept up the glass and wiped the floor with a wet cloth, Charlie returned to his seat.

His mom and dad joined him at the table. His dad was the first to speak up. "Care to explain what you meant by that?"

He inhaled then lifted his glass and took a sip of water. "Olivia filled you in on what happened last week?"

"*She* did."

Charlie ignored the jab and swirled the glass on the table, leaving wet streaks from the condensation. "Yesterday, I went after someone determined to hurt a lot of people. Long story short, I jumped from a plane careening out of control thirty seconds before it hit a gas tank and blew up."

Shock flashed in his mother's eyes, and she covered her mouth. He reached for his mom's hand and squeezed. "As you can tell, I'm okay."

"Why?" his father asked. No, more like demanded.

"Because people's lives were in danger." Did the man think he had a death wish? Why else would he have done it?

His dad's lips pinched into a straight line. "Well, I hope you caught the bad guy."

That was all? He had no concern about Charlie, just the

criminal? Charlie had had enough. Time to lay it out there. He placed his hands flat on the table. "What is it with you?"

"Charles Lee. Don't speak to your father like that." His mother scowled.

"No, Mom. I can't do this anymore. Ever since I broke my leg in that hit and run, Dad has acted like it was my fault. He's been a good dad, but it's like I'm not enough for him."

"Son—"

He ignored his father's attempt to interrupt. Charlie faced his dad and continued before he lost the nerve to speak his mind. "Then after Shana died, you put more distance between us. We used to share funny secrets, be silly together. But something changed. It's like you struggle to even look at me." Charlie finished his rant. His gazed drifted from his dad to his mom and back. The shock on both of their faces almost made him wish he'd just kept his mouth shut.

"I-I'm sorry, Charlie." His father ran a shaky hand over his thinning hair. "I didn't realize."

Charlie used some of Lizzie's calming techniques, not for a panic attack, but to give him a moment so he didn't say something he'd regret. His gaze connected with his dad's. "I know it's been years, but I have to know. What did I do to make you stop seeing me? Why did I become invisible to you?"

His father's face drained of all color and he swayed in his seat. "Charlie...oh, my boy. No. You didn't do anything, son." Dad seemed to fight an internal battle. "It's all me."

"I don't understand." Charlie leaned forward, praying his father continued.

"Go ahead, love," his mother said. "Our son needs to know."

He jerked to stare at his mother. His head spun and he clutched the edge of the table. He wanted to call a timeout, but desperation had him stuffing his emotions away.

His father clasped his hands together. "When that car hit you and the person drove off, I was determined to get justice for you. A week turned into a month, and a month turned into three. By the time I came up for air from trying to find who hurt you, you had retreated in on yourself, and your mother was still with Shana. I didn't know what to do, so I did the only thing I knew...I continued to investigate."

The little boy whose father had ignored him all summer still ached for approval from his dad. "Mom was gone, and Shana had her own stress. I just wanted my dad to pay attention to me."

"I wish I'd been around for you." His mom squeezed his hand.

"No. Shana needed you. We talked every day. I knew the pressure she faced."

His mother's eyes widened. "You did?"

"Of course. It was a mutual check-in call."

"At least Shana stepped up to the plate for you," his father said. "I hope you can forgive me for not being the father you needed." The defeated tone surprised Charlie.

Forgiveness—such a difficult thing to give, but withholding it only harmed the person unwilling to give it. Charlie knew without a doubt that he'd make that step, but he desperately had to know why before he could say the words. "Dad, what happened?"

His father stood and paced the kitchen. "Here I was, the detective who had the best solve rate in the city, and yet I couldn't find the person who hurt you." He stopped and stared at Charlie. "I failed my own son. Then when Shana died... A father's supposed to protect his children."

That's what the years of heartache were about—regret and self-recrimination? "Dad, I've always respected you, always been proud of you. I just wanted the same."

Two strides and his dad was by Charlie's side. His father grabbed his shoulders and leaned down to eye level. "I am proud of you. So incredibly proud. You are a man of honor and have a passion to serve others. Someday you'll make a wonderful husband and father."

For a moment, emotion nearly took him to the floor. How long had he wanted to hear those words from this man? "Thank you, Dad." He cleared his throat. "But what about Susan?"

"Susan." His father scoffed and waved a dismissive hand. "She never deserved you."

Charlie's mouth hung open.

"You gave your all to your job *and* to her. She never was satisfied."

"You didn't like her?" How had Charlie never known his parents didn't approve of his fiancée?

His mother took over. "We liked her, but knew she wasn't the woman for you."

"Why didn't you say anything?"

His dad snorted. "You think you would've listened?"

Charlie couldn't help the smile that curved the corner of his lips. "Probably not, but if I had, it would've saved me a lot of dark days during my recovery."

"Olivia stepped in where we knew we couldn't." Dad tapped his chest. "And that's on me. I'm thankful your sister pulled you out of that depression and gave you a shove."

Yeah, he owed Olivia several times over for what she had done.

"I wish I could go back and do everything over," Dad said, "but since that isn't possible, can we start fresh? From right now, right here?" His father's hopeful tone brought tears to Charlie's eyes.

He blinked the moisture away and smiled. "Yes, Dad, I forgive you. You're not the only one with regrets. It's taken me a lot of years to face you and confront my pain. I wish I would've done it sooner."

His mother leaned across the table and grabbed both of their hands. "I'm so glad you two mended fences. Oh, you're making me cry." She released them then dug into her pocket and pulled out a tissue.

"Mom." Charlie dragged out the word, making her laugh.

"Can you stay for a while?" His dad hadn't found the confidence in his words yet, but Charlie had faith it would come.

"Well, I was hoping to stay at home a day or two, if that's okay."

"More than." His mother jumped up from the table. "I'll get lunch started. You look like you've missed a few meals."

Charlie started to tell her to relax, but his father stopped him. "Let her. She's happy you're back."

The double meaning wasn't lost on Charlie. He nodded to his dad. If his mom wanted to feed him, he'd let her. He missed her amazing cooking since he'd moved out. "Sounds great, Mom."

20

TUESDAY, 3:00 P.M

Lizzie checked her phone for the hundredth time, hoping for anything from Charlie.

She'd brought Addy home and settled in after he'd left the hospital. Since the team knew of her diagnosis of depression and anxiety, she'd filled in her mother. Her mom had smiled and said she'd known for years. Then she'd hugged Lizzie, sending both into tears.

It felt good to not hide her disorder anymore.

Seventy-two hours ago, Charlie had sent a group text. *Trying to rest. Quit blowing up my phone. Turning it off. Now.* He'd added multiple smiley faces. Then she'd received a private one immediately after. *Give me time, please. I need to work through a few things.* The message triggered optimism, and she held on to the hope in his words.

Her phone rang and she practically pounced on it. "Hello?"

"Hey, Lizzie. It's Quinn."

She flopped onto the couch. "Oh, hi, Quinn."

"Sorry to disappoint."

"No, it's not that." Okay, so maybe it was. She threw her head back against the cushion. "What's up?"

"Just checking in and letting you know our boy is back at home."

She straightened. "Any idea where he went?"

"Nope. Only that when I did a drive-by, his truck was in the driveway."

Relief overwhelmed her. He'd left soon after he'd texted everyone and told no one where he'd gone.

The team knew the moment he'd left town. They'd taken turns checking his house, watching for signs of life. Not that they thought he was a danger to himself or that someone else had him in their sights. Parker was dead, Copeland was in custody, and the Drug Task Force had done their job—the drug bust had been successful and the gun delivery had been stopped just in time to prevent the gang war. So there were no more threats on those fronts. But due to Charlie's injuries, his friends wanted the comfort of knowing that he was okay.

Lizzie bit her lip. "Do you think he'll reach out soon?"

"I've never known Charlie to go this far off-grid, but yeah, he will." Quinn grumbled. "When I get my hands on him—"

"Quinn." She waited a beat for him to settle down. "We all need time on occasion. And Charlie's endured a lot lately. Give him that time."

"Fine. But if he doesn't make an appearance by tomorrow, I'm going in."

Lizzie chuckled. When Quinn worried, his grumpy side came front and center. "Sounds like a plan."

Quinn ended the call, and Lizzie stretched out on the couch. Her mom had taken Addy and a friend on a mini vacation to the mountains. Lizzie's worry for Charlie had spilled over onto her daughter, and her mother had suggested a little time away until the prodigal returned.

She missed her daughter and her mom something fierce, but her mother had made the right call. Lizzie's restlessness would've set the whole house on edge. She closed her eyes and let the hum of the refrigerator and the whoosh of the ceiling fan lull her into a fitful sleep.

A knock at the door stirred her from her dreams. She blinked and peered out the front window. A shadow fell across the room. She glanced at her phone and shot to an upright position.

The knock intensified.

"All right already. I'm coming." She dragged her weary body to the front door and opened it. She sucked in a breath. "Charlie." Tears welled in her eyes. "You're here."

He gave her a lopsided smile and opened his arms wide. "In the flesh. May I come in?"

"Of course." Lizzie moved out of his way and ran fingers through her hair, attempting to tame her sleep-mussed mop. "Let's go in there." She pointed toward the couch she'd just vacated.

He nodded and followed her into the living room and took a seat on the sofa. She lowered herself onto the easy chair next to him.

Lizzie wanted to blurt out how she'd missed him and throw her arms around him, but she contained herself and waited for him to take the lead.

Charlie stared straight into her eyes. "I'm sorry I disappeared on you."

Keep it calm, Lizzie. She shrugged. "Not gonna lie. That hurt."

His eyes flickered. "I know. And I'm sorry."

"But you had things to work out."

"I did." He blew out a breath. "I needed time to think. And I had to put the past behind me."

Uncertain where he was going with this, she just nodded.

"I went to see my dad."

Oh wow, the courage it must have taken him to confront the hurt his father's actions had left in Charlie's life. "How'd it go?"

His eyes reddened then overflowed. Tears trickled down his cheeks.

Lizzie couldn't take it any longer. She rushed to his side and wrapped her arms around him.

He buried his face in her shoulder.

Unsure how long they held each other, she finally eased back. "Want to tell me about it?"

Charlie lifted his head. "He apologized. He never realized his commitment about finding the man who injured me had left me feeling abandoned."

Her breath hitched. The one thing Charlie hadn't told her, but she'd known. His fear of being abandoned...forgotten.

"I've been harboring resentment because of a child's perspective. It took seeing it through the eyes of an adult to finally understand. I'm glad we cleared the air. It was good."

"I'm glad."

He swiped his eyes with the back of his hand and huffed out a chuckle. "I'm sorry for falling apart on you."

"I'm not." She bit her lip. How did she make him understand? "I want to be the person you go to—for everything. I want to support you and all your dreams." She took a closer look at the man who held her heart.

His Adam's apple bobbed. "I don't know if I can be the man you need. I'm a cop at the center of who I am."

Now she understood. Charlie worried his career choice

would weigh on her, and she loved him even more for wanting to protect her heart. She started to respond, but Charlie had focused on the far wall, looking lost in thought.

Lizzie dropped her hand and waited for him to come back from wherever he had mentally gone.

Charlie blinked and turned to face her. "I love you, Lizzie. I want to be with you if you'll take a chance on me." He rubbed his jaw. "I'm not sure if I should ask or not, but I promise to be open and honest and not hide my true feelings from you."

She grabbed his hands and held them in front of her. "I got to know the amnesia Charlie—the real Charlie, not the one who hides behind humor to deflect deep feelings—and he was kinda special. The real Charlie has a heart worth noticing. Someone who deserves to come first and not always put others ahead of himself."

"Thank you for that." He pursed his lips and inhaled through his nose. "But there's something you need to consider before you decide where you want this thing between us to go."

Not sure she liked the ominous tone, she hesitated before nodding. "Okay."

"I know you've lost the men you loved. And you're uncertain whether or not to put your heart at risk again. So, I have to lay it out there."

Her heart thundered, and she forced her pulse to slow.

"I won't leave the Elite Guardians. This is God's calling for my life. I can't change that for you or anyone. Until He points me in another direction, I'll always have a job protecting others."

Tears spilled from her lashes. His warning filled her with love. She pulled their hands to her chest. "Charlie. One thing I learned while I was disarming that bomb and you were stopping Parker Stone is that God is in control, and I have to trust

Him. I can't stop people from dying by not caring. I have to let God be God."

The confused look on his face made her laugh.

"All that to say, I love you and will never ask you to quit your job. I'm choosing to trust God with you. He's the one with the plan for our lives and no amount of me trying to control that is going to change anything. So...I decided to accept it."

He cupped her face and covered her lips with his. There was nothing tentative or soft about his kiss. Passion simmered, coming dangerously close to erupting.

She wilted into him and felt wanted, needed, and loved for the first time in years.

They pulled back, breathless.

Charlie rested his forehead on hers, still breathing hard. "You're addictive."

"Right back at ya." She smiled.

"Lizzie Tremaine, will you be my girl?"

She giggled—actually *giggled* like a teenager. "Why, Charlie. You have such a way with words."

"What can I say? I'm talented like that." A grin spread across his face.

"That you are." She sighed, content to remain right where she was.

"Woman, you're killing me here. Are you going to answer me?"

She smacked a kiss on his nose. "Hmm, let me see."

He tickled her and she burst into peals of laughter.

"Okay. Okay." He stopped and she struggled to catch her breath. "Yes, Charlie. I'd love to be your girl."

"Good." He tucked her in beside him, and they relaxed back against the couch. "So, where do you want to go on our first official date?"

She shrugged, not caring if she ever moved from this spot. “You can choose.”

“I know—let’s play mini golf and go go-kart racing.”

She laughed again. Dating Charlie would be terrifying, amazing, and the answer to her dreams all rolled into one.

Lizzie snuggled in. “You’re on, Hotshot.”

EPILOGUE

THREE AND A HALF WEEKS LATER

SATURDAY, 1:00 P.M.

If the last few weeks had taught Charlie nothing else, he'd learned one thing—Lizzie was his future. What had started as a slow burn had turned into an all-consuming fire. He had no more doubts about what he wanted. And it centered around a spunky brunette.

He pulled his truck up to Olivia's house and parked behind Quinn and Maddy's car. The team had gathered to celebrate the first *family* get-together. Today was his birthday, and he had sworn his sister to secrecy. Old habits died hard, and simply enjoying his friends was the only gift he needed.

Well, there was one more. He tapped the ring in his pocket. A sudden rush of nerves had his hands trembling, but Charlie had no reservations about marrying Lizzie. He just prayed she felt the same way.

Charlie slipped from his truck and collected his signature dish, the seven-layer dip that Olivia had asked him to bring. He strode up the walk, entered, and headed straight for the backyard and pool. “Hey, all you lucky people, I’m here!”

“Happy birthday!” a chorus of voices yelled.

He stumbled backward.

Lizzie caught his elbow before he landed on his tush. She leaned in. “Happy birthday, Hotshot. You deserve a day focused on you.”

“I...um...don’t know what to say.”

“Hand me your dish, and go say thank you,” she whispered.

Charlie placed the dish in her hands and a kiss on her cheek. “Thank you.” Charlie had no doubt Lizzie had changed the plans to include a birthday party—for him. One more reason he loved her.

Someone handed him a can of Pepsi and he made his rounds, accepting birthday wishes. He really had great friends. The party hit full swing, and the food and conversation flowed. Lizzie even included a birthday cake. Chocolate with raspberry filling. His favorite.

Two hours later, stomach full of amazing food from Daniel’s restaurant, A Taste of Yesterday, Charlie leaned his hip against the brick half wall. He, Wade, Quinn, Steven, Daniel, and Grey had commandeered the area. Happy screams and laughter from the ladies and little ones floated from the pool. His heart fluttered at the sight of Lizzie and Addy playing in the water.

“You look happy, man,” Grey stated from his wheelchair after ditching his arm crutches a little while ago.

“I am.” A simple statement that encompassed all his emotions.

Steven settled onto a lawn chair next to Grey. “I heard Mayor Baker is continuing Jacob Stone’s Mental Health Awareness project. Too bad his brother killed him before the man got it up and running. It's a great thing he was doing. Did you know the mayor asked Lizzie to help?"

Charlie nodded. "Yup, and Lizzie agreed. I'm proud of her for stepping out of her comfort zone."

Quinn raised his root beer. "That is one strong woman."

Charlie lifted his can in salute. That was his Lizzie. Strong and amazing.

Addy caught his eye and gave him a frustrated look.

He chuckled at the priceless young girl. A few days ago, he'd asked Addy for permission to marry her mom. The girl had thrown her arms around his neck and about choked the daylights out of him. Now, she appeared tired of waiting. Charlie smiled at her and gave a slight nod.

Addy jumped out of the pool. "Come on, Mom. Let's get out."

"Slow down. I'm coming." Lizzie stepped from the pool, water puddling at her feet. Addy gave her a towel, and Lizzie mopped her face then dried off.

"Uncle Charlie, will you help Mom get more chips and dip?"

He rolled his eyes. Subtle the girl was not. "Yeah, we need to refill the snacks." Charlie slapped Quinn on the shoulder. "See ya in a minute."

The group of guys looked confused. He didn't blame them. There was enough food on the table to feed the state of Texas.

"Coming." Lizzie slipped her coverup over her head and grabbed a small bag from her things.

He held the door open for her. "That girl of yours has too much energy. She makes me feel old."

Lizzie's elbow jabbed his gut. "You are old."

"Thanks a lot." He planted a kiss on her. "Call me old once more and I might have to kiss you—again."

"Is that a threat or a promise?" Mischief twinkled in her eyes.

He playfully growled and swept her up in his arms. After a kiss that made them both lose all train of thought, he lowered her to her feet. She swayed and he steadied her. Nice to know he had that effect on her.

He slipped his hand in his pocket and clutched the ring. *Now or never, man.*

"If you'll keep your lips to yourself, I have a present for you." She retrieved the bag she'd dropped when the kissing fest started.

Charlie wanted to close his eyes and let out a frustrated breath, but instead he smiled and snuck one more kiss just to annoy her.

She swatted at him. "Stop that." Lizzie fiddled with the handle of the bag. She looked nervous.

Hand on her cheek, he peered into her eyes. "Is everything okay?"

"Yes." She bit her lip.

Oh yeah, not okay. He rubbed her arms, hoping she'd relax and tell him about whatever was bothering her.

She released a quick breath and straightened. "Charlie, we've known each other for the past three years, and we've spent the last few weeks dating. Words cannot express how much that time has meant to me. You've helped me see that I can have a future. But..." She paused.

His heart dropped to the floor. She was breaking up with him. "It's okay—"

A finger to his lips, she continued. "But, I need you to know where I stand." She pulled out a cross on a chain from the bag, raised on her toes, and slipped it over his head. "Charlie Lee, this cross is my promise to you. You're it for me. I'm all in, and whenever you're ready, I want that future with you."

Had she all but proposed to him, giving him the green light to move forward? He blinked then burst out laughing.

Brows furrowed, she tilted her head. "Charlie?"

"Oh, honey, I'm ready." He pulled out the engagement ring from his pocket and dropped to a knee in front of her. He held up the emerald cut diamond. "Lizzie, I love you and can't think of a better future than with you. Will you marry me?"

Eyes wide, she stared at him then joined him in laughter that filled the room. Once they'd calmed down, he placed the ring on her finger and kissed her to seal the deal.

Addy opened the door and stuck her head inside. "Well?"

Not taking his eyes from his fiancée, he smiled. "Well, what?"

"Uncle Charlie." The exasperation in Addy's voice sent him and Lizzie into another fit of laughter.

He met Addy's gaze. "Yes, Ads, I asked."

Addy threw her hands in the air. "And?"

Lizzie peered around him at her daughter. "And I said yes."

Addy spun around and shouted the announcement to the group.

Whoops and catcalls came from outside.

Charlie wrapped his arms around Lizzie. "I think they're happy."

"I know I am." She smiled and pointed to her daughter. "Are you ready for her? It'll be an adventure."

"Bring it on." He smoothed her wet hair from her forehead. "I love you, Lizzie."

"I love you too, Hotshot."

When Charlie's lips found hers again, he knew he was right where God meant him to be.

CONNECT WITH SUNRISE

Thank you so much for reading *Impending Strike.* We hope you enjoyed the story. If you did, would you be willing to do us a favor and leave a review? It doesn't have to be long—just a few words to help other readers know what they're getting. (But no spoilers! We don't want to wreck the fun!) Thank you again for reading!

We'd love to hear from you—not only about this story, but about any characters or stories you'd like to read in the future. Contact us at www.sunrisepublishing.com/contact.

We also have a monthly update that contains sneak peeks, reviews, upcoming releases, and fun stuff for our reader friends. Sign up at www.sunrisepublishing.com.

OTHER ELITE GUARDIANS NOVELS

Elite Guardians Collection

Driving Force

Impending Strike

Defending Honor

Elite Guardians Series

Always Watching

Without Warning

Moving Target

Chasing Secrets

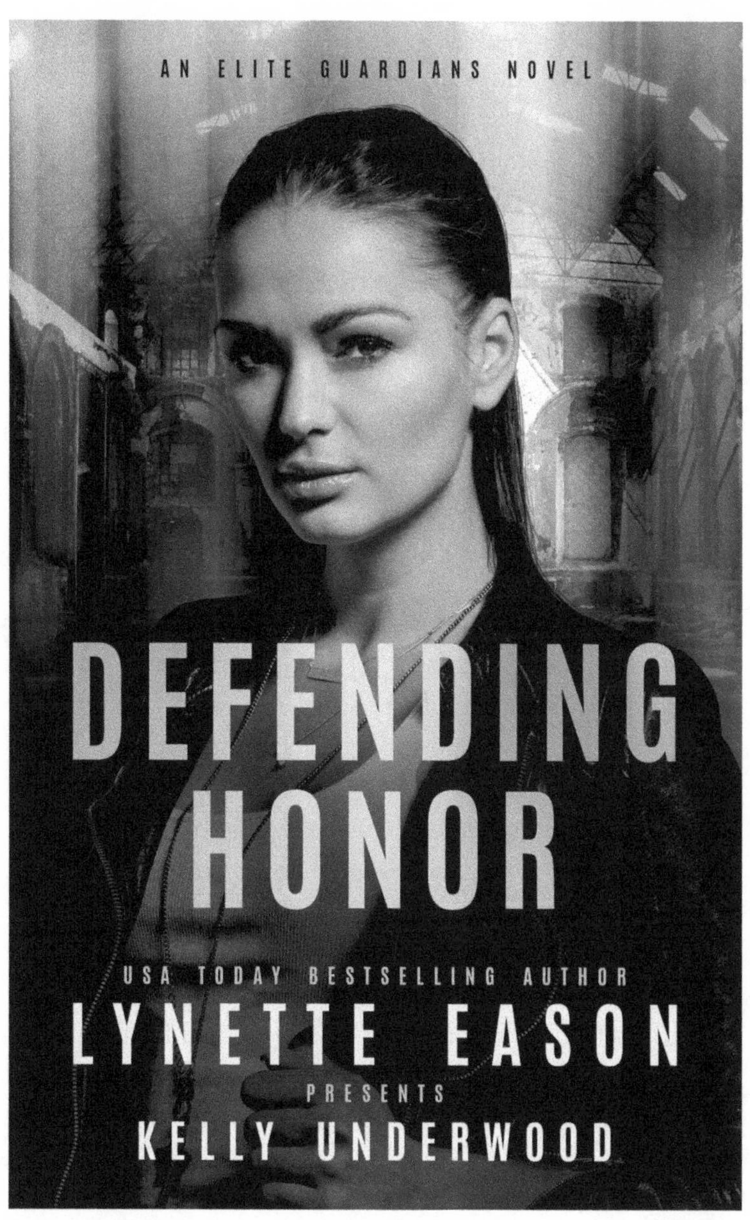

Turn the page for a sneak peek of the next Elite Guardians novel, *Defending Honor* ...

SNEAK PEEK

DEFENDING HONOR

Laila Rabbinowitz tossed the binoculars onto the passenger seat and stifled a shudder. Jesse Cora, the man she was charged with protecting, had turned out to be a lying creep who didn't give a second thought about stepping out on his marriage.

Ten showers couldn't wash off the disgust smothering her like a blanket. But as a professional bodyguard, she didn't get paid to judge people's actions.

She just had to keep the man breathing. Once his wife got a hold of him...well, that wasn't Laila's problem.

Anabelle Cora was the one footing the bill for the protection detail. The wealthy woman's fourth husband had received suspicious text messages from an alleged stalker. When his wife pressed him to be careful, Jesse had dismissed the danger. Worried sick, Anabelle had hired a bodyguard from the Elite Guardians Agency and simply didn't tell him.

Covert operations weren't Laila's favorite. She'd done enough stakeouts in her former role as a Mossad agent. Memories sprang up but were instantly dismissed. She'd long since left that life behind after moving to Columbia, South Carolina to take a job with the Elite Guardians.

"Do *not* let him catch you following him," Anabelle had warned her after their first meeting.

"Of course not," Laila had promised. Which was why she found herself in this unpleasant situation – hiding out in her car, stalking the man she was supposed to protect from a stalker.

Jesse had told his wife he'd be working late, but instead headed to a hotel to rendezvous with a woman who appeared to be a much younger blonde wearing a little black dress and three-inch spiked heels.

Laila sighed. Babysitting the rich and elite ranked right up there with getting a root canal, but she'd found a parking spot in front of the swanky hotel with an excellent view of the penthouse suite and waited. The hotel looked like it would cost more than her monthly rent for a one-night stay. At least they hadn't opted for some pay-by-the-hour seedy place.

Movement from the room made her reach for the binoculars. People should close their blinds. Thankfully, Jesse and his mistress didn't bother. Not that she wanted a front row seat to this show, but another peek through the binoculars confirmed her initial impression. Jesse was a money-grubbing cheat. He crossed through the room and wrapped his arms around the woman who clearly wasn't his wife.

Laila didn't want to watch anymore, but she traded the binoculars for a high-powered zoom lens and snapped a few incriminating shots. If Jesse denied his actions, well...

The philandering trophy husband was half the age of Anabelle.

Again, not your problem, Laila. Do your job and keep your opinions out of it.

Her stiff shoulders begged for a good workout. What she

wouldn't give to be in the boxing ring at the gym, releasing some of her pent-up energy by sparring with anyone who dared take her on. She'd been cramped in the car for close to three hours and just wanted to call it a day. With the pictures as evidence, this case was closed as far as she was concerned. She dreaded telling the sweet but misguided Anabelle that she had bigger concerns than a stalker attacking her husband.

Laila connected her Bluetooth earbuds and snagged her phone to call Olivia Savage, one of the owners of Elite Guardians. When her boss picked up, Laila didn't wait for her to utter a greeting. "Thanks for giving me the worst assignment possible. Of course, he's cheating on his wife. I'm going to stop watching before I see things I can't unsee."

Olivia laughed. "Just make sure nothing happens to our guy. I guess I have the pleasure of informing Mrs. Cora that those texts she found on her husband's phone weren't from an alleged stalker, and close this case. Without an actual threat, we can wrap things up."

"Exactly what I was thinking." A shadow in the hotel room window caught her attention. "Hold on a sec." Laila grabbed the binoculars again and squinted. "Oh no." A different man stormed into the room. He yelled something and pointed at Jesse.

"What is it?" Olivia asked.

"I spoke too soon." Laila scrambled out of her car. "I guess Jesse needs a bodyguard after all." She snapped her gun into the side holster under her jacket and grabbed her phone from the cupholder. "I suspect that the other woman's husband just discovered the affair and decided to put a stop to it one way or another." She jumped out of the car and rushed through the parking lot, the cold fall air stinging her face. "I've got to run, Olivia. I need to check on our client to make sure he doesn't get his head bashed in."

"Do you need backup?"

"I'll keep you posted." She disconnected the phone and shoved it into the back pocket of her jeans.

Jesse Cora had played with fire and she had to keep him from getting burned. She burst into the building and a security guard rose to his feet. "Sorry," she said, "I'm in a hurry." At least she might have some back up if things got hot. She skidded to a stop in front of the elevator and hammered the up button like it would bring the car faster, while she mentally ran through the defense moves she'd use if necessary.

Jesse would not get beat up on her watch, even if the slime ball deserved to be in traction.

Laila pushed a wayward strand of her long brown hair behind her ear to keep her hands from smashing the button again. The drone of classical music drifting through the lobby stole any remnant of patience she had left.

"Oh forget it," she muttered and ditched the slow-to-arrive elevator in favor of the stairs. When she hit the tenth floor, the scent of cheap liquor led her to the room. The door hung open a crack, wide enough for her to observe the unwelcome guest stagger toward her client.

The glint of metal in the man's hand propelled Laila through the door. She rocked the severely inebriated man with a kick to the side and ripped the weapon from his hand before he hit the ground. He went down without a fight.

She looked at the item in her hand. A spoon? Apparently, he'd grabbed the first thing he could find from the dining cart in the hallway. She tossed the flatware on the bed and patted the groaning man down. No weapons. Good. She looked at Jesse and the other woman who were staring, eyes wide, mouths open. "Who . . . who are you?" Jesse asked.

"I'm your bodyguard. Your wife hired me to protect you

from a stalker." Laila nodded her head towards the mistress. "I assume she's the stalker who's been texting you?"

Jesse rubbed his eyes. "Stalker? Texting me? What are you talking about?"

The man on the floor groaned and pushed up to his knees, attempting to stand. "He's cheating with my wife. That's what's happening. I'm going to—"

Laila pressed a hand to his shoulder. "You, stay down," she said. When he complied by stretching out on the floor, she shook her head, then pointed at Jesse. "You, come with me. I'll take you home."

The woman glared at Laila.

"It's not what you think," she said, her voice cool. "Jesse met me here because I'm only in town for a few days. He's planning a sixtieth birthday party for Anabelle. You can check me out online. I have tons of references for my event planning company, and I often meet clients all over the place. It's not unusual. My husband jumped to the wrong conclusions and followed me here."

The lies burned Laila's ears. She held up her hand for the woman to stop. "I don't need the details. What you two do is none of my business. My job is to keep Jesse out of danger." Laila stifled a laugh when soft snores puffed from the man on the floor. She might have over-estimated the threat level a bit.

Laila looked at the attractive blonde and nodded towards the floor. "You good with this guy?" The drunk might be a lightweight, but Laila wouldn't leave the woman if there was potential for trouble.

"He'll understand when I explain this mix up to him." The woman hissed. She glared at Laila, her face redder than her passed-out husband's. "Unlike you."

Laila shrugged and waved Jesse towards the door.

"We weren't doing anything," Jesse sputtered. "We were

going to discuss party details."

"Save it for your wife." Laila paused. "I can't make you go with me, of course, but my agency will need to get back to Anabelle about what I've witnessed. It might be better if she hears it from you."

"There was nothing to witness!" His shout bounced off her ears and she kept her gaze steady. "Fine," Jesse mumbled and turned towards the woman. "Celia, I'll call you later. To plan a party." His last words spit out of his mouth like bullets from a machine gun. He stared down Laila. "Just wait until Anabelle finds out what you've done."

"What I've done?" She scoffed. "I'm not the one lying to my wife and meeting up in the hotel room of some other woman."

Celia pushed forward, her nose practically touching Laila's. "You'll regret this. I won't have you trash my reputation because you can't see the truth. You're mistaken. Nothing happened."

Laila resisted the urge to put the woman on the floor next to her husband. Instead, she motioned for Jesse to go ahead of her. At first, she thought he might refuse, but then he sighed and stomped towards the elevator.

"I don't need a bodyguard," Jesse mumbled like a school kid caught with his hand in the cookie jar. "Why would you think I was having an affair? I love Anabelle. I can't believe this."

They rode the elevator in icy silence. At least the car arrived this time because Laila didn't want to prolong this adventure by even a second. When the doors opened, she marched through the lobby with Jesse in tow. When they got to the parking lot, she turned to him. "Go home to Anabelle. You might not have needed a bodyguard to protect you from a stalker, but who's going to protect you from your wife when she finds out where you've been tonight?"

Jesse's jaw went rigid. "I'm not cheating on my wife." He muttered a few choice words at Laila and headed to his flashy car. Taillights glowed an angry red as he peeled out of the parking lot. Laila watched him go, her disgust with the man sliding into a sadness she had no desire to explore. No sense in following him. The danger wasn't real.

Laila got back into her car and her phone vibrated. She glanced at the screen. Olivia. A swipe to the right connected the call.

"Hey," she said in greeting. "I just finished up here. Jesse is heading home and isn't in danger." She explained the situation.

"Well, that's good news. The not being in danger part, I mean. I'll have to figure out how to tell Anabelle the not so good news about Jesse's infidelity. But for now, I need you for a security job in the morning."

Laila suppressed a groan. Her dreams for a day off evaporated.

"I know you've caught some back-to-back assignments," Olivia said, "but this should just be a one-time thing. I'm sending you the details, but I need to arrange some personal security for a funeral tomorrow. Check your in-box and you'll understand why this is top priority."

With the phone still connected, Laila pulled up her email. A headline from the local paper streaked across the screen. *Walt Whittaker and Son Die in Boating Accident.*

Laila frowned. "Wow. This is terrible news. The Whittakers are treated like royalty around here." They were famous, or more like infamous. The family had become a media spectacle, fodder for tabloids and Internet gossip after Walt Whittaker's start up tech company had hit the big league. Overnight Whittaker Enterprises exploded as one of the nation's leading software developers, and now employed thousands of people. Walt's daughter had even starred in her own reality show, not that Laila had ever watched it. The family had more money than they knew what to do with and every reporter loved to dish on the family's latest exploits. Scandal kept them in the spotlight.

"I got a call from the Whittakers' attorney, Sebastian Coyle," Olivia said. "He's concerned about the family's safety. He has reason to believe Walt and his son Ethan's deaths were the result of an accident. The police are still investigating the scene, and I have a call into Detective Quinn Holcombe for an update. But Walt's company is worth billions, and we know that kind of money is always a good motive for murder. But the biggest issue is that the business now gets left to Walt's remaining son, Preston."

Headlines from news stories flipped through Laila's mind. Preston's antics had earned him a reputation as a playboy, always showing up to fancy parties with a different woman each time. And the women swooned over him, from his good looks to his endless flow of cash. What a waste. Just like Jesse, Preston had paved his way in life with money and privilege, using and discarding people on the way up.

But Preston had disappeared from the limelight after a lawsuit accused him of negligence at a party where a woman had died. "Wait. I thought Preston Whittaker had dropped off the map. No one's seen him in years. I think a few media outlets even dropped rumors that he died. Are you saying Sebastian can locate Preston?" Laila remembered one twenty-four-hour news station had offered a hefty finder's fee to anyone who could help them locate Preston, but the man hadn't resurfaced. "Where has he been this whole time?"

"The family attorney has kept tabs on him, and he's very much alive. That's why we've been called in as additional protection just for the funeral. Sebastian wants someone to watch Preston's back and stick close to him for the day without being obvious about it. Because the long-lost son is coming back for the funeral. Preston Whittaker is your next assignment."

Preston Whittaker hated giving up his beloved anonymity, but his hand had been forced.

He'd been gone for almost five years. And now, his father and brother were dead. He'd contemplated staying away, but grief sealed his decision.

He wanted to attend their funeral. *Needed to attend.*

Very few people knew of Preston's whereabouts. Five years ago, the media had run wild with news of his quick departure, and speculation had spread like crazy, but that was probably nothing compared to the gossip-fueled frenzy his homecoming would generate. He shuddered at the thought.

For now, he'd remain as anonymous as possible. He snuck into the last row of the crowded sanctuary of his childhood church. At least he wouldn't stand out with the room packed full of people. His scruffy beard hid most of his recognizable face, but the reporters were relentless when sniffing out a story. And a double Whittaker funeral would be the biggest story of the year, until someone spotted him. The last thing he wanted to do was upstage his father and brother's funeral, so he kept his head down and hoped he could duck in and out of the service without getting into a single camera shot.

Giving up life in the spotlight had been the best decision he'd ever made. He no longer belonged here, and the sooner he hit the road and headed back to his cabin in the mountains, the better.

He sat against the pew, waiting for the spectacle to begin. Finally, the parade started, with his mother and sister playing the role of grand marshals. The pair entered the main doors, faces distorted in over-exaggerated masks of sorrow. They walked down the aisle to the front of the church. Typical. Instead of shielding themselves from public onlookers, they'd chosen to display their grief for all the world to see. Because grieving in private didn't generate nearly as much attention. As his mother started to take her seat, she staggered a bit before she caught her balance and lowered herself onto the pew. Looked like she still drowned her feelings with a bottle.

Preston bit back the swirl of emotions welling up in his chest. Despite leaving his family behind for a different life, he missed them. Especially his mother. Was someone looking after her now that his father had died? Even with their publicity-hungry antics, his heart still beat strong for the Whittakers. And now two members of his family were gone, leaving a gaping hole in his life that we wasn't sure would ever heal.

Someone bumped his shoulder, and he turned to spot his long-time family friend and attorney, Sebastian Coyle. The man had saved Preston from the repercussions of his many bad teenage decisions. Situations he now tried hard to forget.

"Good to see you, Whitt," Sebastian whispered and slid in next to Preston on the back row. Paranoia over the use of his childhood nickname kicked in, and Preston searched the faces of anyone within earshot. Thankfully, everyone's focus was on the show at the front of the church. Sebastian had kept tabs on him during the years he'd dropped off the radar. Which was more than he could say for his family.

"Relax," Sebastian said. "No one would recognize you in that lumberjack attire. Love the beard, by the way. It gives off a rugged vibe. Not something anyone would associate with you."

Preston glanced at his plaid shirt, black jeans, and cowboy boots. While he'd embraced his casual look, he'd once been known for his three-thousand-dollar designer suits. Which outfit would the paparazzi expect him to wear now that he was back in town? And what would the media think of his transformation from rich party-boy to a small-town nobody?

"I see things haven't changed much since I've been gone." Preston nodded towards his sister, Katrina Pace, giving an on-the-spot interview at the front of the church to the right of the casket. Anything to make sure she placed herself center-stage. Her husband, Derek, hovered behind her, angling himself to remain in the camera frame.

"Actually, you don't know how much things have changed. Overnight."

Preston looked at his aged friend. While it seemed like time stood still in some respects, the man's gray hairs documented the passing years.

"We need to discuss you coming back," Sebastian whispered. The man's eyes darted around the room, as if scanning for any signs of trouble. Was Sebastian worried that Preston's identity might get out?

Preston shook his head. "There's nothing to talk about, because it's not going to happen." He kept his voice low. The service started, ending the conversation. For now. Preston half-listened to the minister give the eulogy about the life of Walter Whittaker. Despite their differences, nothing had prepared him for the finality of never seeing his father again.

He rubbed his eyes, willing this to be nothing more than a nightmare that would vanish the moment he woke. Ethan and his dad were gone. There hadn't been enough space for the grief to register while he'd been making plans to return home, but now...it threatened to rip him to shreds. He'd never had a good relationship with either of them. But reminders of the past flipped through his mind, and he struggled to hold back the tears. No way would he fall apart, not in public anyway.

With a few deep breaths, he regained his composure and let his gaze roam around the room. Lots of familiar faces sat with glistening eyes and tear-stained cheeks while the minister continued. He caught a pretty brunette glancing his way. He didn't remember her and sent up a prayer that she didn't recognize him. She looked away, but for all he knew, she might be a reporter.

He abandoned all thoughts of the mystery woman when his sister-in-law, Veronica Whittaker, took the microphone. Preston had once dated Veronica in high school, until she'd moved on to his brother. But never in his wildest imagination would he have predicted it would end this way. At a double funeral. How could Ethan be gone leaving a wife and two kids behind? He spotted his ten-year-old and seven-year-old nephews towards the front and barely recognized them. Five years now seemed like an eternity.

Grief threatened to consume him at the thought of his nephews growing up fatherless. His head pounded as he held back the tears. Coming back had been a terrible idea. He had to get out of here. *Now*.

Preston jumped to his feet and rushed out of the sanctuary with Sebastian hot on his heels. Anger at the senseless loss fueled his feet and he picked up speed when he hit the parking lot. How could he lose his father when he never had the chance to mend their broken relationship? Now it was too late. He'd waited too long.

"Wait!" Sebastian called. "Don't go."

Preston stopped and faced his friend. "I can't stay. I don't belong. My dad and Ethan are gone. There's nothing I can do to bring them back, and my presence just invites trouble." He perused the area and didn't spot a soul. At least the camera crews were busy inside getting their sound bites of the funeral.

"You have to stay," Sebastian said. "Someone has to take over the business or your father's partner will sell the company.

You're next in line and you're needed here. Don't you realize what this means?"

Preston knew all too well. If they shut down Whittaker Enterprises, thousands of people would be out of jobs and his family would lose everything his father had built. His dad had started the company in his garage and turned it into one of the leading software development companies in the world.

Walt's biggest desire had always been to keep Whittaker Enterprises a private family-run company. While the thought troubled him, it didn't prick his conscious enough to make him accept the position. "There has to be someone else. There are tons of people more qualified than I am to follow in my dad's footsteps. I'm out, remember?"

Movement in the corner of his eye triggered warning sirens in Preston's head. He noted the same woman from the church, standing by the side of the building, out of ear shot but definitely watching them.

Preston turned and walked through the rows of parked cars to locate his truck. Sebastian followed. "You can't outrun your past," the man said. "Or your future, for that matter."

Preston spun around to face Sebastian, but his mind refused to form words in the midst of another onslaught of emotions threating to spill out. Why had he come here?

They stood between two parked cars and the vehicles provided a bit of privacy. "You aren't out," Sebastian said, his voice soft. "You were never out. This is your life. You let one stupid lawsuit take away everything from you."

"I live with that regret every day. I don't expect you to understand."

"I care a great deal about what happens to you and your family." Sebastian scanned the parking area, then locked his gaze back on Preston's. "Look, I don't think your father and brother's deaths were an accident."

Preston froze. "What are you suggesting?"

Sebastian placed a hand on Preston's shoulder. "I think your life is in danger. Once word gets out that you're alive and back in Columbia, it's possible you might be the next target."

"What are you talking about? You really believe that someone wanted both Ethan and my father dead. Why?"

Sebastian shrugged. "I just have a bad feeling about this. I'll feel better once the police conclude their investigation, but your dad had called in extra security at the house a few weeks before he died. He claims that someone had followed him home one night, and there was also a break in at the estate. Now, he's gone. It just makes me think something sinister could be going on. Not to mention that you stand to inherit a lot, Preston. And you've seen firsthand what money does to people."

Preston stared at the man who had been more of a father to him than his own. He knew he could trust Sebastian's instincts.

But murder? His head reeled at the thought. His tarnished family legacy concealed plenty of secrets, and if all their enemies lined up, they'd circle the block. But who would act on the desire to see them dead?

He pressed his thumb and forefinger to his eyes, then dropped his hands. "I can't, Sebastian. I don't want to come back to this life. Being chased by the media, having to live up to other people's expectations. That's not me anymore. I'm sorry."

Preston walked in the direction of his truck, his mind twisted with unanswered questions. Why would he come back to Columbia after making a new life for himself? But could he sit on the sidelines and let his father's company fall apart? And what about Sebastian's crazy theory that the fire on the boat wasn't an accident? Could it be true?

He stepped into the aisle between the rows of parked cars. A revving engine grabbed his attention. The smell of burning rubber hit his nose before his brain registered the van barreling down the lane, aimed directly at him. He pivoted to get out of the way, but the van mirrored his movements and continued to bear down on him.

"Preston, look out!" Everything around him moved as if in slow motion. Before he could run, someone tackled him and rolled him between two parked cars in one seamless motion. A rush of air whooshed past as the speeding van took off, leaving a haze of blue smoke in the air.

His body ached from its impact with the pavement. A groan escaped his lips. What just happened? Sebastian's words flashed through him like a bolt of lightning, sending shivers down his spine. *"You might be the next target."*

He pushed at the weight on his chest and when it didn't budge, he forced his eyes to focus. Two intense dark brown eyes stared back at him for a split second before the woman rolled off him. She was on her feet before he could blink. "Are you ok?" she asked and offered her hand to help him up. He waved her off and stood, swiping his hands over his jeans to wipe off the bits of gravel. Sebastian rushed over, concern etched on his face. Preston stared at the stranger turned rescuer. "Who are you?"

She opened her mouth to respond, but Sebastian jumped in. "This is the woman who just saved your life. Someone just tried to run you over. To *kill* you. Now do you believe me when I say you're in danger?"

Preston raked a hand over his head and let his gaze jump between the two. "I don't know what to believe."

The pretty brunette dusted herself off and said, "I'm Laila Rabbinowitz. Nice to meet you. Looks like I'm your new bodyguard."

Bodyguard? At first glance he never would have pegged this woman as a professional security guard, but maybe that was the point. Despite her petite stature, he was willing to bet she could hold her own against someone twice her size. But he needed to get out of town, not have someone trailing his every move like those paparazzi stalkers.

Preston tried to wrap his mind around the situation while Sebastian rambled. "I insisted on additional security for today and called the Elite Guardians Agency. It's a good thing I did. That van targeted you. Laila came to watch your back for the funeral, but you're going to need round the clock security. I just lost your father and Ethan. I can't lose you too."

His heart warmed at how much Sebastian cared about his family, but if Preston left, there'd be no need for twenty-four-seven surveillance. He turned to Laila. "It's nice to meet you too, but the media hasn't noticed me yet and I'd like to keep it that way. So, if you'll excuse me, I'm leaving town tonight."

"Someone tried to run you over," Laila said. "I'd say that at least one person knows you're here and isn't happy about it."

"Could have been a fluke. I wasn't paying attention when I stepped out. How do I know I was the intended target?" Even as the words left his lips, he knew his rationale sounded pathetic. That van was laser focused on him. What if someone really had murdered his father and brother, and that same person had just tried to take him out?

The church door clanged open, and Preston spotted a reporter heading to one of the parked news vans on the other side of the lot, cameraman in tow.

He looked at Sebastian. "I'll stay in town long enough to sign whatever papers you need from me to forgo any share of the company. Because I'm *not* coming back."

He walked toward his truck, leaving Laila and Sebastian staring after him.

Many people had speculated that he was dead, but could his life actually be on the line after all of these years?

ACKNOWLEDGMENTS

Dear Reader,

Thank you for reading *Impending Strike*. I hope you enjoyed reading it as much as I did writing it.

We saw a glimpse of Lizzie and Charlie for the first time in Lynette Eason's original Elite Guardian series. When I found out I was chosen to tell their story, I was so excited. I absolutely fell in love with Lizzie and Charlie. What a fun couple to follow on their journey.

This book wouldn't have been possible without Sunrise Publishing's Susan May Warren, Lindsay Harrel, and Rel Mollet. You ladies are awesome. I can't thank you enough.

A super special thank you to my mentor, Lynette Eason. Words cannot express my gratitude for all you've done.

And I can't forget my EG girls, Kate Angelo and Kelly Underwood. We connected from the start and our friendship has only grown stronger.

Finally, my family. My husband Darren and adult kiddos Matthew and Melissa. You always cheer me on and remind me that "I can do it." Thank you!

Thanks again for reading Lizzie and Charlie's story.

I'd love to hear from you. You can contact me through my website at samiaabrams.com, where you can sign up for my newsletter to receive exclusive subscriber giveaways.

Hugs,

Sami A. Abrams

ABOUT THE AUTHORS

Lynette Eason is the best-selling, award-winning author of over 60 books including the Women of Justice series, the Deadly Reunions series, the Hidden Identity series, the Elite Guardians series, the Blue Justice series, and the currently releasing, Danger Never Sleeps series. She is the winner of three ACFW Carol Awards, the Selah Award, and the Inspirational Reader's Choice Award, among others. Her Elite Guardians series, featuring strong, successful female bodyguards, has captured readers' hearts and minds. Visit her at www.LynetteEason.com.

Sami A. Abrams grew up hating to read. It wasn't until her 30s that she found authors who captured her attention. Now, most evenings you can find her engrossed in a romantic suspense novel. In her opinion, a crime plus a little romance is the recipe for a great story. Sami lives in Northern California, but she will always be a Kansas girl at heart. She has a love of sports, family, and travel. However, a cabin at Lake Tahoe writing her next story is definitely at the top of her list. Visit her at samiaabrams.com.

Impending Strike: An Elite Guardians Novel

Published by Sunrise Media Group LLC

For more information about Sami A. Abrams and Lynette Eason, please access the authors' websites at the following respective addresses: samiaabrams.com and https://lynetteeason.com

Published in the United States of America.

Cover Design: Jenny at Seedlings Designs

CPSIA information can be obtained
at www.ICGtesting.com
Printed in the USA
LVHW100442210622
721699LV00005B/151